# DOWNLOAD MURDER

*Detective Damien Drake*

Book 3

**Patrick Logan**

# Books by Patrick Logan

## Detective Damien Drake

Book 1: Butterfly Kisses
Book 2: Cause of Death
Book 3: Download Murder
Book 4: Skeleton King

## Insatiable Series

Book 1: Skin
Book 2: Crackers
Book 3: Flesh
Book 4: Parasite
Book 4.5: Knuckles
Book 5: Stitches

## The Haunted Series

Book 1: Shallow Graves
Book 2: The Seventh Ward
Book 3: Seaforth Prison
Book 4: Scarsdale Crematorium
Book 5: Sacred Heard Orphanage
Book 6: Shores of the Marrow

*There is nothing to writing.*
*All you do is sit down at a typewriter*
*and bleed.*

-Ernest Hemingway

# Prologue

THE WHISTLING WAS GENERIC, not representative of anything that either of the girls could recognize. It was just a string of pitchless notes that didn't seem to follow a particular pattern or tune.

Which somehow made it even more terrifying.

Melissa shivered and opened her eyes. Her neck and shoulders were sore from falling asleep with her back against the cold concrete, and her hands, bound tightly behind her, had long ago gone numb.

Her heart rate quickened with the sound of a door opening, and Melissa shut her eyes tightly, trying to will their captor away.

The whistling abruptly stopped, and she somehow mustered the courage to open her eyes again.

A shadowy figure was crouched but a foot from her, head tilted to one side. When a gloved hand moved toward her face, Melissa recoiled so quickly that the back of her skull bounced off the wall hard enough to send stars shooting across her vision.

But the hand didn't grab her as she thought it might; instead, the fingers brushed a lock of a brittle brown hair away from her face.

"Why are you doing this?" Melissa whimpered.

When the figure's only response was to change the angle of the head tilt, rage suddenly filled her.

"Fuck you," she growled. When the shadow didn't respond at all this time, didn't even seem to acknowledge her, she leaned forward and spat.

The spray struck her captor directly in the face, and the figure stumbled backward. The crawlspace couldn't have been more than four feet tall, and for a second Melissa thought that the captor might crack their head on one of the low crossbeams.

The figure ducked just in time.

"Tsk, tsk, tsk; that isn't polite," her captor said. When the fingers extended toward her face again, Melissa didn't cower away. This time, she stared forward, hatred in her eyes.

"That simply isn't tolerated here, sweetie."

There was no anger in the voice—just simple, perfunctory castigation.

The gloved hand slipped out of sight. When it reappeared, the leather fingers were wrapped around the handle of an eight-inch butcher's knife.

Melissa didn't want to show fear, didn't want to feed her captor's sick desires. But when her eyes fell on the blade, she couldn't help it; her eyes widened.

Her captor must have noticed this, as a dry chuckle suddenly filled the crawlspace.

"Oh, it's not for you, hon," the figure said. With that, the shadow spun around to face the other woman.

She had been here when Melissa had first arrived, and even though it was difficult to tell how much time had passed in the crawlspace, Melissa thought it to be around three days.

And in all that time, the other woman hadn't said a single word, hadn't so much as muttered her name. In fact, the only sign that she was alive was her near-constant shivering. Like Melissa, her hair was grimy, covering her pale face in thin spaghetti-like strands. As the figure moved toward her, however, the woman started to animate.

Hope suddenly bloomed inside Melissa.

*She's been saving her energy; all this time, she's been waiting for just the right moment. Together... together maybe we can take the knife, maybe—*

But when the woman simply held her arms out, palms up, all optimism fled her.

There were scars on her wrists, a network of crisscrossing pink lines that stood out on her alabaster forearms.

This woman wouldn't fight, Melissa knew.

"See?" the captor instructed. "This is how you're supposed to behave."

Without hesitation, the blade flashed out and a scarlet streak appeared between the pink scars. Blood immediately spilled forth, coating the lower half of her arm before pooling in her palm. The woman's eyelids sagged, and her neck drooped.

"That's alright, sweetie. You've done your part—I've seen you die."

The figure cleaned the blade on the woman's dirt-smeared shirt before putting it back into the holster. Then a gloved thumb reached out and pressed into the wound, soaking the pad in her blood.

Melissa wanted to be angry, to scream at her captor, to demand, for the hundredth time, the reason why she had been taken, why they both had been kidnapped.

But the only thing she could muster was a muted curse.

"Leave her the fuck alone."

The dark figure turned and moved quickly, half-squatting, half-crawling, over to her.

Melissa tried to turn away, to hide her face, but a hand shot out and grabbed her cheeks tightly, forcing her lips into a pout.

"We don't curse down here," the captor hissed. Melissa struggled, but the grip was too tight to pull away. Her cheeks ached, and even if she wanted to speak then, she wouldn't have been able to.

*The blade is going to cut me now, cut me deep just like the other woman. Then I'm going to die here in this shitty, freezing basement.*

The person squeezed even tighter. Then, with their thumb still dripping with the other woman's blood, the captor smeared it across her lips, crudely painting them with the tacky substance.

Melissa gagged, and her captor finally released her face. She tried to spit without touching the blood with her tongue, without letting any of it into her mouth.

Bile rose in her throat when she tasted the coppery liquid, but she somehow managed to fight the urge to vomit.

Apparently satisfied, the captor backed away, moving closer to the dim bulb that provided the only illumination in the crawlspace.

The gloved hand moved again, but instead of withdrawing a knife, it came back holding a black notepad.

As Melissa watched in horror, the figure flipped to a blank page, and then pressed the gloved thumb against the upper right-hand corner, leaving behind a bloody thumbprint.

"Write what you know," Melissa's captor whispered. And then the whistling started again as the pen started to move across the page.

# First Act

## Chapter 1

**DAMIEN DRAKE HUNCHED LOW**, hiding his six-foot frame behind a parked Lincoln Navigator. He was breathing heavily, and sweat was dripping down his forehead despite the snow that flitted down around him.

*I'm getting sloppy.*

If it hadn't been for his recent health kick—not skipping the booze, but cutting back—he almost certainly would have been seen.

And what had Ken Smith instructed him?

*Don't be noticed. If you're noticed, I will deny ever speaking to you, Drake. And you know what that means.*

Drake grimaced as he recalled their conversation by the fire in Ken's lavish penthouse condo.

*Yeah, I know. I know what that means.*

He instinctively held his breath when he heard the voices, louder now, and he remained completely still, hoping that the two people he had been following hadn't noticed the puffs of warm air filtering up from behind the Lincoln.

"You know what the worst thing is?" the male voice asked.

"What's that?"

"*He's* the one who's dirty; he's the one who bailed his son out of all his problems as a teenager, paid off the cops, reporters, and god knows who else. And yet he's painting *me* as a criminal. If it wasn't so damaging, it would be damn comical."

Drake heard the sound of a car door opening. Taking one deep breath, he raised his head just enough to peer through the Navigator's windows at the two people who were speaking.

One was Dr. Gary Kildare, of course, but the other was a pretty woman he didn't recognize.

"Yeah, but you can't go after Ken, at least not directly. If you do, you might as well just forget about winning the election," the woman said, her bright red lips turning downward into a frown. "After what happened with Thomas..."

Dr. Kildare nodded.

"Yeah, I know. And I feel bad about what happened to his son," he paused. "I know that this is going to sound terrible, but I can't help but think that Thomas's death was the best thing that happened to Ken's election hopes. Seriously."

The woman's frown deepened.

"You're right, it does sound terrible."

Dr. Kildare sighed heavily, then rubbed at his temples with a gloved hand.

"I know; I'm sorry. It's been a long week is all," a weak smile crossed his face, which made him look much older than he did on the large election posters that covered the windows of the building that they had just exited. "Thank you, Mary. Thanks for everything."

Then something happened that made Drake's eyebrows lift, something that convinced him that hanging outside in the freezing cold for the better part of an hour wasn't a complete waste of time.

Dr. Kildare leaned in and kissed the woman, who Drake was now fairly certain was his campaign manager, on the lips.

Only this wasn't one of those European-style exchanges between close friends.

This one lingered.

When they eventually pulled apart, Dr. Kildare wiped his mouth and then his eyes darted around.

Drake dropped a split-second before the man's gaze fell on the Navigator.

*Shit, that was close.*

"See you tomorrow?" Dr. Kildare asked.

"Of course."

"You're sure that we can't meet later tonight?"

There was an inaudible exchange that Drake didn't pick up.

"Alright, tomorrow then," Dr. Kildare said, a hint of solemnity on his tongue. "Goodnight, Mary."

"'Night, Brent."

A car door closed, and then the sound of an engine starting filled the winter air.

Drake finally allowed himself to exhale, and then slumped against the Navigator's wheel well. His relief, however, was short-lived; the sound of footsteps approaching in the freshly fallen snow incited panic.

*What the hell?*

It dawned on him that he had only heard one door close, and then the obvious fact that the doctor and campaign manager had said goodbye *outside* the car came to the fore.

Drake had expected that they would leave together, which was obviously not the case.

*Jesus Christ, I really am getting sloppy. Sloppy and slow.*

The real problem was that there was only one other car in the lot beside Dr. Kildare's Mercedes.

And that car was a black Lincoln Navigator.

Drake swallowed hard and focused on the sound of the footsteps. He was huddled by the rear driver side door, and when he confirmed that Mary was making her way around the front of the car, he slid around the back of the vehicle, staying crouched and out of sight. The sound of a key fob chimed, and then the driver's door opened. Mary stepped inside, knocked the snow from her boots, then slammed it closed

Drake glanced around, desperately trying to find a way out of the situation. He considered running, but there were no other cars in the lot that he could hide behind. And in his black coat, there was no question that he would be spotted in the snow.

*Does it matter? I can hide my face; she'll never know who I am.*

Drake shook his head.

It *did* matter; it mattered because Mary would tell Dr. Kildare, and they would know that Ken was spying on them.

And that would make them cautious, and Drake couldn't afford that. He needed them to be loose, to be free-speaking, in order to get what Ken wanted.

There was only one other thing he could think of to do.

Drake waited for the engine to roar to life, and then when the brake lights came on, he quickly swung around to the passenger side of the vehicle. With a hand on the bumper to gauge the car's speed, he moved with it as Mary backed out of the parking spot. He stared at the side mirror, and realized that he couldn't make out her face; it was bent in such a way that he could only see that Navigator logo embroidered on the passenger seat headrest.

Drake was reminded of the signs that he occasionally saw plastered to the back of transport trucks.

*If you can't see me, I can't see you.*

He wondered if that were true, but then had to focus when Mary put the car into drive.

To make things worse, Dr. Kildare's campaign manager had a lead foot, it appeared.

The car shot forward, and Drake had to jog to keep up with it, which was no small feat considering that he had to remain crouched the entire time.

He slid in behind the vehicle, his thighs burning, the inside of his legs chaffing. Just when he thought he was going to collapse with exhaustion, the car neared the entrance to the parking lot. And there, parked at the side of the road coated with a fresh layer of snow, he spotted his car. As Mary passed his Crown Vic, Drake leaped and landed on the road, barely missing the bullet-ridden hood of his ride.

The air was forced from his lungs, and he gasped, but remained completely still. The snow had looked much more comfortable, more cushioning, than it actually was.

After a moment, he turned his head and peered beneath his car. Breathing heavily, his heart pounding in his chest, he watched as the Navigator turned left and sped into the night.

When he was confident that Mary was gone, Drake started to laugh.

*This is ridiculous. Absolutely fucking ridiculous.*

But as insane as it might be, he finally got something on Dr. Kildare. After all, everyone knew that the good doctor's wife's name was Julia, not Mary.

# Chapter 2

"CAN YOU PLEASE STATE your name and position for the record?"

Chase Adams glanced around briefly before answering. She was sitting on a chair across from two sets of desks: the first was occupied by three men, who had introduced themselves as Officers Herd and Lincoln from internal affairs and Assistant Deputy Inspector Roger Albright. All of the men had matching expressions on their faces as if they had been photoshopped using the same parent image: hard, unforgiving, and unsympathetic.

Dr. Beckett Campbell sat on his own behind the second desk. The man had dark circles around his eyes, which appeared sunken, and his bleach-blond hair was flat against his skull. He was wearing a plain navy suit, which seemed wholly out of place on the man that Chase had come to call her friend.

Beckett's eyes were downcast and when he reached for the glass of water on the desk, she noticed that his hand was trembling slightly.

Chase fixed her gaze on Roger Albright.

"Chase Adams, Sergeant of the 62nd precinct of the NYPD," she said calmly.

"Thank you," Officer Herd replied. "Now, can you please recount the events leading up to your appearance at the derelict domicile that once belonged to the now deceased Dr. Tracey Moorfield."

Chase felt her lips twist into a sneer.

*Derelict domicile? They really brought out the thesaurus for this one...*

"Sure," Chase began, then proceeded to tell them the same story that she had been recounting since this investigation had begun: that she had been off-duty at the time, serving a suspension that had since been rescinded after Sergeant Rhodes himself had been suspended. She reported that she had been at Triple D Investigations, helping out a friend, when a call had come in from Damien and Beckett, asking her to look up news reports about Dr. Moorfield's past. She left out the part regarding Officer Dunbar's involvement, just as they had planned.

Officer Herd nodded when she was done.

"And when you arrived, were you the first person on the scene?"

Chase shook her head.

"No, there were several officers already present, including fire and EMT. I also saw one of my colleagues, Detective Henry Yasiv, on scene."

Officer Herd waited for her to continue, but Chase bit her tongue. She had answered the question, and that was all that was required of her. One of the few things that her father, a litigator, had impressed on her many years ago was that when people started running their mouths, offering information that wasn't requested, they got themselves, and others, in trouble.

And that wasn't a can of worms that she intended to open. Not when her friend's career, and perhaps even his freedom, was on the line.

"Sergeant Adams? Is there anything else that you would like to add?"

Chase shook her head.

"No. Have I not answered your question?"

Roger Albright leaned over and whispered something into Herd's ear. The officer nodded, then turned back to her.

"This isn't a trial, Sergeant Adams. This is simply an inquest to determine probable cause, and to help us figure out the next course of action."

Chase nodded and, again, Herd waited.

Eventually, the officer sighed, and Chase repeated, a little more sternly this time, "Have I not answered your question?"

It was Roger who answered, which surprised her given that she thought it impossible that with his lips pressed as tightly together as they were that the man could actually speak.

"You have, Sergeant Adams. Please tell us what happened *after* you arrived at the scene, leading up to your encounter with Dr. Campbell."

A terrifying image of Beckett stepping out of the shadows, his hands dripping with blood came to mind, and she shuddered.

"I inquired about my ex-partner, Damien Drake, and then about Suzan Cuthbert."

"Who did you inquire to?"

"Detective Yasiv. He said that both were okay and that both were going to make it."

Herd scribbled something on a pad in front of him, then picked up the line of questioning from Roger Albright.

"Did you ask about Craig Sloan? Did Detective Yasiv mention his name?"

Chase shook her head.

"No; I was just happy that my people were going to survive. That was what mattered most."

"And what did you do next?"

"I was distraught, and because I was suspended at the time, I went down the side of one of the houses to collect myself."

Roger Albright leaned forward.

"Please tell us what happened next."

Chase breathed deeply.

*As we rehearsed,* she reminded herself. *Just as we rehearsed.*

"The first thing I saw was Craig Sloan's body, although at the time I didn't know it was him—I had never even seen a photo of the man before. He was lying on his back, and he didn't appear to be moving or breathing. There was a pistol at his side. Then I noticed Dr. Campbell in the shadows. He was… he was visibly upset."

The three men discussed this amongst themselves for several seconds.

"In your initial report, you stated that you saw blood on Dr. Campbell's hands. Is this accurate?"

Chase indicated that it was, and Roger nodded.

"Did you notice anything that might have been used to strike Craig Sloan?"

Chase didn't hesitate.

"There was a rock near his body, which was also stained with blood."

"Thank you. Now, let's get back to the gun for a moment. You said it was near the body; approximately how far was it from Craig Sloan?"

"It was several feet from his hand," she replied instantly.

Again, a short discussion.

"Thank you for your cooperation, Sergeant Adams. You are dismissed."

Chase blinked, thinking for a second that she had misheard.

"Excuse me?"

"You are dismissed," Roger Albright repeated.

Chase simply stared.

*No, this isn't right. I'm supposed to talk about Craig Sloan, about the seven people that he murdered, about how Beckett's insight led to us identifying him as the killer.*

Her father's warning went out the window.

"Craig Sloan... he murdered... there were —" she stammered.

"That will be all, Sergeant Adams," Roger repeated.

"But — but —"

Roger's face twisted into a scowl.

"Sergeant Adams, I want to remind you that while this is not a trial, anything you say here today may be used at a future date. Now, please, as head of this inquest, I would like to ask you again to please step down."

Chase glanced around nervously, her eyes darting first to the three officers, then to Beckett, who didn't seem to realize what was going on.

She swallowed hard and debated saying something else, but eventually decided against it.

As she stood and walked toward the door, she tried to subtly get Beckett's attention, to implore with only her eyes that he should stick to the script.

But Beckett didn't even look up. Instead, he reached for his water, his hand shaking so badly now that it was dangerously close to spilling.

*Stick to what I wrote in the note, Beckett. Stick to the note, or we're all going to go down for this.*

# Chapter 3

"YOU ALRIGHT, HON? YOU look tired."

Colin Elliot lowered his spoon into the bowl of cereal and then proceeded to rub his eyes.

"Was up late last night writing, then went for a run," he groaned as he stretched his calves. "Might have pushed things just a little too hard."

Ryanne walked over to her husband and laid a hand on his shoulder. He leaned into her, resting his head on her hip.

"You've been pushing too hard, Colin. You're going to burn out."

Colin pulled away and looked up at his wife. Her face was round, and while it wasn't entirely unpleasant, it wasn't exactly pretty, either. Her lips were on the flat side and her nose was a little too thin. She had dark circles around her eyes, a matching raccoon set to his own, but this wasn't what caught him off guard.

It was her smile. It wasn't a patronizing grin, but a genuine expression of gratitude or maybe—*maybe*—even affection. He could hardly believe that this was the same woman who had screamed at him the other night, screamed so long and loud that the police had come to the door to make sure that everything was alright.

Colin swallowed hard and tried to put the image of her face, beat red, her mouth twisted in a snarl, out of his mind.

"Had to finish the book," he said quietly. "Need to get it out quickly."

Something flashed across Ryanne's face, something unpleasant, and her hand slipped off his back. She looked as if she were going to say something, but before she had a chance, laughter suddenly filled the kitchen.

"Juliette, have you eaten breakfast yet? We have to leave soon," Colin said with a half-hearted smile.

Juliette bounded into the kitchen, her long blond ponytail swinging side-to-side.

"Nope. Colby took it," she replied, twisting her shoulders as she spoke.

Colin shook his head and turned to his other daughter, who followed Juliette into the room.

"Is this true, Colby?"

"Colby took it," the girl repeated, imitating her sister.

Colin turned to Ryanne, but she had already made her way to the sink, taking his half-finished bowl of cereal with her.

*And Ryanne took mine.*

"Come on, guys. No fighting this morning, okay? Daddy's tired. Just finish your breakfast and then put your shoes and jackets on."

Juliette looked at him as if he had two heads.

"I told you already, I didn't get a chance to eat it. She took it."

Colin turned to Colby who, unlike her sister, had her hair tied on the top of her head in a bun. With a sigh, he said, "Did you, Colby? Did you take Juliette's breakfast?"

Colby shrugged.

"So what if I did? I'm the older sister, and if I want another bowl of cereal, I can have one. If we weren't so poor, then maybe we could all have two bowls of cereal. Carla Banks gets to have as much cereal as she wants, you know."

Colin's eyes bulged.

*How does a seven-year-old get so much sass?*

"You're only six minutes older than me!" Juliette cried, missing the point entirely. "Six minutes!"

"That's enough," Ryanne snapped, as she leaned over the sink, her back to them. "Get your shoes on, and if you keep bickering, then nobody is going to get dinner tonight."

And there it was: the anger from the night before creeping back into her voice.

*She's getting worse,* Colin thought. *It used to only be me she yelled at, but now she's getting short with the kids as well.*

Colby pursed her lips and pushed her chin into the air.

"I'm still older. Six minutes, six hours, what does it matter? I'm the *big* sister."

Colin sighed and rubbed his sore calves.

"That's enough!" Ryanne bellowed. She slammed her hands on the side of the sink and spun around. *"That's enough!"*

Colin cringed, thinking about the neighbors, hoping that they were already at work.

*What had the police officer said? If we come back, we're going to have to keep you separated for the night. Maybe even bring child services in.*

"Please, Ryanne, it's fine. I'll take them to school today."

Ryanne's eyes blazed into him, a scowl forming on her lips. Colin quickly stood and put his arms around his girls and guided them toward the front door before his wife could get her hooks in.

"C'mon girls, put your shoes and coats on quickly, okay? We're going to be late for school."

Both Colby and Juliette looked at him for a moment and he saw something in his eyes that broke his heart.

*Fear,* he thought with a pang of guilt, *they're afraid of her.*

There was something else in their juvenile expressions, too, something that he hadn't seen before.

*Was it anger? No, that wasn't quite right. Disdain, maybe?*

"Please, girls. Hurry."

Without argument, the girls went to the entrance and started to get ready for the cold. Colin followed and slid his own boots on. He turned back to say goodbye and was surprised to see Ryanne standing only a few feet from him, hands on her hips.

"I'm going out today," she informed him. "Don't expect me home until later,"

Colin nodded.

"That's fine. I have writer's group this afternoon, anyway. But do you think you can pick the girls up from school?"

Ryanne's scowl deepened, and he knew exactly what she was thinking because she had made it explicitly clear the other night.

*Must I do everything around here? Can't you get a real fucking job? Or how about you write a fucking book that people actually want to read?*

Colin swallowed hard as he waited for the backlash. But while Ryanne's eyes narrowed to slits, she exercised what was for her unprecedented control, and he turned back to the girls.

"Say bye to mommy," he said softly. "Give her a kiss then let's get moving. The bus is leaving."

# Chapter 4

BECKETT FELT LIKE HE was dreaming. In fact, everything that had happened since the night Dr. Moorfield's burnt colonial had been set ablaze for a second time felt like a horrible nightmare.

Every morning he awoke asking himself the same question: *Did I do that? Did I really do that?*

Everything pointed to the fact that he had: the newspaper reports—although they had thankfully kept his name out of it—this very inquiry, and, worst of all, the memories.

In his mind, he heard the sickening thud of the rock colliding with Craig Sloan's skull, he could feel warm blood first on his hands then coating his wrists, and he could see the man's eyes roll back in his head.

After spending more than a decade surrounded by dead men, Craig was the first he had personally been responsible for.

But there was something underlying all of these sensations that was even more alarming.

Something that truly terrified him.

"Please state your name and position for the record," Officer Herd instructed.

Beckett leaned forward and cleared his throat before answering.

"My name is Dr. Beckett Campbell. I am the Senior Medical Examiner for the NYPD, and I'm also an associate professor of Medicine and Pathology at NYU."

"Thank you, Dr. Campbell. As you overheard me say to Sergeant Adams, this is not a trial, but an inquiry. That being said, please acknowledge that you have waived your rights to having someone from the Royal College of Surgeons or from the American Medical Association to accompany you today."

"I have."

"Good. Then we shall continue. Please, in your own words, tell us what happened on the date in question."

Beckett closed his eyes and scratched his forehead.

"I was with a close-friend—ex-NYPD Detective Damien Drake—and we were looking for the daughter of a fallen police officer whom we believed had been kidnapped by a man who had killed six people over the course of two weeks. I was outside in Drake's car while he was inside a—" *tread carefully, Beckett,* "—a condo building in downtown Manhattan. When he came out, he had identified the kidnapper and murderer. We called Sergeant—"

"Slow down, Beckett," Roger Albright interrupted. "You say you were at a condo in Manhattan. Can you be more specific?"

Beckett shook his head.

"No. It was dark, and I was running on very little sleep."

Roger's frown deepened.

"And did Damien Drake say who he was meeting? Who he had acquired the name of the alleged kidnapper from?"

Again, Beckett shook his head.

"He never told me. Perhaps you should ask him."

"Damien Drake is unavailable for this inquest. Please continue with what happened after you left the condo."

"I called Sergeant Adams with the name and she referred me to a house that Craig Sloan had burned down once before—when Dr. Moorfield used to live there. We believed that this was where he was keeping Suzan Cuthbert. When we arrived, the place was already on fire. As Drake tried to gain entry, he had an altercation with Craig Sloan by the side of the house. Craig was knocked unconscious, and Drake went into the house to see if Suzan was inside. He instructed me to put Craig in the car and to wait for the police to arrive."

"He told you to put Craig in the car? Where in the car?"

Beckett hesitated.

"In the trunk. Drake was driving a civilian vehicle that didn't have a cage between the front and rear seats. He also didn't have a set of handcuffs."

Roger nodded.

"Continue."

"So I put him in the trunk and then started toward the house to see if I could help Drake."

"Did you ever actually go into the house, Dr. Campbell?"

"No. I was going to enter the house, but I never got there. I heard shots fired from inside the trunk."

Officer Herd rubbed his temples before commenting.

"And you… ran? You ran away from the man as he came out from the trunk? I mean, he was, in your words, a murderer and he had a gun."

Beckett thought back to that moment, the fire at his back, the flickering yellow and orange hues illuminating Craig's snarl. The man had one leg out of the trunk when Beckett had picked up the rock.

"No, I didn't run."

"Why not?"

"Because he had a gun, and I thought he was going to take Drake out when he came out of the house. Suzan, too, if she was still alive."

"What did you do next?"

"I grabbed a rock and struck Craig in the side of the head. I think he was disoriented or maybe deafened by the sound of the gunshots inside the trunk, because he never saw me coming."

"How many times did you strike Craig Sloan? Once? Twice? Multiple times?" Roger asked.

Beckett re-read Chase's letter that Screech had handed him back in the hospital in his mind.

"More than once, but I can't tell you how many. No more than three or four, I think. I was just trying to knock him out, but he wouldn't go down; he kept trying to turn the gun on me."

Roger made an *uh-huh* sound. Then he opened a folder on the desk and took out a sheet of paper. He handed it to Officer Lincoln and told him to bring it over to Beckett, which he did.

"Are you familiar with this report?"

Beckett scanned the page quickly.

"Yes. This is the pathology report concerning Craig Sloan's death."

"And do you recognize the ME who prepared the report?"

"Yes, of course. Dr. Henrik Karl."

"And in your professional opinion, is Dr. Karl a qualified ME? A competent doctor?"

"Yes, of course; I trained him myself."

"Very well," Roger continued. "Can you please read the official cause of death out loud?"

Beckett found the line.

"Craig Sloan died as a result of multiple blows to the skull with a hard, smooth object. He—"

Roger held up a hand.

"That's good enough. I'll ask you again, how many times did you strike Craig Sloan with the rock?"

Beckett shrugged.

"Like I said, more than once, but I'm not sure exactly how many."

"And is that congruent with the pathology report?"

Beckett didn't need to read the line again. He knew exactly what it said, in part because he had helped Dr. Karl draft it.

"Yes—multiple in this context means more than one, but the ME could not determine the exact number of strikes."

Roger Albright locked eyes with him for what seemed like an eternity, before speaking again.

"Thank you for your cooperation, Dr. Campbell. My colleagues and I will now hold a brief, private discussion."

With that, Roger turned to Officers Herd and Lincoln. The abruptness with which the questioning had come to an end surprised Beckett, and it took a few moments for his heart rate to settle.

The three men spoke in hushed voices, voices too low for him to hear, and Beckett resisted the urge to try and lipread. It was clear to him now that Roger and his IA posse had come to a conclusion even before this entire charade.

Like Chase had said, if they all stuck to their story, then there was nothing that they *could* do.

"My colleagues and I have decided that we are going to close this case. Craig Sloan murdered seven people, and we have no doubt that without your intervention he would have continued to kill. Although your actions were... how can I put this... *unorthodox*, they do not, in our opinion, constitute either a criminal or negligent act on your part."

Beckett felt a massive weight roll off his shoulders, and he took a deep breath for the first time in what seemed like forever.

*Chase was right... just stick to the script.*

"However, that being said, we recommend that you take some time off, Dr. Campbell. You have been through an incredibly emotional and taxing ordeal, and we believe that it's in everyone's best interest for you to spend several weeks away from the NYPD, NYU, and any other related medical matters. Although we do not wish to tarnish your record by making this a formal request, I strongly suggest that you take our advice and heed our *recommendation*."

Roger Albright adjusted his glasses before continuing. "Speaking plainly, Beckett, I think it's time you took a vacation. A nice, long vacation in the sun. Get your mind off things, come back refreshed."

Beckett glanced around nervously, not quite believing that this was finally over.

"Am I free to go?"

"You are indeed free to leave."

Beckett shot to his feet, holding his hands out to his sides.

"Fuckin' A. Then I'm out of here."

He was halfway to the door, when Roger's voice made him turn back.

"Off the record, Dr. Campbell, were you aware that Craig Sloan's pistol was empty when he climbed from the trunk?"

In his mind, Beckett pictured the five holes in the trunk, and the one that had destroyed the lock.

"I had no idea," he lied, and then left the room.

\*\*\*

Chase was standing in the hallway, chewing her lip when Beckett skipped out of the briefing room. For a split-second he considered messing with her, telling her that he was going to prison, but seeing the concern on her face, he decided against it.

"They said I can go," he said, eyes downcast.

Chase lunged at him and wrapped her arms around his back and shoulders.

"I told you everything would work out," she whispered in his ear. "I told you."

Beckett nodded and gently peeled her off him.

"What are you going to do now?" Chase asked when they were separated.

Beckett shrugged.

"Roger and his goons suggested I take a vacation, so I might just do that."

Chase smirked.

"You lying on a beach? I don't see it."

"Me neither, but I guess this is the new me."

He had meant the comment to be a joke, but there was something unintentionally profound about the comment that made him uncomfortable.

"Anywhere in particular?"

"I have a friend with connections to a very exclusive island in the Virgin Gorda—St. Thomas area. He's always asking me to come visit, so I think it's about time to take him up on that offer."

Chase's smile grew.

"Excellent. I—"

Her phone buzzed and she took it off her hip and stared at the call display.

The smile slid off her face.

"I've got to take this," she said, her eyes still locked on the phone.

"Chase?" Beckett said softly.

"Yeah?"

Beckett opened his mouth to speak, but sensing that she was preoccupied, instead of the words he had initially intended, he simply said, "Thank you."

Chase offered him a tired smile.

"Take a break, Beckett. You'll be fine."

With that, Chase answered her phone and turned, making her way slowly down the hallway as she barked into the mouthpiece.

Beckett watched her go.

Chase was wrong, of course; he wouldn't be fine. In fact, he doubted he would ever be *fine* again. After all, Craig Sloan had changed him.

Beckett had said *thank you*, but what he really wanted to say was, *Craig got what he deserved. I killed him because he was going to kill again. He wasn't going to just hang it up after he completed the pathology exam—the test was only the beginning. I stopped him the only way I knew how: by killing him, by smashing his head in with the rock until it was covered in his brains and blood and bits of skull. And Chase? I liked it.*

It was this last part that scared Beckett most of all.

*I liked it, Chase, and I'm afraid that I'll do it again someday.*

# Chapter 5

DRAKE RETURNED TO TRIPLE D feeling as if he had just run a marathon.

Not that he had any experience with marathons.

"Fuck I'm tired," he muttered to himself as he pulled the front door wide. He stomped his feet on the mat, a strange, beige thing with the words 'Jump to Conclusions' on it that Screech had purchased, then shook the cold from his body like a dog drying its fur.

"Hey, Beethoven, you alright over there?" a voice asked from the darkness.

Drake peered into the dim office, trying to locate the owner of the voice. When he didn't immediately see anyone, he flicked on the lights

Nothing happened.

"Screech? That you?"

The man leaned out from behind a computer monitor, allowing some of the glow to illuminate his face. Screech had grown his hair out, particularly on the sides where it used to be shaved, and he had gotten rid of the peach-fuzz goatee. Drake couldn't decide if his partner looked older or younger with these changes... just *different*.

Almost mature, partway to being an adult.

"Who'd you think?"

Drake ignored the question and turned his gaze skyward.

"What's wrong with the lights? And why is your computer still working if the power's out?"

Screech's face moved back to the screen and out of view.

"It's a laptop, Gramps. And the lights are out because our office is one step up from a trap house."

Drake frowned and took off his coat, placing it on the coat hanger beside the door.

"Or maybe you forgot to pay the lighting company," he grumbled.

But he knew that Screech was speaking the truth. In fact, so many of the frosted letters on the door had fallen off that instead of reading *Triple D Investigations*, it now read: *ri p e  n est ga  s.*

*Ripe nest gas.*

He was sure that Screech might have had something to do with the exact wording, but that didn't change the fact that the place was old, dirty, and smelled like a high school locker room.

And yet Drake was reluctant to move. After Screech had rescued Mrs. Armatridge from… well, herself, their financial issues had suddenly become an issue of the past. But he liked it here. It was like home. Screech could call it a trap house, could call it whatever he wanted, but to Drake, it was an old, worn recliner.

And he liked it that way.

"It'll come back on in a minute or two," Screech said absently. "It's been doing this all day. Speaking of which, I've been holding down the fort while you've been…?"

Drake started toward his office when the lights flickered then came on.

He turned his gaze upward, squinted and then nodded.

"And they're back."

As he passed Screech, the man swiveled in his chair, a worn pen deep in the corner of his mouth.

"Hey? Where you been?"

"Out running errands," Drake replied, trying to end the conversation.

Screech grunted and turned back to his computer.

Drake wasn't sure how much Screech had figured out about his new "arrangement" with Ken Smith, but if his partner had proven anything with the Craig Sloan case, it was that he was more than just resourceful; Screech was smart and had a surprising knack for detective work.

Which Drake would never tell him, of course.

"Anything come in that isn't Mrs. Armatridge related?"

Screech swirled around on his chair and hammered a few keys.

"Yeah; this one guy lost his boat. Wants to know if we can help him find it."

Drake chuckled and continued toward his office.

"No, I'm serious. Buddy lost his boat, needs our help... should we take the case?"

Drake turned and was surprised to see Screech staring back, no hint of a smile on his face.

Apparently, he *was* serious.

"Really? How the hell do you lose a boat?"

"Here, check it out."

Drake walked over to Screech's computer and crouched down to get a better look at the screen.

"A boat? That's not a boat, Screech. That's a yacht."

Screech shrugged.

"Whatever. You say *potahto* I say *patayta*. Forty-feet long, looks like. There was a name here somewhere... ah, there it is: *B-Yacht'ch.*"

Screech chuckled and turned to Drake.

Drake just shrugged.

"Seriously? *B-Yacht'ch*? Like *biotch*? Anyyyyways, the owner, Bob Bumacher wants to meet. Should we?"

Drake observed his partner closely, hoping that he was pulling his leg. Sure, Screech was resourceful, but Drake was starting to reconsider if he was actually as bright as he had first thought.

"Screech," he said at last. "It's a six-hundred-thousand-dollar yacht. Of course we want to meet. Mrs. Armatridge is grateful that you stopped her from Lorena Bobbitting her husband, but her gratitude won't last forever."

Screech blinked long and slow.

"Lorena Bobbitt? Was that a joke, Drake? Did you just... oh my god, you did! You just made a funny!"

Drake flipped him the bird.

"Set it up, Screech."

"Alright boss, will do."

Drake had just opened his office door when Screech hollered after him.

"Oh, almost forgot: a package came for you today. Left it on your desk."

Drake flicked the lights on in his office and was relieved when the lone bulb bled yellow light on the plain package sitting in the center of his desk.

"Any idea who it's from?"

"Nope. No stamp on it either. Must have been hand delivered."

Drake's eyes narrowed as he made his way to his desk. He plopped down in his chair and then picked up the package.

Inside he felt something hard and thin, roughly eight-inches long and five inches wide. With a shrug, he opened the package and pulled out what, to him, looked like a miniature laptop sans keyboard.

He flipped the device over and read the words on the back out loud.

*"E-reader: all your books in one place."*

He turned it over in his hands, trying to find some way to turn the damn thing on.

"What the hell is this?" he grumbled.

When he failed to find a single toggle or switch, he had no choice but to shout.

"Screech come give me a hand with this, would you?"

# Chapter 6

CHASE STEPPED OUT OF her car and immediately looked around. They were an hour from Manhattan, in a rural area that she had never visited before. Her GPS told her it was technically Larchmont Village, but that was the extent of her knowledge, other than the fact that it had been at least fifteen minutes since they had passed a gas station.

Pillowy snow covered the ground in all directions, as high as a foot in some places, Chase surmised. There didn't appear to be any fresh car tracks that couldn't be accounted for by the police vehicles, or any discernible footprints on the road, which indicated that the killer had either walked here or had arrived prior to the most recent snowfall.

She spotted Detective Yasiv by the side of the road, leaning against his car. When he saw her coming, he immediately straightened, moving so quickly that he spilled some of the coffee from a Styrofoam cup on his gloves.

He pretended not to notice as she approached.

"What do we have?" Chase asked, striding forward.

"One dead female, twenty to thirty years of age. Still waiting on an ID. The ME hasn't arrived yet."

Chase frowned, knowing that her friend wouldn't be the ME on duty.

"Where's the body?"

Detective Yasiv pointed to a barn with a partially collapsed roof about forty yards from the road.

"In there. Tucked beneath some hay."

Chase nodded and looked around again. The only tracks leading from the road to the barn were in a neat line that made a wide arc to the latter.

These belonged to the detectives and uniforms, she knew.

Chase moved toward these footsteps and started along their path as Yasiv fell into step beside her.

"Who owns the barn?" she asked as she made her way down the small embankment to what she suspected was a cornfield during the warmer months.

"A, uh, a Mr. Francis Dolan. Detective Simmons has gone to speak to him, but over the phone, he claimed he abandoned it many years ago. He's in his late eighties."

Up close, the barn was in better shape than it appeared from the road. Only a few of the boards were missing on one side, and the part of the roof that had collapsed had done so in a way that maintained the integrity of the structure.

A man in his late eighties would have a hard time carrying a body down from the road, let alone doing so without leaving any tracks.

*And walking forty yards in the heavy snow… in this weather…*

Chase was already starting to rule out the old man as a suspect.

"Sergeant Adams," Detective Yasiv introduced her to the two uniforms standing in front of the barn entrance.

"Gentlemen," Chase said with a nod. They stepped aside and allowed her to enter.

If Francis Dolan had abandoned this place years ago, as he had told Detective Simmons, then it had remained in pretty good shape over that time.

The interior appeared to have been a horse barn before it fell into disuse, divided evenly into eight stalls, four on either side. Chase's eyes went to the floor next, noting that unlike just outside the door, it was fairly dry and covered with a thick layer of hay.

"The body is in the second stall," Yasiv said. Chase followed his finger.

Yasiv was indicating the second on the left.

As Chase made her way over to the stall, she kept her eyes on the ground, trying to identify any recent tracks, broken hay, trace evidence of any sort.

Nothing seemed out of place.

With a deep breath, Chase turned the corner and peered into the stall.

The victim was in a seated position, her legs splayed out in front of her, her back propped up against the back wall. Her hands were at her sides, palms up. Hay covered her midsection and thighs haphazardly like some sort of rough blanket.

Stiff black hair hung in front of her face, obscuring her features.

Chase strode forward.

"The body was moved here after death," Detective Yasiv said quietly.

Chase nodded. She knew that already; the woman's wrists were covered in slashes, wounds both old and new, but there was no blood on the hay or the walls.

Careful not to disturb any potential evidence, Chase squatted on her haunches in front of the victim. She pulled a pen from her pocket and used it to move some of the woman's hair from her face.

The woman's eyes were wide, her expression one of sheer terror. But it was the victim's lips that drew, and held, Chase's attention. They were a dirty brown, a smear that extended a sloppy inch from the corners of her mouth.

It didn't look like lipstick to Chase.

It looked like blood.

A quick glance at the wounds on her arms and Chase realized that there was no blood on her skin at all. She had been wiped clean.

Except for her mouth.

Chase suddenly stood and turned to Detective Yasiv.

"Did you check the other stalls?" she asked quickly.

Yasiv's smooth features contorted.

"I just got here a minute before you, I—" Yasiv, his face turning red, spun around and addressed the nearest uniform, "Officer Hewart did you check the other stalls?"

Hewart's mouth twitched.

"Not yet, just trying to warm up first," after noticing the stern expression on Chase's face, he smiled a gap-toothed grin, "but we're plenty warm now. We'll start right away."

Chase, still frowning, watched him go.

"Who found the body?" she asked.

"A drifter. She was looking for a place to stay, to get out of the cold," Yasiv replied.

Chase frowned, remembering how pristine the snow had been from the road to the barn.

"No footprints?"

"I noticed that, too, and I asked her about it; she said she went around the back, through the forest. Had to walk six miles before she found someone with a phone.

Chase's frown deepened. Like the elderly Mr. Dolan, this drifter didn't sound like a suspect, either.

"Did you take her statement?"

Detective Yasiv nodded.

"Yes. Have her at a halfway house closer to the city, with eyes on her. If she starts to move, we'll know."

Chase nodded.

"Good. I don't think—"

*"Jesus Christ!"*

Chase spun away from Detective Yasiv, and bolted toward the corridor that divided the barn.

"What? What is it?" she asked as she hurried toward the voice.

Chase found Officer Hewart in the last horse stall on the right. He looked up at her as she entered, fear in his eyes.

"There's another one here," the man almost whispered. He leaned to one side, giving Chase a clear view of another woman. Only this victim wasn't propped up like the first; this one was almost completely buried in the hay. Most of her face was covered, including her eyes and chin, and yet Chase could see that her mouth was smeared with what she suspected was blood.

For nearly a minute, the three of them stood in silence, observing the dead.

Eventually, Chase pulled out her cell phone and started to dial.

"Who are you calling?" Detective Yasiv asked after the shock of finding a second body wore off.

Chase turned to him.

"An old friend. We're going to need some help with this one."

# Chapter 7

*THE DETECTIVE STARED DOWN at the body, looking into the eyes of the dead girl.*

What did you see right before you died? *The detective wondered.* Whose face was the last that you saw?

*She crouched down and teased some hay away from the woman's face. As she did, she noticed a brown smudge across her lips.*

*Lipstick? Is it lipstick?*

*The detective leaned closer to investigate, but stood bolt upright when a police officer's shouts echoed throughout the barn.*

*"We've got another body over here! Oh god, there's another body!"*

Drake's phone buzzed and he stopped reading.

"Drake here," he said, his eyes still locked on the e-reader that had been delivered to his desk.

*Why the hell did someone send this crap to me?*

The book, *Red Smile*, was the only one on the device. *Preloaded*, Screech had called it.

*Red Smile*, written by someone he had never heard of: L. Wiley.

Lost in thought, he finally realized that the person on the other end of the line hadn't said anything yet.

"Hello?"

When there was still no answer, he pulled it away from his ear and looked at the number.

*UNKNOWN.*

Thinking that it was a telemarketer, he was about to hang up when the person finally spoke.

"Drake?"

Drake forgot all about *Red Smile* and sat up straight.

"Chase, that you?"

"Yeah, listen, I—"

"Heard about your promotion—Sergeant, huh. Who *wouldathunk* it. Congratulations are in order."

"Thanks, Drake. It's been... well, it hasn't been the most exciting of times. I miss being in the field, mostly. Apparently, promotion is just code for 'more paperwork'. But, hey, I don't want to mislead you... this isn't a social call."

Although Drake figured as much, part of him wished that it was.

"Yeah, I thought not. What's up?"

His thoughts turned to Doctor Kildare and his campaign manager Mary, and briefly wondered if they had seen him after all and had reported him to the NYPD. It would be unusual for such a case to travel all the way up to the Sergeant, but he knew that Chase had his back and would give him the head's up if anything with his name attached to it popped up.

But when Chase spoke again, he realized that his suspicions were unfounded.

"You know how I just said I missed the field?"

"Yeah."

"Well I'm back in it, and I've got a new case, something that I think I could use your help with. You have a few hours to spare? Think you can come aboard as a Special Consultant and help an old friend?"

Drake's ears perked.

*Special consultant?*

He wasn't sure if he was more excited about the prospect of being part of an investigation that didn't involve old ladies or missing yachts, or just the fact that he would be reunited with Chase.

"Hell ya," he said with more enthusiasm than he had intended. "What've you got?"

Chase, her voice clearly expressing relief, told him about the two bodies found in a barn on the outskirts of the city.

"Young females, mid-twenties probably. Cuts up and down their arms. Won't know official cause of death for another hour or so. Bodies weren't quite frozen, but it's cold enough in the barn to mess with determining the time of death."

"Is Beckett with you?" Drake asked.

There was an unusually long pause before Chase answered.

"No—he's... he's on vacation."

The reply struck Drake as odd; for as long as he had known Beckett, the man hadn't taken a single vacation. True, he occasionally liked to head up north to Montreal for the nightlife, but these visits were usually only weekend trips.

And it was a Tuesday morning.

"Vacation? Beckett?"

"Long story—I'll clue you in when you get here. Oh, and Drake? One more thing: the girls, well, it looks like they have blood on their lips, like some sort of gruesome lipstick."

Drake nearly dropped his phone.

"*What?*"

"Blood. On their lips. You okay?"

Drake swallowed hard, his eyes darting to the e-reader on his desk.

*Coincidence; just a coincidence.*

Except the last two cases he had worked on—the Butterfly Killer and Craig Sloan—had taught him that coincidences were rarely just that.

"I'm fine," he croaked at last. "I'll see you in an hour. Text me the address"

"Alright, but—"

Drake hung up the phone and stared at the e-reader until his eyes started to lose focus.

*Coincidence?*

With a shake of his head, he managed to finally tear his eyes away from the damn thing. He reached over and pulled open the top drawer of his desk a little too quickly, and the bottle of Johnny Blue knocked loudly against the wood. He watched as the golden liquid swished back and forth inside the glass.

And like the e-reader, this held his attention for an inordinate amount of time.

*Get a grip. Chase needs you.*

Drake reached into the drawer and grabbed the finger bone beside the bottle and jammed it into his pocket.

After closing the drawer, more carefully this time, he made his way out of the office toward Screech at the reception desk.

The man looked up at him as he neared.

"You going already? Short day there, *pardner.*"

Drake ignored the comment.

"I have something I need to do." He tapped the e-reader in his hand, deep in thought. "Try to find out where this thing came from, okay?"

"I'm thinking you don't mean the manufacturer?"

Drake grimaced.

"You sure you weren't a detective before Triple D, too?"

Screech chuckled.

"You're on a roll today, big fella. I'm liking this new you. Like a younger, more wrinkly Roger Dangerfield."

"Just see if you can find out who delivered it."

"No *problemo*," the man answered, putting the worn pen in his mouth again and turning back to his computer.

*Brown smudges... it had to be a coincidence, didn't it?*

# Chapter 8

THE TEACHER PACED AS he spoke, which annoyed Colin
Elliot to no end. That, and the fact that for someone who was
supposed to be teaching them how to write books that sell,
Colin couldn't find *any* evidence that he had actually sold
anything, put him on edge.

In fact, the only information that Colin could dig up on
Professor Dwight Jurgens was that he had published a shitty-
looking novella that was on limited release and a book of trite
poetry.

*At least it didn't cost me anything,* he thought glumly. This
was the eighth or ninth such 'writer's group' that he had
attended over as many weeks and while he always went in
with high expectations, they never failed to let him down.

But that was okay. After all, he had found other means of
inspiration.

"So how many of you have ever published anything?
Anything at all?" Dwight asked the class. He pushed the felt-
green fedora—which also irritated Colin—back from his
forehead as he spoke, revealing a set of beady eyes.

As Dwight glanced around, Colin did the same. There were
seven of them—there had been eight when the class started,
but a young, pale man with scars on his face had left twenty
minutes ago—not that much different than Colin himself:
tired looking, shoulders slumped, all trying to finish a book
with financial and life pressures squeezing the muse out of
them.

*So you want to write a book, huh?*

"Nobody?" Dwight asked, his mouth twisting into a frown.
"Well, I guess I'm in the wrong place then. I thought this was
a writer's group for *writers.*"

And then, as Colin watched, curious if this was a ruse, Dwight swept his books off the table at the front of the room and into his worn backpack. Then he walked toward the door.

Colin wasn't sure why he spoke up—it wasn't like him. Maybe it was the memory of his wife berating him the night before, or just the weight of the past few years bearing down.

Or maybe it was because he was changing. Deep down inside something was broken, and he didn't know if it would ever be fixed.

Either way, he surprised himself by speaking.

"I'm published," he said. Several of the other class members turned to stare at him, and he felt his face go red. "I have three books out."

Dwight threw his hands in the air.

"There's the ticket! We have at least one writer in the room," he walked back to the table and tossed the bag on top. "I'm not really sure what you other people are doing here, but at least we have *one* writer. Tell me…"

"Colin."

"Tell me, Colin. What kind of books have you written? Novels? Novellas? What Genre?"

Colin felt more heat rise in his cheeks, but now that he had started down this road, he had no choice but to continue.

"Novels, all three. Paranormal thrillers, mostly," he shrugged. "They all have romance elements in them, as well."

Dwight made an impressed face.

"Very nice. And?"

Colin looked around nervously.

"And what?"

"What are they called?"

"Called?" Colin asked, confused by the entire line of questioning. Part of the reason he wanted to write books in the first place was so that he could stay behind the computer screen all day.

No need to interact with others.

"Yes," Dwight said and then sighed dramatically. Colin was beginning to think that the man would be better off teaching the art of over-acting rather than writing. "I imagine that your books have titles?"

Colin shook his head.

"No? All three are untitled?"

His cheeks were so hot now that he wouldn't be surprised if they suddenly burst into flames.

"No... what I mean is, I write under a pen name."

"Ah, a *nom de plume*," his eyes suddenly narrowed and he leveled a finger at Colin's chest. "Wait a second, are you *self*-published?"

Sweat broke out on his forehead and he glanced around nervously, feeling the eyes of the other students on him like laser points.

"Y-yes," he admitted.

Dwight's face underwent a series of expressions that looked to Colin like the iterations of a man undergoing a stroke in slow-motion.

"*Self-published?*" Dwight repeated, his face finally settling on something that was a cross between fury and pure, unadulterated disdain.

"Yes," Colin said again, this time with more confidence. "I self-published all three of my books."

Dwight stared at him for a moment, without saying another word. Then he rose to his feet, picked up his bag and made his way toward the door again. This time he didn't turn.

"I was wrong about you guys," he said over his shoulder. "There isn't one writer in the room. There are *none*."

# Chapter 9

DRAKE ADJUSTED HIS HAT, pulled his gloves on tight, and then stepped out of his Crown Vic. He approached a police officer leaning up against the side of his car, a flutter in his stomach. It was strange for him to feel this way, especially given how little he had cared when the entire 62nd precinct wanted him gone following his expose in the Times. Now, however, after what had happened with Craig Sloan, and how he had saved Suzan Cuthbert's life, Drake had heard inklings that tensions and harsh feelings toward him had lessened somewhat.

And yet Drake knew that they would never dissipate completely. So long as Clay Cuthbert remained dead, there would always be some contempt toward him. But that was to be expected.

He felt the same about himself.

*What's with the butterflies, Drake?*

With an unintentional scowl, Drake approached the officer by the car. He was staring at his cell phone, the top of his hat pointed at Drake.

"Hey, Sergeant Adams around?" Drake said as he stomped through the snow.

The man looked up and Drake immediately recognized him, but couldn't recall his name. He was confident that this was one of the officers that Drake had approached during Chase's press conference for the Butterfly Killer—someone who had ignored him completely.

The officer nodded at him.

"Detective Drake," he said crisply. "Good to have you back."

Drake's scowl became a frown.

*Back? I'm not back, and I'm sure as hell not a detective. Not anymore.*

But rather get into this argument, he said, "Just Drake, please. And I'm only here to help."

The man nodded again.

"Sergeant Adams is in the barn," he replied, hooking a thumb over his shoulder.

Drake thanked him, then walked sideways down the embankment from the road to what was a farmer's field of some sort. As he did, he breathed in deeply through his nose, the bite of the frigid air temporarily numbing the anxiety he felt in the pit of his stomach.

And with that, he started to piece together the crime scene in his mind.

*The killer didn't come from the road. He couldn't risk his car being seen even in a place as desolate as this.*

Drake's eyes lifted to the small forested area behind the barn that was cordoned off with yellow police tape.

*There; he came from there—through the forest.*

He made a mental note to ask if there were any car tracks in the forest.

Detective Henry Yasiv stood by the side of the barn, smoking a cigarette, a far-off look his eyes. As he approached, Drake called out to the man.

"Detective Yasiv?"

The young man lifted his eyes, stared at Drake for a moment, and then something strange and unexpected happened.

Detective Yasiv smiled at him, and Drake found himself smiling back. Henry Yasiv was a young detective, in his late twenties, and although he hadn't been around when the

Skeleton King had taken out Clay, the pervasive hatred at the precinct to Drake had extended to him as well.

But Drake didn't hold it against the man; after all, as a new detective, it was hard to make friends, and being kind to Drake would have made that near impossible.

*But Chase… Chase hadn't succumbed to that pressure. Chase had treated me well, given me the benefit of the doubt.*

Drake held his gloved hand out, and Hank shook it excitedly.

That wasn't fair, though; it did no good to compare people to Chase. She wasn't just a different animal, she was like a goddamn alien species.

Detective Yasiv flicked his cigarette into the snow, exhaled a cloud of smoke, and then grabbed Drake by the arm.

"I'll take you inside," he said. "Bring you up to speed."

As they ducked under the tape across the door, Drake said, "I didn't know you smoke."

"I don't. At least not according to my wife."

The inside of the barn smelled musty, an indication that the doors had been closed for a long period of time before their killer arrived.

"I only smoke at the scene, never at…" Detective Yasiv continued, but Drake found his mind drifting elsewhere.

The barn felt very much like the one described in the book *Red Smile*, and his heart did a strange flutter in his chest.

*Not now. Don't bias yourself. Just take in the facts.*

But instead of focusing on the scene, his eyes landed on Chase as she spoke to a man Drake didn't recognize, her back to him.

For some reason, the sight of his ex-partner caused his heart to skip another beat. Drake subconsciously reached up and touched the area below his left ear, the spot that was a still discolored and rough from where the fire had scarred him.

The last time they had spoken was in his hospital room when she had brought his clothes and had begged him to stay.

He swallowed, feeling a lump in his throat that refused to go down.

"Chase? Or do I just call you boss again?" he said, trying to keep things light.

Chase turned her head, her dark brown hair moving with her. Their eyes met, and then her pretty mouth broke into a smile. He was holding his hand out to her, but she ignored it. Instead, she embraced him tightly, and he hesitated.

It was unprofessional, sure, but what profession was he representing? Triple D? He wasn't on the NYPD payroll anymore—hadn't been in some time, actually.

He hugged her back.

"So glad that you can give us a hand," Chase said as they disengaged.

Drake nodded.

"Just here to help."

He raised his eyes to the man who Chase had been speaking with when he had stepped into the barn.

"FBI Agent Jeremy Stitts," Chase said, "meet Special Consultant, Damien Drake. Shake hands, hug it out, then let's get to work."

Drake smirked and leaned forward to shake the man's hand.

*Special Consultant? I sound like a goddamn henchman.*

And given the work he was doing for Ken Smith, henchman almost seemed like a more appropriate description.

# Chapter 10

THE WRITER'S CIRCLE—CAPITALIZED, likely by Dwight himself—was silent for a good three minutes after the professor stormed out.

A woman with short red hair eventually followed, but the other five students, six including Colin himself, just sat there.

Colin debated packing up and leaving as well, but he wasn't sure where he would go. He didn't want to go home just in case Ryanne was still there, and he had a lot of time to kill before picking up his girls.

*I can just sit here and write*, he thought, and was about to pull out his laptop when the woman next to him turned and addressed him.

"What are your books called, anyway?" she asked. It was an innocuous enough question, but because the room was completely silent, all eyes were once again on him.

Colin was sick and tired of blushing, but it wasn't something that he could control.

"They're part of a series, I've just—"

"You just put 'em up online? That's it?" a rough looking man in his mid-forties hollered across the room. Colin turned to face him.

"Yeah, I mean I had them edited, then I just—"

"Why don't you stand up and tell us?" the first woman, whose face was punctuated by multiple piercings, asked. She had a sparkle in her dark brown eyes and was indicating the front of the class with her chin.

Colin was confused at first, but quickly realized that she wanted *him* to teach.

He shook his head.

"Oh, no. I can't—I came here to learn. I mean, I—I just put the books up there, they don't really sell that well. I haven't sold—"

"If you're gonna keep on talking, do it up there!" another member of the group interrupted.

Colin felt claustrophobia begin to sink in.

"I can't I—"

The woman with the piercings and black hair that was shaved at the sides leaned in close.

"Don't be a fucking pussy. Go stand at the front of the class."

Colin wasn't sure if it was the curse that made him stand, or if it was because the woman was ordering him around like Ryanne. Whatever the reason, he stood and before he truly realized what was happening, he was at the front of the class, staring at the five other students.

He bowed his head and took a deep breath. Blowing the air out slowly, Colin raised his eyes and looked at each of the students individually before speaking.

"If there is only one thing I've learned about writing, it's that you need write about what you know. You need to experience things in order to write about them. That is probably the only universal truth to literature."

# Chapter 11

DRAKE LEANED DOWN TO get a better look. The woman's arms were a mess, slashed so deeply in some spots that he could see gleaming bone peeking through. But the most disturbing aspect was that some of the wounds were old enough to have started to heal.

*This wasn't a crime of passion. This was deliberate. This was torture.*

And that said nothing of the dark smear on her lips.

"This likely wasn't his first kill," Drake said quietly. He hadn't meant to say the words out loud, but when he did, they shocked him a little. He glanced up, and his gaze fell on Agent Stitts. The man was older than Drake, the crow's feet at the corners of his eyes suggested as much, but by how many years, he couldn't tell. Whereas Drake's idea of a good time was a bottle of whiskey and a slice of Key Lime pie, Jeremy Stitts looked like the type of guy who enjoyed pumping iron and being fitted for custom suits.

"How do you know?" Stitts asked. His voice was light and friendly, making it clear that it wasn't an accusation, and yet Drake resented the question.

He rose to his feet.

"Because some of the wounds on her arms have already started to heal—she was held captive for a couple of days, at least. A first-time murderer doesn't hold people captive. He gets nervous, doesn't want to get caught. Kills them, dumps the body. Usually far from their home or the place they killed them."

"Ninety-eight percent of abducted children end up dead if they aren't found in the first twenty-four hours," Agent Stitts offered.

Drake frowned.

"The number isn't that different for adults." He turned to Chase. "And first-time murders don't do two at a time. Where's the second body?"

Chase stepped out of the stall and made her way to the last one on the right.

"We found this one beneath the hay; didn't even know she was here."

Drake walked over to the woman. Unlike the first victim who was propped up, this one was almost completely covered in hay.

*Does this mean she's more or less important than the other victim?*

One thing was clear: they both sported the macabre lipstick.

"We can't disturb the hay—might be trace evidence in it. Sweat, hair, etc. Need to wait for the ME and CSU to get here."

Drake, remembering Chase's comment about Beckett, said, "And Dr. Campbell's definitely not coming?"

Chase's eyes darted nervously over at the FBI Agent, and it looked as if her breath hitched.

Drake had heard about what happened, of course, about how Craig Sloan had blasted his way out of his trunk. About how Beckett had struck him in the head with a rock before Craig could turn the gun on him.

Killed him dead.

Drake hadn't shed any tears for the man, that's for sure.

Not after Craig had gotten people he loved involved with his killing spree.

"No, he's on vacation," Chase said, repeating what she had told him earlier.

"A Junior ME is on the way."

Drake chewed the inside of his cheek, mulling over everything that he had put together since he had parked his car and walked over to Detective Yasiv.

"Doesn't matter. I doubt we'll find any trace evidence here."

Agent Stitts stepped out of the way to allow Drake to enter the main corridor, nodding as he did.

"The killer hasn't been here before. This is his first time, and I doubt he'll be back."

Drake narrowed his eyes at Agent Stitts as he passed. Although he shared the man's opinion, he wasn't too keen on him stealing the words from his mouth.

*Why is he here, anyway? There's no evidence that the killer crossed state lines. Why did Chase bring him in?*

Drake shook the feeling away and started toward the front door. Chase, an annoyed expression on her face, hurried to keep stride.

"Okay, boys, time to come clean... clue the little ol' Sergeant in on your telekinesis, would you? How do you know that the killer's never been here before?"

Drake looked to Agent Stitts, then to Chase.

"Because if he had known, he wouldn't have put the bodies here," he said.

Chase made a face.

"And why not?"

It was Agent Stitts who answered, and Drake's frown deepened.

"Because if he had been here before, he would have known that Mr. Dolan had abandoned it years ago, and, more importantly, he would have known that this barn is often used by homeless people and drifters when the weather gets really cold."

"And this killer didn't want the bodies to be found. Not yet, anyways," Drake chimed in.

"And why not?"

Drake's answer was so immediate that it surprised even himself.

"Because the final chapter has yet to be written. The killer is going to strike again, and soon."

\*\*\*

Eventually, Drake found himself back in the conference room at 62nd precinct where he and Chase had once strung up images of Thomas Smith and the other Butterfly Killer victims.

"Sheriff Roshack of Larchmont County or Village or whatever the hell it is pretty much signed the entire case over to me," Chase said. Drake was barely paying attention; he was too focused on the new images on the board, the photographs that Chase's team had printed of the two dead girls from the barn. "But that doesn't mean he doesn't want this wrapped up quickly. Fact is, there's a lot of pressure to get this thing under wraps with as little media attention as possible. And I think we can all guess why."

This last sentence peaked Drake's interest, and he looked around briefly to see if others picked up on Chase's insinuation.

Detectives Yasiv and Simmons were nodding subtly, but Agent Stitts was staring stone-faced at Chase at the front of the room.

*So that's why he's here,* Drake thought.

*...a lot of pressure to get this thing under wraps...*

Drake wondered if Ken was the one applying said pressure.

It wouldn't surprise him. Fact is, mayoral front-runner Ken Smith seemed to have his thumb pressing down firmly on all the NYPD-related buttons.

*And it's only going to get worse, if—*when*—he becomes mayor.*

What had Screech said?

*Whoever's backed by the NYPD wins,* or something like that.

And Ken Smith didn't so much as have the NYPD's backing as he *was* their back.

"Drake? You okay?"

He shuddered and took a sip of his own coffee.

It tasted like burnt charcoal.

"Fine," he grumbled.

Chase nodded and then continued with her preamble. As she spoke, Drake reached into his coat that he had thrown over the back of the chair, and fondled the e-reader within. He wasn't sure why he hadn't mentioned the story, but something about the timing just seemed off.

Besides, he had driven straight from the barn in Larchmont to 62nd precinct and hadn't had a chance to read the end of it.

"Did the ME clear the body yet?" Detective Yasiv asked when Chase finally finished.

Chase nodded.

"Yes. Cause of death looks to be a combination of blood loss and the cold."

"Any idea how long the victims were held captive? Any missing person reports?" Detective Simmons asked.

Chase shook her head.

"We'll know—"

The door to the conference room opened, and Officer Dunbar entered.

He was young, although not quite as young as Detective Yasiv, and had put on considerable weight since Drake had seen him last. Drake liked the guy; he was friendly, helpful, and kind. There wasn't much to dislike, actually.

But he could also see why the man was stuck down in Records instead of being out in the field.

Nobody that nice could make it out in the open, exposed. They would be eaten alive by the business, torn apart by the atrocities of the crimes, taken advantage of by the Marcus Slasinsky's and Craig Sloan's of the world. People like whoever this new sick bastard was with a fetish for organic lipstick.

"Hi," he said hesitantly, looking first to Chase for support. She nodded encouragingly.

"Come on in," she instructed. "This is FBI Agent Jeremy Stitts—you know everyone else."

Dunbar nodded to the federal agent.

"Officer Robert Dunbar," he said, offering his hand.

"And of course you know Drake."

Dunbar nodded at him.

"Welcome back."

Drake frowned.

*Why does everyone keep saying that? I'm not back...*

"I'm not back. I'm here as a... what'd you call it, Chase?"

Chase gave him a queer look.

"Special Consultant," she said, before facing the rest of the room. "I've brought both Agent Stitts and Drake on board based on their experience with serial killers—and the need to wrap this thing up quickly. Even though there are only two bodies, I think we can all agree that this isn't the act of someone who is going to stop anytime soon. And now that you grinders have gotten acquainted, maybe we can do away with the introductions and start putting out some theories? Ideas, anyone?"

Dunbar strode forward and put a folder on the table in front of Chase.

"That's where I can help, I think."

Chase opened the folder and started to read. Drake watched as her frown deepened.

When she was done, she spun the folder around and passed it to Drake first.

"Melissa Green, 29, and Tanya Farthing, 31," Chase said grimly. She started scribbling on pieces of paper, then put the names and ages on the board beneath the appropriate images.

Drake scanned the file that Dunbar had provided.

"Did they know each other?" Agent Stitts asked.

Drake shook his head.

"Doesn't look like it. Melissa was a young mother of two, Tanya was a Law Student at NYU Law. Lived on opposite sides of town, and opposite sides of the social spectrum."

He continued to read.

"Melissa went missing about a week ago, while Tanya didn't show up to class four days ago."

Silence fell over the group.

"I'm glad you brought me in," Agent Stitts said at last. "Because you're right, Drake. This isn't going to be the last murder."

# Chapter 12

DRAKE LEFT 62ND PRECINCT with more on his mind than he had expected for a lazy Tuesday afternoon. And yet most of his mental acuity wasn't exhausted on the two dead girls, but focused on something else: the strange e-reader loaded with *Red Smile*, which held an odd similarity to the murders in the barn.

But before he relinquished the device to Chase and Agent Stitts, he felt an urge to read more and to learn about the whole eBook business. In his estimation, it was best if he exercised some good ol' fashioned police work first, before he sent the FBI off on some half-baked tangent.

After all, this approach had saved Suzan Cuthbert's life.

As he drove back to Triple D, Drake's mind drifted to Suzan, to the night when he had pulled her smoldering body out of the burning building. And as had become a habit when his thoughts turned to that night, his fingers started to rub the pink scar tissue on his cheek.

After leaving the hospital to deal with a pressing domestic violence issue, he had eventually made his way back to see Suzan. He hadn't wanted her to know that he was there — hadn't expected her to see him, given the hypobaric chamber that she was housed in — but she had.

And her reaction was completely unexpected. Recalling the way she had screamed at him when he had arrived at her house that day to speak to Jasmine, he thought that maybe she would yell at him through her oxygen mask, demand that he get the hell out. After all, Suzan couldn't have known that he was the one that had saved her; she was unconscious and half-dead from smoke inhalation when he had pulled her out.

Instead of anger, Drake had seen sadness in her eyes. A deep, brooding anguish that seemed to transform her entire face.

The only problem was, Drake didn't know if the sadness was directed at him, or if she simply harbored it for herself.

Drake reached up and wiped a tear from his cheek, and then his hand snaked its way into his pocket and fondled the finger bone within.

*I'll find out who did this to you, Clay. I'll find out who killed you—for Suzan, for Jasmine, and most of all for me.*

But first he had another crime to solve, and as much as he hated to admit it, he couldn't help but think that Agent Stitts was correct.

Their killer would strike again. It was only a matter of time.

Drake pulled into the parking lot of the strip mall that housed Triple D, noting with a frown that it hadn't been plowed yet. The snow was coming down heavier now, and even though it didn't feel that cold—it had to still be in the thirties—it was only a matter of time before the snow turned to ice. And given their most common clientele—octogenarian's courtesy of Ken Smith—they had to make sure that the next lawsuits they filed weren't against Triple D.

Drake opened the door, knocked the snow from his boots on the stupid Jump to Conclusions mat, then tried the light.

It didn't go on.

"Fuck," he grumbled. "Screech? You still here?"

There was no answer. It was dark inside Triple D despite being midday, and Drake was forced to turn on his cell phone to be able to navigate his way. With a dissatisfied grunt, he flicked the light a few more times, once again admonishing himself for not moving before winter hit. He had originally leased the place for a year, and now, nine months in, he knew that it would be impossible to get out of their lease. Subletting in the dead of winter? Fat chance. And while the influx of capital from Mrs. Armatridge was plenty sufficient, he was reluctant to just throw it away.

Things could change, could become lean very quickly, he knew.

"Screech?"

To his surprise, his partner seemed to have finally left the confines of the office.

He tried the light switch a final time and was about to remove his coat when he spotted something that caused him to freeze.

The door to his office was open. He never left it open, and Screech had been given explicit instructions to make sure that it was closed in the event he ever left Triple D.

"Anyone here?" he said, slipping a hand under his armpit out of habit.

It had been a long time since he had carried a gun, especially one in the armpit holster, but old habits died hard. And as a PI, he wasn't permitted to carry. He wondered briefly if Chase could approve a handgun based on his 'Special Consultant' status, then swept the thoughts away—it was too late for that now.

That didn't mean that he didn't have a gun—he did, of course—but he just didn't have it *on* him.

It was in his office.

"Anyone?"

He moved silently across the front entrance, passing the vacant maroon chairs against the wall. With his eyes locked on the door to his office, he walked to the reception desk and reached below the cheap plasterboard material. His searching fingers found the baseball bat strapped beneath and tried to pull it free without making a noise.

He winced as the Velcro that Screech had used to hold it in place tore away, and he silently cursed the man.

It sounded like someone with incredible dry mouth eating a Dorito inside a vacuum.

And yet there was still no movement from the office, despite the sound.

Imbued by confidence that only the heft of an aluminum Louisville Slugger could afford, Drake strode forward. When he reached the partially open door to his office, however, a sudden sense of dread overcame him.

His first instinct was that he would find Dr. Kildare sitting inside, waiting to confront him about the other night, threatening to report him to Ken Smith.

But he quickly vanquished this notion.

It didn't make sense.

The doctor who, aside from his fidelity transgressions, was morally perfect broke into his office? To confront him? To what end?

No, it had to be something else.

*Someone* else.

The real Skeleton King, perhaps.

A flash of anger suddenly washed over him as he pictured Clay's face, blood and spit clinging to his beard as he drew his final breath.

Drake used his free arm to throw the door wide and then lunged forward, leading with the bat.

"Whoever the fuck—" he stopped short. "You? What the hell are you doing here?"

# Chapter 13

COLIN ELLIOT LEFT THE writer's group with an unexpected spring in his step. He had gone into the endeavor the way he always did: fearing that he was wasting his time, that he would be better off just writing, while at the same time scared of doing just that. Finishing another novel would mean publishing it, and publishing it meant that he was opening himself up to the reviews of others. Sure, his pen name allowed him some insulation from public scorn, but it still hurt him deeply when someone wrote something negative about one of his books.

His books, after all, were his babies.

*"You need to extricate yourself from your work,"* an old tutor had once told him. But this was in direct contradiction to what he had just instructed the writer's group: write what you know, write about your experiences, write about your life.

It wasn't quite three yet, but he was in such a good mood that he thought he would pick the girls up early from school and take them for ice cream before going home. Juliette and Colby typically finished at three, then had after-school program until five.

Colin was still smiling when he pulled up to Hockley Elementary school. And the smile remained as he walked up to the chubby woman manning the desk just inside the school doors.

Shivering slightly as he approached, he absently dusted snow from the shoulders of his coat.

"It's getting cold out there," he remarked.

The woman looked up at him and grinned, her cheeks forming apples.

"Yeah, and it's only going to get colder." The woman replied, squinting as she spoke. "You are… Mr…"

"Elliot," Colin confirmed.

"Yes of course; Juliette and Colby's father. They'll be happy to see you. Mrs. Ross mentioned that they both fell asleep during math today."

As she reached over with a chubby hand for a walkie on the desk, Colin felt his smile falter.

*Did they hear us fighting the other night? Did we keep them awake?*

He knew that his girls, Colby in particular, was a very light sleeper. It was possible—no, it was *likely*—that she had heard their fighting and had stayed up listening.

He hoped to god she hadn't, but knew deep down that this was just wishful thinking.

The woman at the desk grunted, and her splayed fingers brushed up against the walkie, but failed to grab hold.

Colin grasped it and handed it to her.

"Thank you," she said. "The cafeteria food seems to be taking its toll." Her thick thumb pressed the side of the walkie-talkie. "Mrs. Ross? Can you please send Juliette and Colby Elliot to the front? Their father is here to pick them up."

She let go of the button and waited. A second later, a staticky voice replied, "Sure thing. They're just putting on their coats and hats then they'll be right out."

The woman nodded at him and then put the walkie-talkie down. Colin shifted uncomfortably for a moment as he stared at the plump woman.

*Should I say something? I already mentioned the weather… what else can I say to make idle conversation?*

For close to a minute, the two of them just stared at each other. Colin swallowed hard, and then, deciding that he couldn't handle the uncomfortable air for any longer, fell into the role of one of the characters in his books.

"So," he said, leaning forward. He tried to put a wry grin on his face, but it fell short and he let it slide. "What are you doing after this?"

The woman blinked several times in succession.

"Pardon?"

"After all of this. You busy? Got a—"

The woman again blinked her fish-eyes at him, and although the grandiose smile remained on her face, it seemed forced now, as evidenced by further creasing on her otherwise smooth forehead.

Colin suddenly caught sight of Juliette and Colby running down the hallway toward him, their heavy backpacks causing them to sway back and forth as they did.

"No running!" Mrs. Ross shouted after them. "No running, girls!"

Juliette instantly slowed to something that fell between a jog and a walk, but Colby continued running and slid in front of her sister.

"Hey!" Juliette cried. She moved to one side to try to regain the lead, but Colby shifted in that direction and blocked her with her backpack. "Get out of the way, Colby!"

Colin walked around the desk and waved.

"Hi girls!" he cried, trying to distract them to pre-emptively stop what was destined to escalate into a spat.

Colby looked up, and Juliette seized the opportunity to slide in front of her.

"Na-na!" Juliette teased.

Colby shoved her sister to one side, and Juliette stumbled, barely keeping her footing.

"Hey!"

Colin shook his head as he moved toward them, bending to one knee and holding his arms open.

Both girls reached him at the same time, and he embraced them awkwardly.

Then he stood and started toward the door.

"How was your day, girls?"

"Fine," they replied in unison.

Colin sighed, and offered a parting smile to the woman at the desk as he passed. She blinked at him, but didn't say a word.

"Just fine, huh? Well, maybe we can change that. Who wants some ice cream?"

"Me! Me! *Me!*"

\*\*\*

"Make sure you lick all the way around. I don't want you to drip in the car," Colin said as he sat in the driver's seat.

"Yes, dad," his daughters replied in unison.

It was only a short drive from Baskin Robbins to their apartment, but during that time Juliette and Colby both managed to break into tears.

Twice.

Colin was barely holding it together when he finally put the car into park, any semblance of pride or esteem from his time at the writer's group having long since fled him.

"Please, guys. No more fighting. *Please.* You know how it upsets your mother."

There was a pause and he glanced up into the rearview.

Colby stared back at him, her eyes oddly vacant. Then she turned to Juliette.

"Gimme a lick."

Juliette pulled the ice-cream away from her sister, inadvertently rubbing a multicolored swirl on the inside of the door.

"No way, you have your own."

"Yeah, but I want to try yours!"

Colin rubbed his temples and got out of the car, hesitating before opening the door for Juliette.

"No way!" Juliette whined. "And your breath stinks! Eat your own!"

Juliette jumped from the car, knocking snow across Colin's running shoes. Colby quickly followed.

"Alright guys, go on inside."

The girls hurried toward the front door, Colby with her tongue out trying to slurp her sister's ice cream. They were halfway to the door when Juliette suddenly stopped.

"Hey," she said, pointing to a light that was on in the second story window. "Isn't that your room? You said mommy wasn't going to be home until later."

Colin squinted upward, confirming that the light, one that he had turned off before leaving, was indeed on.

He shrugged and gestured for them to continue toward the door.

"That's what she told me."

Once inside, Juliette slipped off her backpack and then sprinted toward the stairs.

"Mommy! Mommy! Daddy got us ice cream!" she hollered, taking the stairs two at a time.

"Juliette! Your shoes!" Colin shouted after her. "Take off your shoes! You're going to track snow through the house!"

The girl didn't even look back. Somehow, even the sway of her pony-tail seemed sassy.

Colby started after her sister, but Colin grabbed her backpack before she could get away.

"Take off your boots first, Colby."

The girl whined and grunted, while at the same time trying to remove her boots without untying them, using the toe of one to drive against the heel of the other.

"I can't! They're too tight! How come Juliette gets too—"

Colin dropped to a knee.

"You have to undo them first. Here, I'll help you."

With numb fingers, he started to untie her first boot. When he was done, she shook it off, flinging snow onto the carpet. He had just started with her second boot when there was a scream from upstairs.

Colin immediately whipped around and ran toward the stairs.

"Juliette? *Juliette!*"

Colin spotted his daughter in the doorway of his bedroom, her back to him.

"Juliette? What's wrong?"

Walking briskly now, Colin made it to his daughter and grabbed her, trying to spin her around to look at her.

"Juliette? You okay? What's wrong?"

Colin looked at his daughter, trying to figure out what was going on. His first thought was that she had dropped her ice cream, but it was still clutched tightly in one hand, the melted pink and blue liquid coating her fingers.

"Juliette?" he repeated.

A sound from the bedroom drew his gaze.

Colin turned and saw his wife sitting on the side of the bed, a cigarette dangling from her lips. She was wearing only a pair of underwear and a plain gray t-shirt, the outline of her small breasts clearly visible through the thin material. Ryanne clicked her lighter and lit her cigarette.

After taking several puffs and exhaling a thick gray cloud of smoke, she raised her gaze to Colin.

"You're getting the carpet wet," she said.

Colin's eyes went wide and he stumbled into the hallway. If it hadn't been for his daughter, and the fact that his hand was still on her back, he would have fallen.

Behind Ryanne, a man stood, his back to Colin. Like his wife, he was in his underwear, and as Colin watched, the man stretched and put on a t-shirt.

# Chapter 14

Sergeant Chase Adams slid into her BMW and waited for FBI Agent Jeremy Stitts to get into the passenger seat before she started it up.

"Nice ride," Agent Stitts commented as he lowered himself into the creme-colored seat.

"Thank you," Chase said as she reversed out of the precinct parking lot, wondering if she was going to have to explain, as she had to Drake long ago, that she had bought the car from Internet poker earnings.

*And how will that go over with the feds, Chase? Hmm?*

But Agent Stitts's next question made it clear that he wasn't preoccupied with the vehicle.

"Melissa Green or Tanya Farthing first?"

Problem was, Chase didn't know how to answer that either. With the suicide killer, she hadn't had to speak to the victims' families; either they couldn't be located or simply didn't care, or in the case of Eddie Larringer, Drake had done the honors. But she vividly recalled speaking to Clarissa Smith, and was keenly aware of how awkward and terrible an experience that had been.

*I should speak to her, reach out,* she thought suddenly.

A sense of *déjà vu* overcame her then, as she realized that she had had this thought before. Only it had been in reference to Drake and not Clarissa Smith.

*It's happening again. I'm getting obsessed with the job, forgetting the human element.*

"Sergeant Adams?"

Chase shook her head and looked over at Agent Stitts who was staring back at her, a concerned look on his face. He was handsome, she realized, if a little clean cut for her tastes.

"Sorry, it's just that the last few months have been a bit of a whirlwind."

Stitts nodded.

"I've read your file. A transplant from Seattle Narc to NYPD Detective, then to first grade in record time. And now Sergeant. You've made quite the impression, it seems."

Chase tilted her head to one side.

*He's read the file; that's good.*

Part of the reason why she had been so quick to get the FBI involved in this case, despite her previous unproductive interactions with them in Seattle, was to get noticed, to get on their radar.

And, to her surprise, Agent Stitts seemed not only to know what he was doing, but also seemed respectful. He didn't strike her as the type to flash his badge like his pecker and scream *FBI, I'm taking over this case!*

Her thoughts turned to Sergeant Rhodes and how cocky the bald bastard had been before he had gotten in her way.

"Either that or it's just good timing; rotten eggs above me, if you catch my drift."

Agent Stitts grunted and he turned his attention to the snow that the windshield wipers worked fruitlessly to wick away.

"Maybe," he said absently.

They drove in silence for the next few minutes.

"Green," Chase said at last. "Let's go see Melissa Green first. See if we can figure out how and why the killer targeted her, if she had any enemies, and if she knew Tanya Farthing."

Agent Stitts nodded.

"Sounds good. You want me to lead the discussion or do you want to?"

Chase pressed her lips together. Although she didn't share Drake's extreme revulsion at the idea of breaking terrible news to loved ones, she wasn't a fan of doing it either. But it was her case, she was the Sergeant, and it was her city, dammit.

"I'll do it," she said without hesitation. "I'll speak to the family."

\*\*\*

The address listed in Melissa's file—which they had procured from a shoplifting arrest a few years back—was a trailer park at the eastern border of the city. They gained entry to the compound by calling ahead, and the manager, a portly man named Hector, directed them to a trailer toward the back of the compound.

The trailer itself was old, the corners that rested on cinderblocks starting to rot. Chase noticed that the blinds of the other trailers surrounding Melissa's were open just a little, and the suspicious eyes that peered out were trained on her. For once, she wished that she hadn't insisted on driving. She had no idea what Agent Stitts drove, but guessed that it had to be less... *expensive*... than her BMW.

"Ready?" she asked.

Agent Stitts nodded and Chase opened the door and stepped into the cold.

The screen door to the trailer was torn, and Chase put her fist through the hole to knock on the wood behind it.

"Comin'," a husky voice called from within.

Chase glanced furtively at Stitts and was about to say something when then the door suddenly opened. A woman in her mid-forties sporting a long t-shirt that came to her knees,

stood in the doorway. She stared at them with deeply sunken
eyes.

"Yeah? Who are you? What do you want?" she snapped.
Her eyes flicked to the BMW behind Chase. "You cops or
something? Cuz he ain't here, if that's who yer looking for."

*He? Who's he?*

"No, ma'am. I'm here with some very upsetting news. May
we come in?"

The woman observed Chase for a good minute, taking
several hauls off a hand-rolled cigarette during this time.
Eventually, her eyes narrowed and she repeated her initial
query, "You cops or something?"

Chase nodded.

"My name is Sergeant Adams and this here is FBI Agent
Stitts. Are you related to Melissa Green?"

The woman put the cigarette between her thin lips and
crossed her arms over her chest.

"I don't got nothing to say to cops. If Melissa got herself in
trouble again, then that's her problem. I ain't paying for bail. I
told her that I wasn't gonna bail her out no more. Didn't do
her no good last time, and it won't do her no good this time."

"Ma'am, it's not—"

A toddler wearing only a sagging diaper suddenly
appeared beside the woman, and she ushered him away.

"What's this about, then?"

Chase sighed, a cloud of fog forming in front of her face.

"Please, can we come in?"

"Nuh-uh, not 'til you tell me what this's about."

A quick glance at Stitts, who raised an eyebrow, and Chase
just came out with it.

"I'm very sorry to tell you this, but Melissa's dead," she
said flatly.

# Chapter 15

DRAKE LOWERED THE BAT to his side and stared at the man sitting in the chair behind his desk. He was short and unimpressive, and yet every time he saw him, Drake felt unease wash over his soul.

"What do you want?" Drake snapped, the words coming out more harshly than he had intended.

Raul stood and Drake felt his hand tighten on the bat.

"He wants to see you," he said flatly in a thick Spanish accent.

"What does he want?"

Raul said nothing. He simply moved toward Drake and the door.

"You don't need that," Raul instructed, his eyes flicking to the baseball bat.

*Don't go; tell Raul to fuck off. Tell him to relay the message to Ken Smith that I'm not his errand boy.*

But he couldn't do that. He owed the man. If it weren't for him, Suzan would be dead right now, burnt alive by a psychopath hellbent on recreating deaths from Beckett's forensic pathology exam.

Drake frowned, the scarred skin on his cheek crumpling uncomfortably. He leaned the bat against the wall by the door and shrugged.

"Alright, let's go then."

\*\*\*

As expected, Raul said nothing during the drive to Ken Smith's condo. This, unfortunately, left Drake with time inside his own head, which soon became a messy bog of emotions and memories.

He was glad that Chase had brought him on the case, even if his position as 'Special Consultant' was ambiguous at best. And he was pleased that the harsh feelings that his ex-colleagues in the force had once harbored toward him, seemed to have eased. Yet being back in the fold meant that his memories returned, that Clay was once again front and center in his mind.

And this made him want to drink again. He hadn't sworn off the sauce completely, but it was more under control than it had been for as long as he could remember. No drinking in his car parked outside a high school, for instance. But now, in this moment, sitting in Raul's midnight black Range Rover, he wished that tucked inside his jacket pocket was a miniature of Johnny Walker.

Just one. Just enough to take the edge off.

But the only thing in his pocket was a mysterious e-reader.

And a finger bone. There was that, too.

As they pulled up to the condo in downtown Manhattan, however, Drake knew that he only had to wait until he made it to the 80th floor—the penthouse—before he would get his fix.

Drake exited the car first and hurried across the parking lot to the glass doors at the front of the building. He knocked once and a security guard with a thick brown mustache waddled over. There was immediate recognition on his face, but to Drake's annoyance, he didn't open the door. Instead, he just stood there, his hand on the keys at his belt.

"Open up," Drake barked.

The man didn't acknowledge him.

"Hey, you deaf? Open the—"

The security guard's eyes darted over Drake's shoulder, and he followed the man's gaze. Raul was suddenly beside him, forcing him to do a double-take to make sure that he had left footprints in the snow, that he hadn't just materialized like a damn apparition.

"Ah, I see," Drake grumbled. "Waiting for your boss."

Raul nodded, and the security guard returned the gesture before immediately unlocking the door.

"Thanks," Drake said sarcastically as he passed. He didn't bother to knock the snow off his boots.

Like the front doors, Drake was the first to the silver elevator, but once again had to wait for Raul to flash his key card for it to open.

Drake took note of the card that he used: a plain, white key card that was attached to a cable extending from his plain, black belt.

*It might come in handy to have one of those,* Drake thought absently.

The elevator chimed and they stepped inside.

Something occurred to Drake as the silver coffin ascended, a conversation he had had upon first meeting Raul.

He turned to the man then, who was staring blankly at the doors, paying Drake no heed.

"I thought you worked for Clarissa Smith?"

Raul said nothing and Drake pressed harder. He was annoyed by the man's affect, and was going to try his best to break through his frozen demeanor.

"What? She turn you down after Thomas died?"

Drake thought he saw the man's mustache twitch.

"Ah, I bet that's it. I bet you tried to slip it in as Thomas was lowering into the ground, didn't you?"

Nothing this time.

"How's she doing, anyway? You still in touch?"

Raul turned to him then, his dark eyebrows furrowing so much that they nearly covered his beady eyes.

"Clarissa is—"

The elevator pinged, announcing their arrival, and Raul's mouth suddenly clamped shut. The doors started to open, but Drake's hand shot out and hit the close button, halting their progress.

"Clarissa's what? Just a pawn in your boss's game? Is that it?"

Raul looked at his hand, then the doors at half-mast. For a second, Drake thought that he was going to slap his finger away from the button, and something inside of him clenched.

But Raul did nothing.

"You know what I don't understand about this whole thing, Raul? I get what Ken Smith is up to—he wants to be mayor. Will do anything to be mayor, evidently. But you? What do you want out of this thing? Why are you so loyal to this prick? Me? I owe him… but you? Do you owe him too?"

Raul looked him straight in the eyes then, and Drake thought he detected a hint of a smile on the man's dark lips.

"We should go. Mr. Smith will be waiting," he said calmly.

Drake scowled and took his finger off the button. The doors slid open, and he was surprised to see Ken Smith standing just a few feet away, dressed in what looked like another bespoke suit.

He was smiling, revealing a row of perfectly straight, perfectly white teeth that stood out on his tanned face.

"Drake, so glad that you could make it."

"Like I had a choice," Drake replied, stepping past Raul and into the lavish penthouse.

"Please, come in," Ken said with a hint of sarcasm. "We need to chat."

"What I need," Drake began, stamping his feet, leaving wet footprints on the marble tiles, "is a drink. Then maybe we can talk."

# Chapter 16

"Mrs. Green, I know this is hard, but I need to ask: did your daughter have any enemies? Anyone that might want to do her harm?"

Abigail Green took a drag of her cigarette, her hand trembling as it brought the white cylinder to her lips.

"Enemies? How about the bastard that knocked her up? The one that punched her in the face when she was still pregnant? Does that count?"

Chase let her vent. She understood the woman's anger. People dealt with grief in different ways, but anger was one of the most common responses.

"The father of her children?" Chase asked, her eyes darting to the two toddlers in diapers—a boy about two years of age and a girl who was at least four—who were giggling as they played with a cardboard box.

"One of them," Abigail replied. "Brent Doakes was his name. Little prick, if you ask me."

Chase turned to Stitts, who nodded back at her.

"Alright, just a few more questions then we will be out of your hair, Mrs. Green."

"It's Ms. Green," she corrected, glaring at Chase.

"Sorry, Ms. Green. Do you know if your daughter was friends with a Tanya Farthing?"

The woman's face screwed up.

"Melissa didn't have no friends. All she had time for is her damn books. That's it. Nothin' else. I wish she would stop reading and look after her kids. Told her that all the time."

Abigail's eyes started to water as she spoke, but Chase saw the woman's jaw clench as she fought back the emotion. This was a hard woman who had led a hard life, and while she was understandably angry, she was also clearly upset.

As she should be.

Chase stood, and out of the corner of her eye, she saw Stitts do the same.

"Thank you, Ms. Green. And again, please accept my sincerest condolences for what happened to your daughter."

Abigail Green grunted as she reached for another cigarette.

"A uniformed officer will be by tomorrow with some further instructions and paperwork," she said as she made her way to the trailer door.

"I don't want no cops back here. People start talking, make things hard for me 'n the kids."

Chase nodded.

"I understand, but it's procedure. I'll tell them to be discrete."

With that, she opened the door and was met by a blast of cold air. She was partway to her BMW, feeling the full brunt of the irony of telling Mrs. Green about discretion while driving a car that probably cost twice as much as her trailer, when the woman's voice drifted to her through the falling snow.

"Catch the bastard who did this to Melissa," Mrs. Green called after them, her voice unexpectedly soft. "Catch the bastard."

Chase turned back and nodded once to the woman, and then got into her car.

When Agent Stitts took up residence in the passenger seat, she moved her hands to the wheel, only now noticing that they were shaking slightly.

"You okay?" Agent Stitts asked, looking over at her. His hazel eyes were soft, caring.

"I'm fine," she replied, putting the car into drive. She exhaled sharply. "One down, one to go."

\*\*\*

Tanya Farthing's home was the opposite to Melissa Green's in pretty much every way possible. Located in the heart of Manhattan, Tanya lived in a meticulously maintained brownstone. Relatively new to New York, Chase wasn't up-to-date on the real estate minutia of the city, but she knew enough to recognize that this area was expensive.

Like seven figures expensive.

She and Agent Stitts made it to the door together, and just before she knocked, he asked her again if she wanted him to do the talking.

At this point, Chase wasn't sure if he was just genuinely being a nice guy or if it was all some sort of a test.

She shook her head.

*It doesn't matter*, she surmised.

This was her gig, and she would see it through.

*Find the bastard who did this to Melissa*, Ms. Green had said.

Chase hadn't answered, not because she didn't want to, but because she didn't have to.

She *would* find the killer. It was only a matter of time.

"I'll do it," she said as she knocked.

The man who answered the door was short, bald, and had teeth that seemed slightly too large for his mouth.

"Yes? Can I help you?" he asked with a slight accent that Chase couldn't place.

"Is this Tanya Farthing's address?"

Concern suddenly formed a shadow on the man's face.

"Yes—I'm her father. What's this about?"

"My name is Sergeant Chase Adams, and this is FBI Agent Jeremy Stitts. Can we come in?"

The man hesitated, but then nodded when Agent Stitts produced and displayed his badge. He stepped to one side, and Chase could see that his breathing had become labored.

"Honey? Who is it? It's a little late for clients, isn't it?" a female voice drifted down to them from the staircase off to Chase's left.

Tanya's father swallowed hard.

"Tiffany? I think you should come down. The police are here and they want to speak to us. It's about Tanya."

# Chapter 17

"AND MRS. ARMATRIDGE, HOW is she?" Ken asked between puffs of his cigar.

Drake took a swig of his whiskey, marveling again at how smooth the Johnny Walker Blue was. His thoughts turned to the video feed of the elderly woman removing the knife from the butcher block while her husband was being satisfied by the maid in the bedroom above. As she walked slowly to the stairs, slowly, as if sleepwalking, Screech and his curly hair suddenly came into the frame. His partner had grabbed Mrs. Armatridge by the wrist before she did something truly terrible.

Drake shook his head.

"She's fine," he replied flatly.

"Good to hear. And business at Triple D? Still steady?"

Drake frowned and sipped his drink.

"Just get to the point, Ken. You want to know what I found out about Dr. Kildare."

Ken smirked.

"You know what I like about you, Drake?"

"That I do your bidding?"

Drake was hoping that the man's smile would falter and was disappointed when it didn't.

"I like your no-nonsense attitude. Directness is a virtue that has been lost in a world of emoji's and abbreviations," he took a haul of his cigar, then exhaled the smoke through his nostrils like some sort of dragon. "And you are correct: I've brought you here to learn what you've uncovered."

Drake hesitated. For some reason, he was struck by the impulse to lie, to tell Ken that he had found nothing, that Dr. Kildare was as perfect as he seemed.

But he couldn't bring himself to do it. After all, whatever his feelings for the man, he owed Ken Smith. Besides, he was only reporting facts. He never coerced, entrapped, or even suggested anything to Dr. Kildare.

"Dr. Kildare is having an affair," he said after a short pause. "He's sleeping with his campaign director."

This, at last, got a reaction out of the man.

Ken chuckled and took another puff.

"Raul? Can you please come here?"

Raul appeared beside Drake and slid an envelope onto the table beside his whiskey glass.

Drake looked at it with a sense of loathing. And yet, when he finished his drink, he picked it up. It was heavy; heavier than he expected.

He stood and slid it into his jacket pocket.

"Raul please give our guest a ride to wherever he wants to go."

Drake frowned at the use of the term 'guest'. Was he really a guest? Something told him that if he had declined Raul's offer—however enticing—to come see Ken Smith, then there would be repercussions.

Raul led the way to the elevator, but before it arrived, Ken Smith added, "Get your partner to set up one of those cameras, would you, Drake? Get Dr. Kildare on tape with his manager."

Drake nodded, but didn't turn.

"And remember, it doesn't do either of us any good if you're seen."

Drake was scowling when he entered the elevator, and this expression remained etched on his face during the silent drive all the way back to his Crown Vic at Triple D.

"Thanks for the ride," he snapped as he left Raul's Range Rover.

Predictably, Raul said nothing before driving off, leaving Drake standing with the snow falling around him.

He felt the weight of the two objects in his pocket; in his right was the e-reader that he felt compelled to continue reading, while the left housed the envelope that Raul had given him.

And he was tired, too. The day had started with the lights being out at Triple D and only went downhill from there.

Drake's hand slipped into the pocket with the envelope, and he wrapped his calloused fingers around the material, feeling the thick stack of bills within.

The dead women and *Red Smile* would have to wait. He had his priorities, and there was something he had to do first.

# Chapter 18

COLIN COULDN'T BELIEVE WHAT he was seeing. His wife of eight years was in bed with another man—an older, fat man, whom he had never laid eyes on before.

But that wasn't the worst of it. The worst was that she didn't seem to give a shit that he had caught her.

In fact, Ryanne's entire being seemed to be dripping with contempt as she sat at the edge of their bed in her t-shirt and underwear.

"Juliette, go take off your boots," she instructed.

Juliette didn't move. Colin wasn't sure that, at seven, she understood what was going on, but she knew given his reaction that something wasn't right here.

Colin reached down and patted his daughter gently on the shoulder. Juliette looked up at him with wide eyes.

"It's alright, sweetie, head downstairs with your sister."

Juliette nodded and then fled the hallway without a word, leaving Colin with his wife and the stranger.

"Don't look at me like that," Ryanne spat. She reached for her pants and put them on, then grabbed her pack of cigarettes off the bedside table. As she did, the man turned around, and Colin felt his jaw drop.

He *did* know the man, after all. It was their landlord, a man who Ryanne had repeatedly referred to as a scumbag.

"You," was all Colin could manage.

The man glared at him. In his mid-sixties, he wasn't an imposing figure despite his burgeoning belly; short in stature, with thinning grey hair and a gap-toothed smile, and yet Colin was none-the-less intimidated.

Ryanne lit another cigarette and inhaled deeply.

"I said don't look at me like that," she repeated.

Colin shook his head.

"Like what? How the hell do you want me to look at you? Is this a joke? What the hell is going on?"

Ryanne took a long drag of her cigarette.

"What was I supposed to do? You can't pay the rent, and we need somewhere to live."

Colin gawked.

"So, you're what... *whoring* yourself?"

The landlord, who Colin in his fury couldn't remember was named Gerald or Gary or Glenn, moved toward the door.

"I'ma leave now," he said, fists and jaw clenched. "See you next month, Ryanne."

Colin was so floored by the man's audacity that he didn't even flinch when G-whatever his name slipped by him and down the stairs.

"Grow up, Colin. Bills needed to be paid, so I got it done. If you could just get a real job, then we wouldn't be in this mess in the first place."

Colin whipped his head around to stare at his wife.

"Are you serious? Are you—" he lowered his voice an octave —" are you *fucking* serious?"

Ryanne nodded.

"As a heart attack."

Colin raised a hand, and only then realized that it was so tightly clenched that his knuckles were white.

He relaxed his grip and pointed a finger directly at Ryanne's chest.

"You're going to be sorry, Ryanne. You don't know what I'm capable of. I've..." he let his sentence trail off.

Ryanne's face broke into a grin and then she threw her head back and laughed.

"What? What are you going to do about it?" her face grew serious. "You're too much of a pussy to do anything. Don't be fake; I hate fake people. Fucking poser."

"Oh, you're going to be sorry. My next book... you'll see. My next book isn't just going to sell, but it's going to be a fucking phenomenon. You'll see Ryanne. And you're not going to get a goddamn dime."

Ryanne looked away and ashed her cigarette in a can of Coke on the night side table.

"Whatever," she grumbled. "Your books never sell."

Colin, on the verge of seeing red, of losing control, spun on his heels. His equilibrium was suddenly off and he stumbled, and was forced to brace himself against the wall to avoid falling.

In a daze, he made his way down the stairs.

"Where are you going?" Ryanne yelled after him.

"Out! Make sure that the girls get dinner!"

With that, Colin threw the door to their apartment open so violently that the doorknob put a dent in the drywall.

*She'll pay — that bitch is going to pay for everything that she's done to me. She will pay.*

# Chapter 19

CHASE'S HANDS WERE VISIBLY shaking when she returned to her car after visiting with Tanya Farthing's hysterical parents. Ms. Green and Mrs. Farthing's reactions to the news of their daughter's deaths were as opposite each other as their abodes.

But it was their eyes that got to her. Their eyes were wide, they were moist, but they had a quality of emptiness that she only knew from dead bodies.

"Fuck," she swore, momentarily forgetting that Agent Stitts was in the car with her. And when she realized that he was, she repeated the curse even louder this time and hammered the steering wheel with the heel of her hand.

She wasn't sure why these murders affected her when the victims of the Butterfly Killer and Craig Sloan's twisted acts hadn't, but the fact that they did remained.

She took a deep breath and then turned to Agent Stitts. He was looking at her again, but there was no judgment in his face.

"Sorry," she grumbled.

Stitts shook his head.

"Don't apologize. You know what the difference between you and I is?"

Chase remained silent as she started the car.

"I'm better at internalizing the pain I see in others, pushing it deep down in my gut where it toils with my own anguish. That's all. But don't let it fool you; I feel it. I feel it with every breath I take. One of the worst things that has happened to society is the pervasive notion that showing emotion, of being vulnerable, is a weakness. It's not. It's a strength. You're stronger than me, Chase. That's the real difference between you and I."

The candid speech took Chase by surprise. For as long as she could remember, she wanted to be an FBI agent. But in all that time, she had thought of it as a cold, hardened institution set on solving the most difficult, and the most heinous, of crimes.

In her mind, the FBI was uncaring, unforgiving, and above all else, infallible.

And maybe that's what drew her to it in the first place.

But the front that Agent Stitts was presenting... was, well, unnerving to say the least.

And Chase wasn't sure how she felt about it.

"Where should I take you?" she asked dryly. "You staying in a hotel?"

Stitts nodded.

"Yeah, but you can just drop me at the precinct. I've got my rental there. Do you want to talk about the case? We can wait until morning, if it suits you better."

Chase chewed her lip. She wanted to wait until tomorrow, but thoughts were already festering in her head. If she went home and tried to sleep now, it would never come, she knew.

She checked the clock on the dash. It was almost ten.

"It'll take about forty minutes to get back to the precinct. We can talk as I drive."

Agent Stitts agreed.

"Good," he said softly. "I'll start. There's no way that Tanya new Melissa. No way. Not even in some sort of bizarre tutoring relationship. And although the reactions of Melissa's and Tanya's parents were very different, they were both genuine. They had nothing to do with either of their deaths."

*"Hmph,"* was all Chase could manage. This was another twist that she hadn't expected: such *conclusiveness,* and at such an early stage of their investigation. And yet, Agent Stitts had just verbalized her very thoughts.

"So, if they didn't know each other, how did the killer pick them?" she asked. "They're both young women around thirty years of age. But Melissa was plump, out of shape, and Tanya was thin, on the verge of being skinny. Melissa had black hair, Tanya blond."

Agent Stitts hesitated before commenting.

"Random?"

Chase mulled this over for a moment.

Unlike the man's previous comment, his voice had wavered slightly while uttering the word 'random'.

*Is this a test? Did he see something and wants to know if I saw it, too?*

Chase shook her head and decided then and there that she would just be herself, do whatever she did that got her to this position in the first place.

She wasn't about to change who she was or become preoccupied with what others thought about her. Not now. Not after all she had been through.

"Honestly? I've never heard of a truly random killer. There's a connection between them, between Tanya and Melissa. Two women, around the same age, murdered in tandem? Can't be a coincidence."

Agent Stitts nodded.

"So, what's the connection then? It's not their socio-economic status, that's for sure. Their looks, then? Maybe. A general hatred toward women of child-bearing age? It wouldn't be the first—"

"Shh," Chase said without thinking. Her cheeks started to flush, but she forced this feeling away.

*Don't blush—you're a fucking police sergeant for Christ's sake. Act like one.*

"There's something... something..." she let her sentence trail off.

There *was* something, something in common between the two women. It wasn't something that she saw, necessarily, at least, not at Melissa's, but something her mother—

"Books," she said. The word came out more as an apology than an exclamation as she had intended.

"Excuse me?"

"Books—that's the connection. Ms. Green said that Melissa was too busy reading or going to the library to look after her children," her words sped up as she gained confidence, "And Tanya's mother—remember when she took us up to Tanya's room? There were books everywhere, but not just law books. Novels. There were dozens on the shelves. Did you see them?"

"Yeah, I saw them."

And with that unenthused response, Chase's confidence was suddenly shot.

*Books? How many people have books in their homes? And the library? How many thousands of people go to the library?*

"It's somewhere to start, I guess. Might be nothing, but..."

"No, it sounds... I think there might be something there."

Chase shrugged and took the off-ramp.

"Let me ask you something," Stitts continued in a softer tone. "Why didn't you ask about the lipstick?"

The question took Chase by surprise.

"The lipstick?"

"Yeah, the bloody lips... the lipstick spread over the dead girls' mouths. You didn't ask either of the mothers about makeup at all."

Chase vividly recalled the dark maroon smudges coating the corpses's otherwise pale lips.

"I... I don't know."

"Don't sell yourself short, Chase. You *do* know. You know it in the same way that you know the books are important."

The first thing that popped into Chase's head was so embarrassing that, despite her previous promise to stay true to herself, she couldn't bring herself to say it out loud. It was trite, it was clichéd, and it was borderline demeaning: *a woman's intuition.*

In the end, it didn't matter; Agent Stitts said it for her.

"Intuition, that's why."

Chase suddenly felt tired and decided then and there to put an end to the discussion.

"It doesn't matter anyway, books or no books. Gaining access to library records is almost as difficult as breaking into the Pentagon. Homeland security and Mein Kampf and all that."

Stitts chuckled.

"Yeah, well. That's where I come in, I guess. This badge carries some perks, after all."

# Chapter 20

DRAKE OPENED THE BLACK mailbox and then pulled the envelope from his pocket. He weighed it in his hand for a moment, and then put it inside. He closed the lid and then was about to flip the small red flag up when he saw a door opening and froze.

"Drake? Is that you?"

Drake debated not saying anything and getting back into his car, but realized that this would hardly keep him anonymous.

After all, he drove a conspicuous Crown Vic. Besides, Jasmine had to know who was putting the money in her mailbox all these months... didn't she?

Drake turned around and put on his best fake smile.

"I was just leaving, Jasmine. Don't mind me."

Jasmine Cuthbert tugged the robe of her belt tight and stepped onto the porch. She was only wearing slippers, he noted.

"What... what are you doing here?"

Drake took a step toward the house.

"It's cold out, Jasmine. Why don't you head inside and get warm?"

Instead of listening, Jasmine did the opposite and took another step onto the porch. After a glance back at his car, Drake finally made up his mind and walked toward the house. When he reached Jasmine, he put an arm around her shoulder and spun her around, guiding her toward her open door.

She didn't resist.

Once inside, he shut the door behind them and immediately started to warm up.

"Is... is Suzan home?" Drake asked hesitatingly.

Jasmine shook her head.

"She's at a friend's house, studying for an exam."

Her response surprised him.

*Suzan's back at school? Already?*

Drake knew that the girl was strong, but this was unprecedented. After what happened to her...

"You want some tea, Drake?"

What Drake wanted was to go home and sip from the bottle of Johnny Red that he had waiting for him until he passed out.

"Sure," he replied.

Drake followed Jasmine to the kitchen, watching her as she went. She set the kettle on the stove and then reached up to grab a mug from one of the upper cupboards. As she did, her robe lifted slightly, and Drake looked away when a bare ass cheek came into view.

He blushed.

"What were you doing out there, Drake?" Jasmine asked as she grabbed two mugs and turned back to him.

Drake stared at her for a moment, trying to figure out if she was being facetious or not. He decided not — in her sleepy state, he doubted that she could be anything but honest.

"I was... I was just passing by," he lied; he didn't feel up for a discussion about the envelopes, where they came from, why he left them.

Now it was Jasmine's turn to squint at him.

She opened her mouth to say something, but was cut off by the scream of the kettle. A small smile formed on her lips, and she turned her back to him again.

Something came over Drake then. Without thinking, he moved behind her and slipped a hand around her waist.

*Pull away,* he urged her. *Pull away, slap me, call me a bastard and I'll leave.*

But Jasmine didn't pull away. Instead, she shifted her hips backward ever so slightly, pressing her ass against him.

Encouraged by her movement, Drake spun Jasmine around. And then he kissed her. Softly at first, but when he felt her tongue probe his lips, he kissed her more forcefully.

He felt Jasmine's hands wrap around his waist and pull him even closer. Drake lifted his hand from her hip and slipped it beneath the collar of her robe. His searching hand found her breast and he squeezed, feeling her nipple harden between his fingers.

Jasmine moaned, a sound that was barely audible over the kettle's high-pitched squeal, and Drake suddenly pulled back.

He blinked rapidly, and as he did he felt light-headed.

*What am I doing? This is… this is* wrong.

Jasmine looked up at him and ground her hips against the front of his pants, which had become uncomfortably tight.

She tilted her chin upward, her mouth open slightly, and a split second before he leaned down to meet her lips, something changed.

Drake was no longer staring at Jasmine Cuthbert's pretty face, but someone else's. Someone with short brown hair and smallish features.

He was staring at Chase Adams.

"What the—"

Jasmine suddenly yanked him forward and, eyes wide, Drake found himself kissing her again, tasting her sweet scent, feeling the moistness on her lips and down below.

*What the fuck am I doing? What the* fuck *am I doing?*

# Chapter 21

CHASE FINALLY MADE IT home around midnight. It was dark, it was cold, and the exhaustion that she had felt in the car with Agent Stitts had only grown in his absence.

As had the cloud of… what was it that she felt, exactly? Doubt? Discomfort?

Whatever it was, it gnawed at the lining of her stomach.

With a sigh, she exited her car and made her way toward the door. As was her habit, she tried the doorknob before inserting the key and was surprised to find it unlocked.

Shaking her head in frustration, she knocked the snow from her boots and stepped inside.

A flicker of movement from down the hall caught her eye and her hand went to the gun on her hip.

"Chase? That you?" a groggy voice asked. Chase took a deep breath and relaxed.

"Yeah, it's just me. Listen, Brad, you left the door open again. You *have* to remember to lock it."

"Sorry, I was beat. Fed Felix dinner and then fell asleep on the couch watching the Yankees game. There's some left, you want?"

Chase removed her coat.

"The Yankee game's over by now. Unless they're playing the Red Sox, then it'll probably last until tomorrow afternoon."

Brad tousled his short brown hair and chuckled.

"Not the game, you puffalump; I meant dinner. Made a chili-slash-stew. Pretty good, if I do say so myself. Felix thought it was too spicy, but you know how he is. Garlic is too spicy for him."

Brad slid an arm around her waist as he spoke, and while at first Chase leaned into him, she eventually pulled away.

The thought of meat suddenly made her feel queasy.

"Thanks, but I'll pass. Could do a beer though."

Brad frowned, his brow furrowing.

"I'll join you," he said as he made his way to the fridge.

After removing her coat and boots, she flopped down on the couch. A smirk crossed her lips when she realized that not only was the TV still on, but so was the game. The Yanks were playing the Sox and it was 7-7 in the bottom of the fourteenth inning.

Chase was just getting comfortable, feeling her eyes droop, when Brad slid in beside her and handed her an ice-cold beer.

She took a large gulp, wincing as the cold stung her throat. Beer probably wasn't the best thing for her suddenly unsettled stomach, but then again, when was beer a bad idea?

Thoughts of alcohol brought an image of Drake to mind, and she wondered briefly what he was up to at this very moment.

*Probably elbows deep in a bottle of scotch*, she reckoned.

Brad took a sip of his own beer then turned to face her, concern etched on his handsome face.

"You alright? You seem quiet, even for you."

Chase stared at her bottle of beer for a moment, before taking another swig.

"It's this case," she admitted. "There's something about it that… that…"

"Reminds you of your past? Of your sister?" Brad offered, his voice so quiet that the words bordered on inaudible.

Chase ground her teeth and ignored the comment.

"It's just getting to me. I think I'm just tired, is all."

"Ever think of taking a break? A week off maybe? I mean, we haven't even been in New York for a year yet, and you've led two, and now three, major cases. Not to mention being promoted to Sergeant, and all that bullshit with Rhodes. And how can we forget about the fact that you were *kidnapped*. Jesus, Chase, take a break. It'll do you good," Brad sighed heavily and averted his eyes. "It would do *us* good, Chase."

Chase's eyes shot up.

"What? What do you mean?"

Bard picked at the label on his beer bottle.

"You know what I mean. Look, I'm not saying you didn't warn me—you did. I knew that moving to New York would mean that you would be busy. I also knew that it was a career move, that starting as a Detective would eventually take you to the FBI, but—"

Chase opened her mouth to interrupt, but Brad continued quickly, not giving her a chance.

"But, we also know what happened in Seattle when you were overworked, how…" his eyes darted to her arms, which were thankfully covered by a dark sweater, and his sentence trailed off.

Chase hated how Brad couldn't bring himself to say the words, as if she were so fragile that just mentioning what had happened in Seattle when she was undercover would set her off.

She wasn't that person anymore. She was someone different, someone stronger.

Besides, there was only one thing that she refused to talk about, and he had already broached that subject, if only in passing.

*So why is this case getting to you, then?* A nagging voice inside her head demanded.

"Well, you know," he said at last.

Chase's eyes narrowed.

"Say it. Say it, Brad."

He shook his head.

"No, I'm not going to say it. It'll do no good to say it—I just—I just think it's important to let you know that Felix misses you, that I miss you."

Brad looked down as he said this, making it clear that it wasn't intended as a guilt trip. It was just him being honest, which was admirable. And Chase couldn't help but think that she was probably working too hard.

Even poker was failing at taking her mind off her work, which was the main reason why she played.

An image of Melissa Green, her face barely peeking out from beneath a thatchwork of hay, her lips a crusty brown, flashed in her mind.

"After this case, Brad. After this case, I'll take some time off," Chase thought of Beckett and his vacation in the Virgin Gorda. "We can go away somewhere, maybe. Somewhere hot."

She smiled, and while Brad returned the gesture, it also somehow seemed sad.

He patted her knee gently, then stood.

"Come to bed soon, Chase," he said, finishing his beer. "You look tired."

"I will," Chase lied. "I'll be there in a minute."

# Chapter 22

"I CAN HELP YOU with those."

The woman looked over and offered a tentative smile.

"No, that's okay. I can manage."

"You sure? They look heavy."

The woman glanced down at the bags, one in each hand, both bursting at the seams with books. They *were* heavy.

"Sure, my car is just over there," she said, indicating a gold minivan a couple of spots over.

She sighed as she relinquished her hold on one of the bags.

"Normally I have my son here to help me, but he's... well, he needs extra help and stayed late at school. Grade four, and already they're trying to tell me that he's falling behind in algebra. Algebra! I mean, I don't know about you, but I didn't take algebra until at least high school," she chuckled dryly. "And even then, I'm not sure I had any idea how to solve the damn—excuse me, *darn*—equations. I mean, letters and numbers are like liquor and beer. They just shouldn't mix, if you know what I mean."

They were almost at the minivan now.

"You like books?"

"Oh, I love them," the woman said cheerily. She moved the bag to her other hand, flexing her sore fingers.

"Let me ask you something: do you ever leave reviews for the books you read?"

The woman hesitated before replying.

"Reviews? S-s-sure, every once in a while. Why do you ask?"

Her pace slowed slightly as she neared her minivan, and the hand no longer gripping the plastic bag clenched. It was only a subtle gesture, but it didn't go unnoticed by either party.

*Something doesn't feel right.*

"I can take it from here," she said quickly, abandoning her previous line of questioning.

A strange, tuneless whistle suddenly filled the air.

"Oh no, allow me. Here, I'll grab your keys."

# Second Act

## Chapter 23

"Is HE COMING BACK, you think?" the woman with the piercings in her face asked.

Colin shrugged.

He was still so furious about Ryanne that he could barely believe that he had actually made it to the writer's group.

There were six of them again, and ten minutes into the class, there was still no sign of the douchebag Dwight Jurgens.

"Can someone email the guy? Cuz if he ain't coming, I want my money back," a young man with a toothpick dangling from between his lips asked from the back of the room.

"Already did. No answer. And the class was free," a plump woman who had introduced herself as Missy P —*why only use a pen name for your books? Why not have one in real life?* —replied. "Tried calling him, too, but went straight to voicemail."

"Whatever," toothpick boy said as he started to pack up his things.

"Why doesn't Colin teach again?" the girl with the piercings offered.

Colin's ears perked, drawing himself out of the scene that replayed over and over in his mind of his wife with the landlord.

"What? No, I don't—"

Missy P interrupted him.

"I thought what you said yesterday was interesting," she offered with a shrug that sent her entire body quivering. "I'd stick around if you want to teach again. I mean, you don't have to."

"Me too," someone else chimed in.

Toothpick boy strode toward the door.

"No offense, buddy, but I'm out."

Colin watched him go. The last thing he wanted was to teach these people about something he himself had limited knowledge of.

What had Ryanne said?

*If you didn't write your shitty books... If you got a real job.*

Or something like that.

And as much as he hated to admit it, Colin was beginning to think that she was right.

Irrespective of his new life experiences.

"I don't think I can teach you anything. I don't—" he felt his voice hitch and fought back tears. The woman beside him with the piercings lay a comforting hand on his back. Colin regained control just in time. "I—I don't know any more than you do. I self-published three books, but they don't sell. Anybody can do what I did. I'm working on something new, something written to market that I think will do better, something dark, more visceral, but really guys, I'm nothing special."

The hand on his back squeezed gently, and he turned to look directly at the woman. Her eyes were small and dark, and while he sought comfort and compassion in her expression, he didn't find any.

But after a moment of contemplation, he thought that maybe this is what he needed all along.

"What you told us yesterday—about writing what we know, about our experiences—I tried that last night," an older gentleman to Colin's left said in a dry voice. "It was my best writing session in years."

Colin raised an eyebrow.

"Come on, impart us with your knowledge, oh wise one," Piercings joked.

Colin sighed, and reluctantly stood and made his way to the front of the class.

"To write about experiences, the first thing you need to do is to *really* experience something. Something that affects you so deeply that it changes who you are."

\*\*\*

Colin was still out of breath even after all the other members of the writer's group had left the classroom. He had been up there for nearly an hour talking about...

*What the hell was I talking about?*

It had all been such a flurry that he couldn't remember. At one point, he thought he had mentioned Ryanne and his landlord, but couldn't be certain.

*What the hell does it matter, anyway?*

He was in the process of shoving his notepad into his messenger bag, when someone approached.

"You really have no idea what you're doing up there, do you?"

Colin turned in the direction of the voice and was surprised to see the woman with the undercut and tattoos standing in the classroom doorway.

Despite her condescending words, he was surprised to see that she was smiling.

"I thought everyone was gone... was it really that bad?"

Taking several steps forward, the woman said, "Naw, I'm just fucking with you. It wasn't that bad at all. Better than anything that prick Dwight could do, I bet."

Colin took her words as a compliment, although he wasn't sure that this had been her intention.

"Like that shit about, 'write what you know'?"

"What about it?"

"Sage advice. But makes me wonder... what have *you* experienced?" she asked, moving closer to him.

Colin's eyes narrowed and he felt his heart thud loudly in his chest.

"What do you mean?"

She moved closer still, until she was within several feet of him, and for some reason Colin started to get nervous.

"I mean, we all have our dark side, you know? What's that pen name you were telling us about? I am really, *really* interested in reading your work."

Colin felt uncomfortable and was about to say as much when the woman suddenly sidled right up next to him. Before he had an idea of what was happening, her hand was already at the front of his jeans.

His eyes bulged and he tried to swipe her hand away. Her grip, however, had a hold of him, and it was firm.

"I'm... I'm—" *married*, he wanted to say, but an image of his wife smoking a cigarette, her sagging breasts pushing up against the cheap t-shirt, Gary or Gerald or Glenn the landlord standing behind her in his stained tighty-whities came to mind and he stopped himself.

The woman, sensing his apprehension, smirked and leaned in close. She snaked her tongue over her lips, which, with a flash of excitement, he realized was pierced.

*Fuck Ryanne*, he thought suddenly, and this time when she squeezed the front of his pants, he pushed against her hand encouragingly.

Their sex was sloppy and uncoordinated, but it thankfully only lasted a few minutes. Sweating, his breath coming in short bursts, Colin turned away from the woman whom he had propped up on the desk and pulled up his pants.

He could feel his face flush from his embarrassing performance.

It had been a long, long time since he had had sex.

Ryanne, on the other hand...

When he turned around, he saw that the woman, whose name he still didn't know, had hopped off the desk and was in the process of pulling up her own pants.

"I'm sorry..." he began, but stopped himself when she chuckled.

Without comment, the woman buttoned her jeans and then quickly grabbed a piece of paper and a pen from the desk and started to write.

"Wh—what are you doing?"

Again, no answer.

Colin repeated the question, and this time the woman looked up at him.

"I'm doing what you said. I'm writing down what I know, my experience, so that I can recreate it later."

# Chapter 24

DRAKE AWOKE FEELING MORE refreshed than he had in months. Slightly disoriented, certainly, but his head felt clear and his thoughts were crystal.

And when he leaned over and saw Jasmine's face pressed against the pillow, her caramel-colored skin a stark contrast to the crisp white pillow, he felt his heart drop.

*What have I done?*

He slid out of bed and then moved toward his clothes that had been thrown on the chair the night prior. Walking as quietly as possible, trying to overcome his typical elephant-like grace, he somehow managed to put his pants and shirt on without waking Jasmine.

After a final glance at her peaceful face, accompanied by a well-deserved pang of guilt, Drake left the room.

Despite everything that had happened, he was beginning to think that perhaps his luck was changing. He managed to make it downstairs and slip on his boots in near silence, and he was within seconds of heading outside and forgetting all about the horrible mistake that he—that *they*—had made when the door suddenly flung open.

Suzan stood in the entrance, a bookbag dangling from one hand.

Their eyes met, and it was as if time itself had stopped.

For twenty seconds neither of them so much as breathed. It was only when Suzan's bag fell to the ground, did either of them react. Drake poised himself, ready to run by her if she started to scream again.

But to his surprise, she didn't scream. Instead, she simply nodded at him, then slipped by without a word.

Drake followed her with his eyes. She knew what had happened, knew the only logical reason why he was here so early in the morning.

She was bright and intuitive.

And yet Suzan didn't seem angered by this fact.

Drake was happy to see that most of her burns had healed, and aside from a slightly rosy complexion and a small patch of missing hair near her temple, she looked pretty good given what she had been through.

As if reading his thoughts, Suzan turned from the first step.

"Is my mom still asleep?" she asked in a soft voice.

Drake gaped, and couldn't bring himself to answer. It was probably for the best; he didn't want to risk breaking the unusual calm by speaking. Besides, the question was likely rhetorical, because Suzan didn't wait for an answer.

She started up the stairs, with Drake watching on.

"Mom?" she hollered. "You awake, Ma?"

Just before he turned and pulled the door wide, Drake spied something peeking out from the pocket of Suzan's jeans. It was only the tip, and he couldn't be positive, but he thought it was the same yellow as the envelope he had placed in the mailbox last night.

Outside, he noted that the little red flag on the side of the black mailbox was down again.

***

Drake entered Triple D and immediately reached for the light switch, only to realize that the lights were already on.

"Screech?"

The man popped out from behind his desk.

"Wassup?"

The man's goatee looked more like a beard these days, and his hair, normally short on the sides, long and curly on top, was beginning to form a tennis ball shape.

"You ever go home?" Drake asked, unable to help the smile that crept onto his lips. It faded when he remembered that the last time he had been here without Screech, Raul had been present.

"Nope. Never. I'm that dedicated to our noble cause, sire," Screech said with a mock bow.

"Speaking of which, did you ever talk to the guy about the yacht?"

"Mr. Bumacher? Meeting with him today. Speaking of which, I think it would be best for you to be there. Says it was your name who brought him to Triple D."

Drake removed his hat and coat and put them on the rack by the door.

"You can handle it, *pardner*," he offered.

Screech opened his mouth to say something, but then his eyes narrowed and a smirk crossed his lips.

"You're being unusually cordial this morning. Maybe even polite. I've only seen you like this once before, when—"

Drake's expression suddenly soured.

"Drop it, Screech."

Screech laughed.

"It's true, isn't it? You—"

"I said, drop it!"

The smile fell off the man's face and he dropped back down behind his computer screen.

"Sorry."

Drake marched past him.

"Did you find out anything about the e-book thingy? Where it came from?"

Screech shook his head and when he spoke, his tone had become serious. Drake immediately regretted snapping at him as he had.

"No idea who it came from. Couldn't link the registration number to anyone, and when I asked around the building, no one saw anyone deliver it. You think it's important?"

Drake hesitated, his hand on the handle to his office.

"I think it is," he said more to himself than to Screech.

"I'll keep digging then. But I looked into the book that was loaded on there—*Red Lips* or whatever?"

"*Red Smile,*" Drake corrected.

"Yeah, sure. Anyway, it looks like it's published online, but hasn't sold much. I tried to find out about the author, L. Wiley, but it's clearly a fake name. L. Wiley doesn't seem to exist."

Drake frowned. It wasn't just the similarities between the book and the murders that bothered him, but also the fact that while it was undoubtedly an important piece of the puzzle, it had taken him so long to look into it.

With Dr. Kildare, Chase, Ken, the man with the missing yacht, and now Jasmine of all people occupying his thoughts, his life had suddenly gone from simple to impossibly complicated seemingly overnight.

*I wish Clay was here… he would know what to say, what to do.*

An image of Jasmine on top of him, her head thrown back in ecstasy, her hard nipples pointed toward the ceiling suddenly flashed in his mind. Only as the scene played out, her pretty features slowly morphed into Ken Smith's, and he shuddered.

Except despite the vision, he couldn't fight the creeping sensation that he was the one getting fucked by Ken and not the other way around.

With a sigh, he turned back to Screech for a final time.

"Can you do me a favor?" he asked.

"Sure. What is it?"

"I need a couple of those cameras," he chewed his lip for a moment. "And set one up by the front door in case any more packages arrive."

Screech stared at him and Drake was certain that he was going to say something about home videos or offer some other lewd comment, but thankfully his partner bit his tongue.

"No problem. I'll have them on your desk by noon."

Drake closed the door to his office harder than he had intended and then slumped down in his chair.

A second later, he pulled the e-reader from his pocket and started to read.

# Chapter 25

CHASE STEPPED OUT OF the shower and dried her hair. With the fan above her head sucking out the moist air, she started to apply her makeup, trying her best to cover the dark circles beneath her eyes.

It had been a long, long night, one that had consisted mostly of Internet poker. She had done well, raking in well over three grand, but it hadn't helped distract her the way she thought it would.

And she had had only an hour of sleep, maybe two.

After Chase had done her best to make her face look halfway presentable, she dabbed concealer on the pale pink scars on the inside of her elbows.

She did this without thinking, the habit so ingrained that it no longer even registered in her brain.

That part of her life was behind her, long gone. And yet she doubted that the scars would ever heal completely.

Someone knocked on the bathroom door.

"Chase? You almost done in there? I have to piss!"

Chase made a face, and after quickly making sure that the track marks on her arms were barely visible, she tucked the towel up under her armpits.

"All done," she replied, pulling the door wide.

Brad was standing in the doorway, his eyes wide, clutching the crotch of his blue and white pin-stripe pajamas like a child.

"Gotta go!" he said as he hurried past.

Chase chuckled and started toward the bedroom, only to stop when Brad's voice drew her back.

"You still taking Felix in today, right?"

Chase frowned. She had forgotten all about her promise that she would take Felix to school today.

"Yeah, shouldn't be a problem," she replied. Her meeting with Drake and Agent Stitts to discuss the book lead that she had come up with wasn't scheduled until ten.

"Great," Brad said with a sigh as pee started to splash loudly in the bowl.

"Groo," Chase muttered, "I hope you put the seat up."

After dressing, she was surprised to see that not only was Felix already wearing his uniform, but he had poured himself a bowl of cereal and was sitting at the kitchen table, munching away.

*All grown up already... nine going on twenty-two.*

"Morning," she said.

Felix looked up at her, milk dripping from his lower lip.

"Good morning, mom!"

Chase smiled and kissed her son on the forehead. As she did, she smoothed a cowlick on the top of his head.

It stood straight up again the second she pulled her hand away.

"Let me get some water for that," she said as she made her way to the sink. "Looks like I'm taking you in today."

Chase put her hand under the tap and wet it, then made it back to her son and smoothed his hair again.

"Wanna stop for a donut before school?" she asked in a quiet voice.

Felix stopped slurping the milk in his bowl and looked up at her grinning.

"You sure? Daddy says I can't—"

Chase raised one eyebrow.

"Well daddy isn't taking you in today, is he? And when you're with—"

Her phone buzzed on her hip and she glanced down at it.
A frown formed on her lips.

"I'm sorry, Felix, I need to take this," she said as she lifted
the phone from her belt.

She turned just as the smile slid off Felix's face.

"Sergeant Adams," she stated.

"Chase, it's Agent Stitts. You need to come out to the barn
immediately."

Chase moved out of the kitchen and lowered her voice.

"Why? Did we miss something? Did CSU find trace
evidence?"

Agent Stitts sighed.

"Call Drake. We're going to need him, too."

Chase felt frustration rising in her chest.

"What? Why? What'd they find?"

"We didn't miss anything, Chase. But the killer returned.
And there's another body."

Chase felt her blood run cold.

*The killer returned...*

"Are you serious? The same barn?" she nearly gasped.

"Yeah. I'm on my way now. Want me to pick you up?"

Chase pictured her BMW in the driveway. She wasn't sure
what Agent Stitts drove, but it was more than likely a rental.

Her car would be faster.

"No, I'll meet you there. And I'll call Drake."

Before Stitts could protest, she hung up the phone and
started toward the door. She had only just opened it when she
heard Brad's voice from the upstairs landing.

"Have a good day at school, Felix!"

Chase cursed silently.

"Mom? Where're you going?" Felix called from the kitchen.

"Brad, can you get down here for a sec?"

"I'm in the middle of shaving."

"Brad, please."

Her husband appeared on the top landing, half of his face covered in shaving cream. He was topless, while his waist was covered in a towel. His upper body was softer than Chase remembered, and wondered briefly if this was a consequence of age or neglect. He was still in good shape for someone his age, nearing forty, but just wasn't as ripped as he usually was.

"What? What is it?" he asked, seeing the expression on her face.

Chase looked away.

"I have to go."

"Chase? What is it? Everything all right?"

Chase continued to stare into the kitchen, unaware that Felix had since come into view.

"Everything's fine, but I can't take Felix in. I have to go—I have to go now."

"What are you talking about? I have a meeting in fifteen minutes. I can't miss this, Chase. Please. Not today. You promised."

Chase looked up at her husband, at his pleading eyes, his cheeks and chin half covered in thick shaving cream.

But then she pictured the faces of the two girls, of Melissa Green and Tanya Farthing, dried blood smeared on their dead lips.

"I'm sorry," she said quietly. "I love you both and I'll see you tonight. I'll make it up to you."

Chase exited into the cold before either her husband or son could say anything that might draw her back.

# Chapter 26

"YOU WERE GONE ALL night again," Ryanne said with a scowl.

Colin ignored her and sipped his orange juice.

"Hey, I'm talking to you," she snapped. When Colin still didn't answer, she slapped his arm with the back of her hand still holding a cigarette. A shower of sparks erupted from where it struck his sweatshirt.

He jumped to his feet.

"Shit!"

As he swatted at the still glowing cherry that threatened to set him alight, he spilled orange juice on his jeans.

Ryanne laughed.

"Serves you right. Answer me next time."

Colin ground his teeth and fought the urge to respond.

That was, after all, what she wanted. And he refused to give in. He turned to his daughters instead, both of whom had their backs to him, their faces locked on the colorful cartoon that exploded across the TV screen.

"Juliette and Colby, grab your boots. I'll take you to school again today."

Neither of the girls acknowledged him.

"Juliette? Colby?"

Still nothing.

Ryanne walked over and swatted Colby in the back of the head.

"Ow!" the girl whined, spinning around. "What'd you do that for?"

"Get your fucking boots on. *Now!*"

Colin cringed. He hated when Ryanne swore at the girls, let alone smacked them. And yet in her backward sort of way, he could tell that Ryanne was trying to be helpful.

Which meant that she felt guilty.

*Good. She started this.*

Colin, on the other hand, felt nothing about his little tryst with the girl with the piercings.

"Time," Colby whined,

Colin's heart nearly broke at the sight of tears in his daughter's eyes. He quickly moved between her and Ryanne, and draped a hand over the little girl's shoulder, noticing as he did that there was a small black hole on his sleeve.

"And turn off those damn cartoons. I want to watch the news," Ryanne spat.

Colin eyed his wife.

*Since when is she interested in the news?*

"Come on," he said, guiding Colby toward the door. Juliette had since risen with the commotion and hurried after them.

With their boots laced, their jackets done up tight and hats pulled down low, Juliette and Colby stepped outside.

"You have to pick them up again today!" Ryanne called after Colin as he closed the door. "I'm doing my yoga class this afternoon!"

Colin closed his eyes and shook his head.

"Do whatever you want," he said under his breath. "We both know you're going to anyway."

When all three of them were finally in the car, he felt the tension in his shoulders release.

Ryanne was right; he had been out all night. He'd been out all night writing.

And gaining experiences.

*If only she knew...*

With a smile, he turned to his girls in the backseat, who had started to fight over who got to pick what they were going to listen to on the radio.

"Hey, you guys wanna do something different today?"

Colby scrunched up her forehead.

"We have school today."

Colin shrugged.

"You can skip school today. There's something that I want to show you guys. What do you say?"

# Chapter 27

CHASE COULDN'T BELIEVE THAT she was back here less than two days since she had left.

It was like a horrible case of déjà vu, only this time it was a different girl in the barn. There was an officer on scene, cordoning off the area, and Detective Yasiv was standing by the car smoking a cigarette.

His hand was trembling as she approached, but he made no move to throw it away this time.

"Sergeant Adams," he said softly.

Chase was furious and fought back the urge to yell at the man. She had put Yasiv in charge of the details, had left it up to him to make sure that everyone dotted their i's and crossed their t's.

To ensure the chain of custody was *never* broken.

Despite her promotion to Sergeant, Chase had no illusions that the Deputy Chief himself was unaware of the errors that had been made during the Butterfly Killer case. She was no fool; she knew that her tenure would last only as long as Dr. Mark Kruk—Marcus Slasinsky—was institutionalized and unable to stand trial.

This wasn't Mark Kruk bad, but discovering a third body in the barn? That was bad. There was no denying it.

She sighed.

"How the hell did this happen, Hank?"

The man took a drag of his cigarette.

"I have no idea," he said, while turning to look at the barn. "This is fucked up."

"There's an understatement."

"After the ME cleared the bodies, CSU came and took all of the evidence they could find. They gave the go-ahead, and I called Tommy Wilde and he must have cleaned the place in record time. After that, it was released back to the owner. I told a uniformed officer to keep watch, but he must have been called to another crime scene."

"And you're sure—you're *absolutely positive* that the body wasn't here with the others?"

Detective Yasiv shook his head.

"No, ma'am. We had over twenty people comb the place. It wasn't here. It's new."

Chase wanted to chastise the man, to yell at him, but couldn't really fault him. It was protocol to hold a scene for at least a week, but with CSU and Tommy Wilde coming in, there was no chance that anything would be left behind, let alone a body.

She opened her mouth to say something when the sound of a car approaching drew her attention. A Taurus pulled up behind her BMW and Agent Stitts stepped out, dressed in a crisp black suit and tie. He strode over to her, his expression grim.

"Sergeant Adams," he said with a nod, then turned to Detective Yasiv. "Detective."

"I called Drake, he's on his way. Just had to wrap a few things up first."

Chase thought she detected a small scowl appear on Agent Stitts's face, but it was gone before it fully formed. He tilted his head and stared at the barn.

"Let's see what we've got."

As Detective Yasiv led them to the scene, Stitts posed the question that was on all their minds.

"Why'd the killer come back?"

Chase thought about this for a moment.

"It's fairly common for a killer to revisit the scene of their crime. Murderers are addicts of a sort; like a heroin junkie looking to recreate the thrill of their first injection, they come back to try and recreate the feeling of their first kill."

Agent Stitts nodded.

"True. But rarely are new victims dumped in the location that has already been found by the police." He offered a sidelong glance at Detective Yasiv before continuing. "Too dangerous. Too risky."

They made it down the embankment in silence. As they neared the door with fresh crime scene tape, Agent Stitts continued.

"And yet, even knowing what we know, none of us thought that the killer would return here. Otherwise, we would have made sure that an officer remained stationed."

Chase frowned.

"Detective Yasiv volunteers to stay here day and night from now on."

Detective Yasiv clenched his jaw, but didn't protest.

"Returning to a crime scene once is one thing, but three times? I highly doubt that," Agent Stitts added. "But that's not the question I asked. I want to know why none of us thought that the killer would return to this particular scene."

Chase didn't know why she had felt this way, but she most definitely had. To be honest, she hadn't extended much thought on the issue, but now that Agent Stitts had verbalized his point...

*It's the same reason that I didn't ask about the lipstick on the other victims. Because of... what had Agent Stitts called it? Intuition. Because of intuition.*

Only, in this case, her intuition was wrong.

And it wasn't the first time, either.

Chase resisted the urge to look down at her forearms, even though they were covered by a thick coat and a sweater beneath.

It was Detective Yasiv who answered.

"I guess it was because I thought the killings were random. My thinking was that if the killings were random, then the drop location might also be random—holding no value or meaning to the killer."

Chase found herself nodding subconsciously. She shared Hank's sentiment, she realized.

"I'll buy it. Only now we don't think that the victims were entirely random, do we?"

Again, Chase nodded.

"Wait—we don't?" Detective Yasiv asked.

"No," Chase replied, lifting the tape covering the doorway and stepping into the derelict barn. "We don't."

*\*\**

The victim, whom they had already identified as Charlotte Banquise based on a recently filed missing person report, wasn't buried as Melissa or Tanya had been. The killer had taken a calculated risk coming back here, but he hadn't been so bold as to take the time to even pull the hay over top of her body.

Like the other two victims, her face was pale, her lips a deep maroon. Only this time, there weren't multiple cuts on her arms. In fact, her arms were pristine.

Instead, her throat had been cut in a ragged gash that ran from ear to ear.

"He's speeding up," Chase said as she surveyed the scene. "With the first two, he had taken his time, cut them slowly, let them starve to death or freeze or bleed out. With Charlotte, he was much quicker."

Agent Stitts got a far-off look in his dark hazel eyes.

"Which is the opposite that usually happens. Typically, the first kills are fast, the killer worried that they would either be caught or that they would lose their nerve. But not in this case." He paused. "Why?"

Chase mulled this over.

"Maybe she fought? Maybe the local PD was closing in? Perhaps they had caught wind of him for an unrelated crime and he had to get rid of the body quickly?"

"Maybe," Stitts replied. "But then why this location? Detective Yasiv, did the uniforms comb the adjacent woods?"

Henry nodded.

"There were some tire tracks off the road about a mile down. They made some casts, but the falling snow already obscured anything of use. They know that it was a car, front wheel drive, likely nothing bigger than a sedan. They also found some disturbed areas where it looks like a body might have been dragged, but, again, the snow makes it next to impossible to draw any strong conclusions."

"No cabin in the woods?"

Yasiv nodded.

"They found an old hunting cabin, but it hasn't been used in years. Cobwebs everywhere. CSU cleared that as well."

"What about the old man who owns this place? Doesn't he live nearby?" Agent Stitts asked.

"Yep—five miles down the road. He's been cooperative, and we've gone over his house with a fine-toothed comb. He's been ruled out, and it is highly unlikely given the state of his house that the killer was using it with or without his knowledge."

As was her habit, Chase crouched low and stared into the victim's eyes. They were open slightly, revealing the bottom crescents of what she suspected had once been vibrant green eyes.

Green eyes not that unlike her own.

"And Brent Doakes?" she asked.

"Doakes?"

"Melissa's boyfriend."

Yasiv cleared his throat.

"Cleared. He's been locked up for possession for the past week."

Chase nodded and returned her attention to Charlotte's body.

"The killer was rushed with the murder, but not with the body drop. He came here specifically, but why?"

There was no response, and she hadn't expected one.

There was only one person who could answer that.

The killer.

Chase sighed and started to stand.

"Get CSU in here," she said. "I doubt they'll find anything, but I want them to scour every inch of this place. Again."

# Chapter 28

DRAKE COULDN'T BELIEVE WHAT he was reading. While at first, he had doubted that the story on the e-reader and the bodies in the barn was a coincidence, now he was absolutely certain that it wasn't.

The similarities were uncanny.

Two bodies, both dead from a combination of blood loss and exposure, half-buried beneath piles of hay in a broken-down barn.

And it didn't stop there.

In the book, like in life, the women's lips had been stained with blood.

"Jesus," he whispered, exhaling slowly.

There were even details about Chase and himself, only the names were different. What they hadn't included, however, was FBI Agent Stitts. With shaking hands, he finished the book—more of a short story, really—which concluded with fictional Chase and himself wondering who the killer was.

There was no real ending, so to speak.

When he had finished reading, there was no question in Drake's mind that the only person who could have written this was the killer.

*I have to tell Chase,* he thought suddenly. And then, as if on cue, his phone started to ring.

He picked it up and was only half surprised that it was Chase.

"There's been another murder, Drake. And the body was dropped at the barn. Again."

Drake's eyes bulged.

"What? The same barn? Nobody was watching it?"

Chase's reply was strained.

"No. They wrapped up and then relinquished custody back to the owner."

"Are you out there now?"

"Yes, as is Agent Stitts and Detective Yasiv. We need your help, Drake. Can you make it here?"

Drake glanced at the e-reader on his desk.

"On my way. And there's something that I have to show you."

\*\*\*

Drake pulled up behind a Ford Taurus and slammed his Crown Vic into park.

Thankfully the snow had stopped falling, but the temperature had continued to drop. He pulled the neck of his jacket closed as he walked through the snow to the barn.

Inside, he was met with an eerily similar scene to the one that he had observed the other day.

Detective Yasiv and Chase hovered over the body, while Agent Stitts stood back, his eyes moving about the dimly lit barn.

Drake announced his presence, then went directly to the corpse.

The victim was a woman in her mid-forties, her throat slit, blood on her lips. He swallowed hard, and then instinctively reached into his pocket and fondled the rubber backing of the e-reader buried within.

This was a cluster fuck, the story notwithstanding.

"Did you speak to the parents of the first two victims?" he asked, breaking the silence.

Chase admitted that she had.

"And? Anything of use?"

"Sergeant Adams thinks it might have to do with books...
that the victims are somehow connected through books?"

All of sudden Drake had trouble breathing, as if the air had
suddenly been sucked out of the barn.

"Wh—what?" he stammered.

Chase gave him a strange look.

"Books—Melissa was an avid reader, and Tanya's room
was filled with them. All types of novels."

Drake felt dizzy and put a hand on the wooden stall to
keep from falling. Chase was on him in an instant, putting an
arm around his shoulders, bracing him.

"Drake? You okay?"

He shook his head and found that he was unable to speak.
The burn on his cheek itched horribly, but he couldn't even
muster the strength to scratch it.

"Drake?"

With considerable effort, he managed to straighten himself.

"Books? You sure?"

"No, not sure. Just a hunch. But I bet that Charlotte here
liked to read as well."

He slipped a hand into his pocket and pulled out the e-
reader.

"There's something you need to see," he said quietly.
"Something you need to read."

***

"I managed to pull up Melissa Green's library records—the
woman took out a lot of books. I've also acquired Tanya
Farthing's bank records, and have singled out her purchases
at bookstores and online. Problem is, there's so much data that
it's going to take a while to process," Agent Stitts said.

Drake looked around the conference room, feeling more comfortable than he figured he deserved. There were five of them in the room: himself, Chase, Agent Stitts, Detective Yasiv, who had since stationed two uniformed officers at the barn, and Officer Dunbar.

"I'll have a go at that. I have a program that can look for similarities in purchases. Shouldn't take that long."

Chase nodded.

"Good. I'll go with Agent Stitts to speak to Charlotte's family, see if we can find a connection there, confirm that she was also a reader."

Drake looked at the e-reader that had been placed in the center of the table like some sort of modern golem.

"And the book? What about the book?"

Officer Dunbar cleared his throat.

"I already downloaded all the data I could from it. So far as I can tell, the IP that sent the book to the reader was scrambled. Pinged all over the Middle East, then Asia. I'll keep plugging away, but I doubt I'll get any hits."

Drake nodded. Screech had already told him as much.

"And the book itself?" Detective Yasiv asked. "Where'd it come from?"

"Screech looked into it. Said it was written by a pen name, untraceable. Right now, it's hidden in the ranks, even though it's available online at most retailers. Should we ask them to pull it?"

Drake bit his tongue, stopping himself from asking the next question that was on his mind.

*Why the hell was it sent to me?*

Chase chewed the inside of her cheek.

"No, not now. All we need is some book selling gunslinger to let something leak, and we'll have a media shitstorm on our hands. For now, have Screech see if he could dig deeper into the bigger retailers, Amazon, Barnes and Noble, Kobo, see if he can find out any connections between Also Boughts, tweets, Facebook posts, etc. We *have* to find out who wrote the damn thing."

When she paused to take a breath, Detective Yasiv spoke up.

"What about the media in general? I mean, it wasn't hard to keep them out given the remote location of the crime scene, but now with a third victim... if even one friend or family member of the deceased goes to the press..."

"For now, we keep it under wraps," Chase replied. "Nobody's to speak to the press."

Silence fell over the room, and their eyes skipped across the images of the three women on the board at the head of the room.

"On second thought, I'm going to set up a press conference. Nothing specific, just to remind women between the ages of twenty to fifty not to accept rides or help from..." She let her sentence trail off, then turned to Stitts. "Agent Stitts, can you help us out here? What sort of profile are we looking at?"

Stitts flipped through a pad of paper before stopping on a page full of notes.

"I've generated a preliminary profile, given the ages of the victims and their cause of death. That being said, it's only a loose profile given the differences in the vics's socio-economic backgrounds."

"Shoot," Chase said.

Agent Stitts cleared his throat and then started to read.

"Based on historical precedence, we are looking for a male between the ages of thirty-five and fifty—just a few years older than the first two victims. Has to be in pretty good shape to have carried the bodies through the woods, and judging by the lack of hurriedness of the first two kills, this is likely someone who has no conscience whatsoever. They are doing this as a means to an end, not necessary just to extract pleasure from the act. The killer likely keeps a low profile, is a middle to high-income earner who, if he had previous encounters with the law, would only have been convicted of some minor crimes. Given the violence of the kills, and the prolonged period of capture for the first two victims, the man is trying to exercise control; he was likely emasculated in his youth, abused by a mother figure, perhaps. A nurse, a nun, something like that. We'll know more after we speak to Charlotte's family, but knowing that at least Tanya appears to have been abducted in broad daylight, the man would be physically unassuming and is likely friendly, handsome, or in the very least charismatic."

The FBI Agent's speech left Drake unimpressed. He wasn't so naive or old-school to believe that FBI profiles had no value, but this one held about as much truth as a horoscope: it was ambiguous to the point of nearly being impossible to be proven wrong, but on the same token, it wasn't all that useful either.

"You're right," he said with a scowl. "It isn't much to go on."

"Still, it's something," Chase said, eying him suspiciously. "When I speak to the press, I'll advise women to stay away from men who approach them outside of malls, grocery stores, and, most importantly, bookstores. We are going to be bombarded by calls, but we can't have another murder on our hands while we just sit on them."

Drake nodded.

"I still have a contact or two in the publishing world I can approach, see if they can find out who this author—this L. Wiley—might be. It's a stretch, but…"

"Anything might help," Chase said, reaching across and grabbing the e-reader. She held it out to Drake, who didn't immediately take it. "Hold on to it, Drake—the killer might send you another story. For whatever reason, he's taken a liking to you. If he does send something else, maybe you can learn from it."

Drake reluctantly took the e-reader. It felt warm in his hands, but he wasn't sure if it was running hot or if it was just his mind playing tricks on him.

"Oh," Officer Dunbar interjected. "Almost forgot; I sent the entire file to our forensic document examiner. Although he specializes in analyzing handwriting, he might have some insight into the background of the author based on word choices, etc." He shrugged. "Not an exact science, but you never know."

Chase stood, and the others followed her lead.

"Good. Dunbar, do you have someone in records you can trust? Someone who might be able to scour perps with criminal records that might have a link to the book publishing business?"

Dunbar thought about this for a moment.

"Yeah, I can ask Pauley. He might be able to do it. Good with computers, and better at being quiet."

"Fine, get him on it. I'll set up a press conference after visiting Charlotte's family. Everyone else, let's keep this book idea under wraps. The last thing we want is to turn this sick bastard into a bestselling author."

With that, Chase made her way toward the door, Detective Yasiv, Officer Dunbar, and Agent Stitts in tow.

Before leaving the room, she turned back to Drake, who remained seated.

"Let's catch this bastard before he kills again."

And then they were gone, leaving Drake to his own thoughts. He looked up at the horrific images of the three dead women, a feeling of disgust working its way deep in the pit of his stomach like food poisoning.

Chase was right, they had to catch the killer before they struck again. Except that wasn't their only problem here.

Chase was going to go public about another set of murders, only a few months removed from Craig Sloan's killing spree and ultimate demise.

And there was one person who really, *really* wasn't going to be happy about it.

It just so happened that Drake also worked for this man.

# Chapter 29

"WHAT IS THIS PLACE, daddy?" Colby asked from the backseat.

Colin stared at the cabin before replying. It wasn't much from the outside—in fact, it needed quite a bit of work—but he could see deeper than the peeling paint, the lifting roof shingles, the rotting porch.

He could see a future here, one where he would spend his days fixing up the place, his evenings at the computer typing away.

The best part about the place was how far it was from any neighbors. It was at least fifteen miles from the nearest farm, and twice that from the closest real suburb.

Seclusion, freedom, but most of all it was *quiet*.

It was a place to gain the experiences he so adamantly espoused the importance of to the writing group.

"Right now it isn't much," he admitted. "Just a cabin, a cottage."

He unbuckled his seatbelt and started to get out of the car.

"Looks like a dump," Juliette replied.

Colin shook his head and sighed as he opened the door for his girls.

They hopped out and immediately started bickering on the front lawn.

Colin ignored them and stared at the cabin, imagining what it might look like with a new coat of paint, fresh window treatments.

The back and sides of the cabin were flanked by heavily wooded areas, adding to the feeling of seclusion. The front lawn, which extended for thirty or so feet until it met the worn path that his car had made, kept it from feeling claustrophobic.

Colin turned his gaze in the direction that he had come, noting that it seemed to disappear when it cut through a section of trees. From the main road, the path was nearly impossible to find, especially with the blanket of snow coating everything.

If you didn't know the path was there, you would drive right by it without a second thought.

"That's mine!" Juliette shouted, bringing Colin out of his head.

He looked over to see Colby holding her hat just out of reach. Juliette stood on her tippy-toes, but Colby turned her back to her sister, preventing her from grabbing it.

"Give it back, Colby," Colin instructed. Either Colby didn't hear him, or she simply chose to ignore him.

"Na-na-na boo-boo," she said, sticking out her tongue.

"Guys, just stop fighting, would you? Let's just enjoy the weather and take a look around. There's a really cool and creepy basement you have to see."

Juliette looked at him and blinked several times before speaking.

"It's freezing out and this place looks like a dump. Can't we just go back to school?"

Colin felt anger start to build inside of him, and for a split second, he debated throwing them both in the basement.

He shook the thought from his head.

"Fine," he muttered. "I just need to get something from inside. You guys stop fighting and wait here?"

"Whatever," they responded in unison.

Colin hurried through the snow to the back door, and then reached on top of the door frame for the key. When his fingers felt nothing, he stared upward.

"I know I put it here—I *always* put it here."

Colin ran his fingers across the entire edge of the rotting wooden frame, but still came up empty.

"What the hell?" he said to himself. His frustration was reaching the point of no return, an apex from which no number of controlled breaths would bring him back.

"Where the *fuck* is the goddamn key?"

Colin tried the door handle, and while it rattled in his hand, it remained locked.

He ground his teeth and pursed his lips.

"Where the fuck did it go?"

Without thinking, his right foot shot out and connected with the bottom of the door. A resounding thud echoed off the trees behind him, and when he pulled his boot away, he saw that he had taken a chunk out of the wood.

"Goddammit," he swore.

Colin moved away from the door and went to the window, trying to peer inside.

A white curtain blocked his view.

"Shit!"

Blood rose in his cheeks, making them tingle. Just as he concluded that the only way to get inside would be to drive his shoulder into the door, he spotted a small indentation in the snow to his left.

Bending down, he felt relief wash over him. In a tunnel of snow lay a silver key.

*It must have fallen off with the snow and wind,* he thought as he picked it up.

Colin unlocked then opened the door, his nose immediately crinkling at the smell. He debated opening the windows and airing the place out, but a shriek from the front lawn nixed that idea.

*Always fighting… always goddamn fighting… will it ever stop?*

Colin spotted the worn black notepad on the counter and scooped it up.

With one final, wistful look around, he exited the way he had come, locking the door and making sure that the key was firmly butted up against the wall atop the door trim.

Book in hand, he hurried back to the front just in time to see Juliette whack Colby upside the head.

Colby stumbled, and Juliette continued with the blow, landing on top of her.

"Get off her! Juliette, get off your sister!" Colin shouted, running over to them.

Juliette didn't listen. Instead, she grew more furious, scooping up snow in both palms before pouring it over Colby's face.

Both girls were shrieking now.

"I said, *get off her!*" Colin bellowed. He ran to Juliette and grabbed her jacket, yanking her to her feet.

"*Stop fighting!*" he yelled in her face, his hand still gripping the hood of her jacket. His fingers twisted in the material, causing it to tighten around her throat. Juliette's eyes started to water and her breath came out in raspy gasps.

"Next time, you listen to me," Colin hissed, staring into his daughter's eyes. "You got it?"

When Juliette didn't answer immediately, he squeezed the coat even tighter.

"Got it?"

Juliette nodded and Colin finally let go. He turned to Colby, who had since gotten to her feet, her face red and wet from the snow that Juliette had piled on top of her.

"That goes for you, too—both of you. Now get in the car. And don't you even think about telling your mother about this place."

# Chapter 30

THE LAST THING THAT Drake wanted to do was to personally head to Dr. Kildare's campaign office—his first choice had been Screech to do it for him, but he was meeting with Mr. Yachty—let alone go there in the middle of the day. Especially given the warning that Ken had issued about being seen.

To make things worse, ever since what had happened with Craig Sloan, and even before that with the Skeleton King, Drake was finding remaining anonymous to be increasingly difficult. The media had done a one-eighty on him when they reported that he had saved Suzan's life, turning him from a heel to a hero.

All the media wanted was a good story, and there was no better tale than a detective who had cost his partner his life, only to save the man's daughter who was kidnapped by yet another serial killer.

*You know what else makes a good story? Red Smile…*

Drake pulled his cap down low and strode across the parking lot. It was quiet, which he found surprising considering that it was a Thursday afternoon. From what he knew about politics, which was admittedly little, he figured they usually ran twenty-four seven this close to the election date.

*Maybe they're all out for lunch.*

There were still plenty of cars in the parking lot, but the interior of the building, despite being brightly lit, appeared completely empty.

Drake's brow furrowed as he approached. His mind was flooded with the idea that this was all a trap, that for some strange reason Ken wanted him to get caught, to be arrested. It didn't make sense, but he couldn't be this lucky.

He never was.

But as Drake came right up to the door and he still saw no movement inside, he simply shrugged.

*The door will be locked and I'll have to break in. And that's when the police will show up.*

When he tried the door and found that the knob turned easily in his hand, however, the fantasy grew less likely.

Drake tucked his chin into his coat and lowered his head. He slid his hands into his pockets, feeling the objects in each that were roughly the same size: the finger bone and the button camera.

Regardless of whether it was luck or a setup, Drake knew that he had to work quickly. He glanced around, his eyes skipping over the many desks covered in election posters, all bearing Dr. Kildare's smiling face, as he tried to locate the best place to put his camera.

The most likely location to record the good doctor doing the bad thing with his campaign manager.

There were several offices near the back, and Drake quickly made his way toward them. The first clearly belonged to a secretary or statistician of some sort based solely on the presence of the massive stack of files on the desk, but the second one gave him pause. Unlike the rest of the warehouse, this office was clean, immaculate even. There was no other evidence that this was the doctor's office, but something in his gut told him that it was.

Only a doctor would be this neat, this fastidious. Again thinking that his luck was about to run out, he reached for the door handle and was surprised when it turned with ease.

His heart rate quickened with the realization that he had probably already broken a half dozen laws, but before his conscience took over, he stepped inside Dr. Kildare's office.

The best location, he figured, was in the corner behind the desk, up near the ceiling. That would offer a clear view of the computer screen and the desk.

Drake grabbed a leather chair and wheeled it to the corner, and then stood on it. He pulled his right hand from his pocket and reached up high, only to realize that he had grabbed the wrong object.

Cradled between his fingers was the finger bone that Ivan Meitzer had given him in the diner what felt like ages ago.

Drake cursed and went to put it back in his pocket when the chair unexpectedly swiveled, and he was forced to reach out and brace himself with his hand. As he did, the bone slipped from his fingers and clattered to the linoleum floor below.

"Shit," he said as he watched it slide under the desk.

Drake quickly pulled out the button camera and pressed the sticky back against the wall near the ceiling. He leaned back slightly, observing his handy work. It wasn't completely unnoticeable on the white wall as it had been beneath Mrs. Armatridge's stairs, but a passive observer would likely just think it a hole or chip in the paint.

Or at least that was what he hoped.

He was about to hop off the chair when a sound from behind him caused him to freeze.

"Roger? That you? What are you doing up there?"

For several seconds, Drake could do nothing but stand frozen on the chair, his back to the man who had entered the office behind him.

His mind was racing as it cycled through every scenario he could think of from knocking the guy out, to making up some elaborate lie to get him out of this jam, all the while Ken's voice provided a soundtrack to his thoughts.

*Whatever you do, don't get caught. Don't be seen.*

Drake settled for the latter, giving up the hope of not being seen.

That ship had sailed.

He turned slowly, almost robotically, so as to not alarm the man behind him.

With the most genuine smile he could muster, he said, "No, not Roger. But close."

The man in the office doorway couldn't have been older than twenty, and even that must have been a stretch. With shellacked hair and a doughy face, the boy was staring at him with wide eyes. "The name is Robert Watts—building superintendent."

He lowered himself off the chair and then strode forward, hand outstretched. The man—intern, he had to be an intern—looked at his hand suspiciously and Drake withdrew it before it became awkward.

"We've been having some problems with the drop ceiling in the other units—especially in the Subway 'round back. The heavy snow has been causing some water damage. I was just checking for any sign of moisture. Can't risk having mold in here."

The man squinted at him.

"I ran it by Mary," Drake said quickly, surprised that he had remembered the woman's name. "Said it wasn't a problem to come in and check it out."

"And?" the man asked, his eyebrows rising.

Drake's smile grew.

"And you—heh, *we're* in luck. It's all dry up there. Should stay that way, too, if there's no more snow, that is."

When the man continued to stare, Drake made his way toward the door.

"Sorry if I startled you. Can't be too careful with these things. Once there's one spot of mold, there's a dozen."

As he passed the intern, he observed him closely, trying to get a read on him.

It wasn't too late to use the Armstrong method, as much as he knew that would only end badly for both of them. Thankfully, the man's wide cheeks suddenly tightened in a smile.

"Well that's good news, I guess. Just make sure that you vote Kildare."

Drake chuckled and walked into the main portion of the campaign office.

"Of course. Here's to hoping the good doctor comes out on top."

"Thanks."

"No problem," he said over his shoulder.

Less than a minute later, Drake was back in his car, breathing heavily in the front seat, his heart still racing.

"Jesus Christ, what the hell are you doing, Drake? Whose side are you on?"

But before he could answer his own question, a strange chime from somewhere in his thick coat interrupted him. At first, he thought it was the smartphone that Screech had given him, but then remembered that had set it on silent. Drake patted his chest, and then pulled out the e-reader.

His heart sunk when he turned it on and saw that there wasn't just one book cover on the home screen, but two. The second also showed the pale face of a woman, her lips painted in blood.

*Red Smile PART II,* the title read.

Drake swallowed hard and opened the book.

It was only later that he realized that he had forgotten to grab the bone that he had dropped in the doctor's office.

# Chapter 31

THE MAN PUSHED THE camera lens through the open window. He waited for the image to focus, then snapped several shots of the building, making sure that most of them included the campaign posters with the smiling doctor's face in the background.

Satisfied that he wasn't too far away to capture the details he needed, he waited.

He didn't have to wait long.

A man in a navy coat, his chin tucked low, made his way toward the door. When his bare hand reached for the handle, he paused, turning to look around.

The camera shutter fired rapidly, capturing more than a dozen pictures of the man's face in just a few seconds.

Zooming in, he captured several more pictures of the man inside the campaign office, and then of him exiting no more than five minutes later.

When Drake made it to his car and slumped in the front seat, the man captured a final image, then pulled the camera inside the vehicle and closed the window.

# Chapter 32

"**WHAT DID YOU THINK** of the profile?" Agent Stitts asked as Chase drove toward Charlotte's last known address.

Chase shrugged.

"To be honest? It's pretty vague. In a city as large as New York, you pretty much described a third of the male population. Shit, even in Larchmont, you only narrowed it down to a couple hundred people."

There was something else that bothered her about the profile, something that she kept to herself for the time being. Agent Stitts had said that the suspect was likely emasculated, probably at the hands of a female superior of some sort. And yet none of the bodies they had recovered showed any signs of sexual assault. She was no expert, of course, but something felt fundamentally wrong about their assumptions.

Agent Stitts turned his eyes to the road.

"That's fair. There's something in my gut that's telling me it's not quite right, that I'm missing something."

Chase nodded, and Agent Stitts faced her again.

"Thinking the same thing?"

"Yes—there's something that we're just not seeing."

"Agreed. Let me ask you something: do you trust your gut?"

The question caught Chase by surprise.

"My gut? Like a gut feeling?"

"Sure."

Again, Chase wasn't sure if this was some sort of test, if Agent Stitts was trying to work his way into her mind. But, as before, all the second-guessing was exhausting. She had a murderer to catch, and couldn't be concerned with whether her hair was straight or if she used proper grammar.

The FBI could wait until this was over.

"Do I trust my gut? Sometimes… the fact is, sometimes my intuition's right, and sometimes it's just dead wrong."

Her thoughts turned to the scars on the inside of her elbows. Intuition had told her that she should gain the trust of the mid-level dealer they were pursuing by taking a hit of heroin. The same intuition had left her with a deadly habit and a whole division of Seattle Narcotics officers looking for her.

And long before that, her intuition had cost her something even more important.

"Nowadays I try to rely on facts and not feelings."

Agent Stitts continued to stare out the window, and Chase worried that she might have said something that offended him.

"I can see how —"

"Millions of years of evolution," he said absently.

"Excuse me?"

"Don't ignore your intuition, Chase. Millions of years of evolution served to develop an inherent defense mechanism in all of us. Call it gut feeling, intuition, a hunch, whatever you call it, it's a valuable asset in the field. Trust me on this one. Sometimes your eyes see things, but your conscious mind is too busy or too tired to take notice. Your gut, however, is pre-historic. Listen, you ever waited for an elevator and when the door opened, you just had a bad feeling about the guy inside waiting for you to enter?"

Chase tilted her head to one side.

"Maybe."

"Maybe's good enough. Everyone has had these experiences in their lives, but there's a selection bias at play. People who listen to these urges? They don't think twice about them later because nothing happened. In fact, they might even convince themselves that they were being foolish, childish, even. But it's the time when you feel something's wrong, that something's just not right, and you don't listen to it and something bad happens? That's what we remember. Over time, if this job has taught me one thing, it's to trust my instincts."

Agent Stitts peered over at the GPS mounted on the dash.

"We've got another ten minutes at least in New York traffic before we arrive at Charlotte's house," he informed her. "Mind if I tell you a story? About why I decided to pursue a career in the FBI? In profiling?"

Chase wasn't in the mood for fables, but couldn't think of a good reason for Stitts not to continue.

"Sure, go ahead."

Agent Stitts looked up and to the right when he spoke next, a tell from poker that suggested that he was remembering something from his past and not just making it up.

"I was young, maybe twenty years old," Stitts began in a monotone voice, "just starting out as a real estate agent. I was also with this girlfriend who was... well, *demanding*, let's say. She was constantly pissed because of the long hours I worked. This one night, after she had just told me that she was getting fed up, a client felt the need to inspect every single floorboard in the house that he was thinking of putting an offer on. I could literally hear my girlfriend getting angrier the longer she waited for me at home. By the time my client was ready to leave, I was already twenty minutes late for dinner. And I still had to drive home, which, in Houston traffic, was going to take at least double that. Anyways, on the way home I thought it would be a good idea to grab a bottle of wine to smooth things over, you know? There was this store that I usually went to for wine and beer that wasn't too far from my place. So, I'm in a hurry, thinking about what I was going to say, what joke I could make in order to make sure my girlfriend didn't bite my head off, and I headed into the store. As soon as I opened that door, I felt that something was off. And I'm not talking about something flitting like, 'oh, I should buy this lottery ticket, it's a winner,' no bullshit like that. This was a strong feeling in my gut that almost made me throw up. And you know what I did?"

Chase shrugged.

"You walked out?"

"That's right—I walked out and went home. Skipped the wine altogether."

"And? What happened?"

"Found out on the news later that the proprietor had been shot dead and his store had been robbed. At first, I couldn't believe it. In fact, I was so shocked by the ordeal that I actually went back to the store and found out that it had been robbed minutes after I had left. I know what you're thinking, it was a coincidence, which is fine, because that's what I thought, too. But, long story short, I managed to get a hold of the security tape from the store. I must have watched that video a thousand times."

Again, he paused.

"What was on the tape?"

"I saw what I already knew, but hadn't registered. At the time, I was living in a rough-ish part of Houston and every single time I walked into a convenience store or liquor store— and I do mean *every time*—the guy or girl behind the counter gave me the good old fashioned up down. It's like part of their training, I guess. Anyways, this time, the guy only glanced over at me and then looked away. In the video, you clearly see me stare at the guy behind the counter as this happens, then I follow his gaze to a man perusing the shelves wearing a parka. A parka in Houston in the middle of summer. I knew then that this is what my 'instincts' had picked up on. They saved my life."

Chase thought about the story for a moment. There were many times in her life when something like this had happened, not as serious as what Agent Stitts described of course, but similar, but she also figured that there was an equal number of times in which her instincts were just dead wrong.

The killer returning to the barn, for instance. In the end, Chase decided to try and lighten the mood as opposed to challenging him.

"And what did your girlfriend say?"

Agent Stitts laughed.

"Ha, she dumped my ass. Made me think I would have been better off getting that bottle of wine after all. Well, that's my origin story, what's yours? Why did you get into the police force and why do you want to join the FBI?"

Chase frowned. Perhaps it was her intuition that had told her that this question was coming, which was why she wanted to avoid the discussion in the first place. Or maybe it was just plain common sense.

"Well," she said, turning into the driveway of a brightly lit bungalow, "would you look at that."

Agent Stitts followed her finger.

"What? What is it?"

"Charlotte's house. Come on, let's get this over with."

# Chapter 33

"C'MON, CHASE, PICK UP the phone," Drake grumbled. He waited for the answering machine to roll before hanging up. Pulling into the strip mall that housed Triple D, he drove right up to the doors and parked his Crown Vic. Then he hopped out, e-reader in hand.

"Hey Screech?" he said as he entered Triple D. He noticed that the door to his office was closed and inside he could make out the silhouettes of two men: one small, with a q-tip shaped head, and the other a massive, boulder of a man.

Drake strode over to the door and pulled it open.

Screech startled and leaned back in Drake's chair as he entered.

"Drake, this is Bob Bumacher," he said after collecting himself, "He is the one whose boat—"

"—yacht—" Drake corrected.

Screech nodded.

"Whose yacht has gone missing. We were just working out the details of our arrangement. Apparently, there is some precious cargo on board," Screech's face twisted slightly as he said this, which gave Drake pause.

*Precious cargo?*

But Drake didn't have time for this. He needed to contact Chase, to tell her about the new story. About part II. And he needed to figure out who the hell was writing the morbid tales.

"Alright, sounds good. I hate to be rude, Mr. Bumacher, but I really have another matter that I have to discuss with my partner."

Bob Bumacher stood, and Drake instinctively leaned away from him. He wasn't just a large man, as Drake had suspected based on the outline, he was *huge*. Six-six if he was a foot, with shoulders like watermelons. He was wearing a tight-fighting t-shirt with Arnold Schwarzenegger's face across the chest and the words, "Come with me if you want to lift" written on top.

He nodded to Drake and then scratched his bald head.

"You've come highly recommended, Drake. I expect that you and your partner will use the utmost discretion in your search for my vessel. Me and Screech have already worked out the details, and I'm sure that you'll find them more than satisfactory."

Bob held out a giant hand and Drake didn't so much as shake it as was swallowed by it.

After Bob regurgitated his hand, he turned and left the office, leaving the door open behind him. When he was gone, Drake shook his head and looked over at Screech.

"What the hell was that all about?" he asked, but when Screech opened his mouth to answer, Drake held a hand up. "Never mind."

He hooked a thumb, indicating that Screech should get out of his chair. Screech nodded and stood, and Drake slumped into it.

"What's up?"

"There's been another murder and another story," Drake replied, tossing the e-reader roughly on the desk.

Screech frowned.

"For real? Fucking hell. I couldn't find anything about the author... about L. Wiley online. Literally nothing. The man's a ghost. No posts on any of the popular writing boards, no website, no email address, no nothing. But I'm no expert when it comes to online publishing. You know anyone who might have experience?"

Drake closed his eyes and pinched the bridge of his nose between thumb and forefinger.

"Dammit," he muttered.

"What's wrong?"

*Not him, I can't go to him again.*

"Nothing."

But he had to go to him, he was the only person who Drake knew had experience with this sort of thing.

His mind turned to the envelope that he had put in Jasmine's mailbox, which he was sure he had seen in Suzan's pocket later when she bounded upstairs.

"I might know somebody, but I'm going to need a favor."

"Another camera?" Screech asked.

Drake shook his head.

"No, no camera—I need you to make sure that the one that I put up is recording, but this is something different. I need some cash."

Screech's face contorted.

"Money? For what?"

"I can't tell you that. I just need some cash."

Screech chewed his lip as he thought this over.

"How much?" he said at last.

Drake thought about it. It was usually him who was getting paid, and that was usually in ten thousand dollar increments. Only after what had happened...

"Twenty grand," he said flatly.

Screech's eyes bulged.

"Twenty grand? Shit, you lose a bet?"

"You'll get it back after Meathead Bumacher settles. But I'm going to need it today."

Screech shook his head.

"No can do. I don't have that kind of scratch lying around. Just bought a new computer set-up for the ol' homestead. Wish I could help you out, but..."

Drake groaned in frustration.

*Not only do I have to meet with him, but now I'm going to have to make a stop along the way.*

"Alright, thanks anyway," he said as he stood.

" You just got here —where're you going?"

"Out for a bit."

Drake's phone buzzed and he answered it.

"Drake here."

"It's Chase. We just got finished talking to Charlotte's husband. He was... he was *destroyed*..."

Drake remembered how much he hated that part of the job, how hard it was for him to tell a loved one that their husband or father was never coming home.

"You alright?" he asked.

"I'll be fine. But get this, it looks as if Charlotte was abducted outside a bookstore."

Drake was leaning down and reaching for the top drawer of his desk when she said this, and he stopped.

"Really? Any video?"

"Haven't had a chance to review the tapes yet. They're on the way back to Dunbar to take a look. And Agent Stitts is getting a record of all the books that Charlotte has bought in the last few months, going to have Dunbar run that, too, cross-referenced with Melissa and Tanya's purchases. Anything on your end?"

Drake pulled the bottle of Johnny Red out of the desk and poured himself three-fingers. He downed half of it in one sip.

"Yeah, got another story—*Red Smile* Part II."

Chase was incredulous.

"What? What'd it say?"

Drake finished his drink and closed his eyes.

"Just that there was another body found at the same scene as the first. You're in it again, too, and the narrative doesn't mince words when it describes that the killer returned to the scene of the first murders to leave another body. Shit, it's like this person is predicting the goddamn future. Are we really that predictable?"

"Maybe—procedure is pretty standardized. What about the end?"

"Just like the first. Stops abruptly, no real ending, no clues as to who or where the next victim is going to be. But there's no *THE END*—the killer isn't done yet. What the fuck is his endgame, anyway?"

Chase stayed silent long enough that Drake had enough time to pour another drink.

"Get it over here as soon as you can," Chase said at last. "Did Screech manage to find out anything about the author?"

Drake lifted his eyes and stared at Screech who was looking at him with a queer expression on his narrow face.

"No, nothing. He tried, but says that L. Wiley is like a ghost."

Another pause.

"Keep on digging, use any contacts that you have. We've got to find this guy before he kills again. I gotta go, I have a press conference to prepare for. Once this drops, we are going to be overwhelmed with tips again."

Drake nodded to himself.

"Good luck," he said, then hung up the phone before uttering the next phrase that popped into his head: *are you sure, Chase? Things can get dicey if I go meet him again.*

Drake finished the rest of his drink and then headed to the door, leaving a stunned-looking Screech standing in his office.

"Can you look after the place for a while? Have to do this Special Consultant shit."

Screech said nothing, but Drake took this as an affirmative.

He was nearly out of Triple D when he turned back.

"Oh, and find Meathead's yacht for him, will you? We're going to need the cash—I don't care what kind of 'cargo' he has stashed on it."

# Chapter 34

IT WAS STRANGE FOR Chase to be standing at the podium again, speaking with the media who had hastily arranged themselves with only minutes' notice. She kept peeking over her shoulder, expecting to see Rhodes's bespectacled face staring back, his cheeks slowly turning a darker shade of red.

But it was only Chase up there today, and she felt oddly comfortable. Agent Stitts and Detective Yasiv were standing in the crowd off to one side, ready to come forward if called upon, but Chase thought it more prudent to be alone in front of the media and discuss how women should protect themselves.

Show them a face of a proud, confident woman.

"Good afternoon, New York. My name is Sergeant Chase Adams, and I've asked the media to congregate outside 62nd precinct so that I can make the public aware of some distressing news: over the past few days, there have been three murders on the outskirts of our city. Three young women were ruthlessly murdered and the suspect is still at large. At this time, we are not releasing the names of the victims or any details about the horrible crimes that were inflicted upon them."

Chase looked down at the paper on the podium with the rest of the speech that she had written, but while it had sounded fine when she was writing it down, it sounded trite and robotic now.

She quickly scanned the paper for what to say next. One of the audience members took this as a pause intended for questions and piped up.

"Are there any leads? Any suspects? Why were the women murdered?"

Chase held up a hand and lifted her head.

"I stand here today not only as a police sergeant, but as a woman," she said, deviating from her script. It was best to sound genuine, to say how she really felt. She could deal with the consequences, if any, from higher-ups later. "Ask a group of men if they've been afraid, really afraid, of being assaulted in the past month and one, maybe two hands might go up. Ask a group of women? All of them will raise their hands. Now, this isn't a gender comment, a political outcry or even a motto; this is just reality. And the new reality is that women are currently being hunted. We will catch the person responsible, this is my promise to all of New York. But in the meantime, women should be cautious. Don't walk alone at night, don't accept rides from strangers. In fact—" Chase bit the inside of her lip and for some reason, her eyes drifted to Agent Stitts's. He had a slightly startled expression on his face.

*Instincts...*

"—don't be afraid to be a bitch. This goes for all women; if you're in a situation that makes you uncomfortable, or someone is offering to help you with your bags or your car, don't be afraid to tell them flat out that you don't want their help."

Chase gripped the sides of the wooden podium and leaned into the mic.

"Don't be afraid to be a bitch," she repeated, her eyes skipping across the floating heads of the media.

Their reaction was confused, at best. Some of the men were looking up at her with dumbfounded looks on their faces, while the women seemed to be smirking at her.

Chase used this to her advantage and quickly said, "be safe, New York," before turning back toward the police station behind her.

This incited the crowd and she heard them shout out questions like sport slogans for a moment before they melded into one incomprehensible cacophony.

Chase moved quickly, suddenly finding it difficult to swallow with the lump in her throat.

*Did I really just say that? Did I just—*

Agent Stitts sidled up beside her, matching her step for step.

"Wow," he whispered, "that was interesting."

Chase felt her face flush and was about to answer when Detective Yasiv appeared on her left.

"Did I just tell the women of New York to be bitches?" she asked as she grabbed the metal door handle and pulled it wide. Before either Yasiv or Stitts could answer, she said, "Yeah, I think I did. I really think I did."

*What in god's name was I thinking?*

# Chapter 35

DRAKE WASN'T SURE HOW Raul knew that he had arrived at Ken's condo, but before he even made it to the door, he saw the man's hunched form appear in the lobby.

Drake raised his fist to knock on the door, but Raul saw the gesture and came to him with the security guard in tow. They opened the door, and he stopped inside.

It was strange coming here, as even though he had a light buzz from the scotch he had drunk at Triple D which made things familiar, it was early.

The sun was still out.

And everything just seemed so damn shiny in the lobby.

"I'm here to see Ken," he said sharply.

Raul moved in front of him.

"Ken isn't here."

For some reason, this surprised Drake, and for a moment he thought that Raul was lying. But it made sense; after all, Ken was a partner at the law firm Smith, Smith and Jackson, and was in the middle of a mayoral race.

Why would he be home on a Friday afternoon?

"I need to speak to him."

Raul looked him up and down. Even though the security guard at his side appeared nervous, his eyes darting from Raul to Drake and back again, Raul's demeanor, as always, was implacable.

"He's not here."

Drake frowned, no longer bothering to disguise his discomfort in the man's presence.

"You said that already. Is he at his office? I'll visit him there."

Raul shook his head.

"I don't think that's a good idea."

Drake's frown deepened.

"I didn't ask you if you thought it was a good idea," he snapped back. With that, Drake turned to leave, except he didn't make it very far. Raul's hand came down on his forearm. Even through his jacket, the man's grip was tight, iron-like.

Drake turned back around and violently shook Raul's hand off.

"Don't touch me," he hissed, glaring at the little man before him. If the security guard had been nervous before, he was now sweating bullets.

"Why don't you just—" the guard began, but stopped speaking when Drake took an aggressive step forward.

"Don't touch me again," he warned, aiming a finger at Raul's chest.

Adrenaline flowed through Drake, and he felt his body primed to act, the fight impulse coursing through his veins.

But Raul dissolved this notion by smiling.

"My apologies, Damien. Please, come up to the penthouse. I'll call Ken and see if he can come meet you."

Even though his mouth was smiling, his eyes weren't.

*You weird little fucking man*, Drake thought. *What the hell is your deal?*

"Is that fine?"

Drake nodded.

"Fine."

The security guard exhaled audibly and Drake shot him a look.

"I'll just go back to my desk," he said, mostly to himself.

Raul, the creepy smile still on his face, turned and started toward the elevator.

Drake, adrenaline surging, followed.

\*\*\*

"Ken said he can meet you in twenty minutes. Would you like a drink while you wait?"

Drake checked his watch. It was nearly one in the afternoon now.

"Make it a double," he said. The way that Raul had switched from aggressive in the lobby to downright obedient upstairs, subservient, even, only added to the discomfort he felt in the pit of his stomach.

He didn't feel like waiting for a minute, let alone twenty, especially not in the company of Raul.

The man returned with a heavy glass of Johnny Blue, and Drake took a sip.

It was like liquid honey cascading down his throat, and in that moment, a sort of bliss came over him and he forgot all about the creepy manservant, about the dead women with the blood on their lips, the books documenting their deaths.

*Why can't life just be like this all the time? Just sheer enjoyment that doesn't involve sleeping with your dead partner's wife?*

Drake shook his head and put the drink down on the table more forcefully than he had intended. The mirage was gone.

A pinging noise from inside his jacket, which he had refused to remove despite Raul insisting, drew his attention.

Brow furrowed, he pulled out the e-reader and turned it on.

"What the hell?" he muttered.

There was a third cover beside the other two now.

*Red Smile Part III.*

Drake swallowed hard, opened the file and started to read.

# Chapter 36

"GODDAMMIT!"

Colin threw up his hands as he stared at his computer screen.

The entire monitor had gone blue.

His eyes bulged.

"What the hell just happened?"

He had been in the middle of a chapter, just wrapping up what was to be his masterpiece, the one that would finally put him and his family in the black.

The one that would finally get Ryanne off his back.

And now *this*.

"What did you say, daddy?" Colby asked from the other room.

"Nothing," Colin replied. "Just keep watching your cartoons."

Colin tried jamming CTRL-ALT-DEL, but nothing happened. Eventually, he held his finger down on the power button.

He counted to three in his head and then turned the computer back on. It took longer than usual to start up, and when an image finally appeared on screen, he was surprised when the Windows logo and the words "Welcome to your new computer" floated by.

"What the fuck?"

Colin jammed the "Next" button in the right-hand corner and the image flicked to another welcome screen, one that asked him to name his computer.

His heart was pounding in his chest now.

"This can't be happening."

He pressed ESC a half-dozen times, but an error message popped up, stating that he had to enter a time zone.

*It can't all be gone... it can't... the hard drive couldn't have been completely erased. That's impossible.*

He turned the computer off and on a second time, but was met again with the *Welcome to Windows* screen.

Colin could feel his chest tightening, his breath coming in bursts.

*I was... I was nearly done with the series, let alone the book. It can't be gone... it can't! Not after all the work I've put into it!*

Sweat started to bead on his forehead, and Colin felt his limbs go numb. He tried to stand, but feared that he might collapse to the Parquet floor and remained seated.

The front door suddenly opened, and Ryanne burst through. She too was sweating, despite the cold air that she brought in with her from outside.

Wearing a purple, low cut top and tight black workout pants, she stormed into the entrance, scowling at the girls' shoes that were strewn across the floor. She kicked them to one side and then pulled the yoga mat from beneath an arm and then tossed that to the ground.

She looked up, the glower still etched on her lips.

"What's your problem?"

Colin's face, which he assumed was as white as the snow outside, went blank. He barely recognized the woman before him.

She *looked* the same—same long brown hair, pulled up into a ponytail, same striking eyes—but there was something different deep down. Ryanne had taken their money problems to a whole other level.

Colin felt bile rising in his throat as the image of the landlord, his back to him, the gray hair on his shoulders standing up like dryer lint, flooded his mind.

"M—m—my computer," Colin stammered. "It just *broke*."

Ryanne stormed over to him, and up close he realized that while she smelled strongly like sweat, there was something else underlying the funk. Something muskier.

"Did you try restarting it?" she asked.

"Of course I did."

Ryanne leaned over and held down the power button anyway. When she pressed it a second, the Welcome screen appeared.

"See? It's like a brand-new computer?"

Ryanne shrugged and leaned away from the table.

"You lose any work?"

Colin gaped.

"Did I lose any work? Seriously? I lost *everything*! Everything was on there. All of my books."

Ryanne shrugged again, and Colin felt his blood pressure reaching dangerous levels.

"Should have backed it up. I told you to back it up."

"Thanks, Ryanne. Thanks for the fucking tip. I *should* have backed things up, but I didn't. And now it's all gone."

To make things worse, Colin would be damned if he didn't detect a hint of pleasure in his wife's voice.

Nonplussed, Ryanne turned her back to Colin and then made her way into the other room to where the girls were sitting watching TV.

"Turn this crap off. I want to watch the news."

Neither girl looked up.

"Colby! Juliette! I said, turn this off!"

"Ryanne," Colin said almost absently. "I need to get my files back. I have a book to publish."

Ryanne stiffened, but she didn't look at him. Instead, she reached down and swatted Colby in the back of the head.

"Ow!" Colby cried. "Why'd you do that?"

"Answer me next time I speak to you!"

Colin's legs finally felt strong enough to stand, and he did.

"Ryanne, leave them alone," he ordered. "They haven't eaten yet. I've been trying to get my computer to work."

Ryanne spun around, eyes blazing.

"You want your computer fixed? Huh?"

Colin recoiled from the unexpected anger in his wife's face and voice.

"Yeah, I want—"

She smiled.

"Oh, I can get it fixed; Gary can fix it. He's good with computers."

And there it was again, the image of the man who had just had sex with his wife, his back to him, pulling his white underwear up to his waist.

He thought he was going to be sick.

"Well? You want me to get him to fix it or what?" Ryanne demanded, her smile growing.

Colin hated her in that moment. He hated her, and he wanted to hurt her.

Badly.

Instead, he closed his eyes and took a deep breath. If he didn't know any better, he would have thought that she had planned this whole thing.

Either way, he was trapped, and Ryanne knew it.

He opened his eyes, and his wife looked watery.

"Yes," he whispered. "Please get it fixed."

# Chapter 37

"CHASE? YOU OKAY? IT sounds like you're running," Drake asked.

"I'm just walking fast. Did you catch the news? My press conference?"

Drake shook his head, glancing around Ken's penthouse, his eyes moving from the wood fireplace, which Drake was ninety-percent certain was illegal in a new building such as this one, to the gold-framed oil paintings on the walls.

He didn't see a TV.

"No, haven't seen it. How did—"

"Don't. Do yourself a favor and don't watch it."

The exasperation in Chase's voice caused him to sit upright and to stop slouching in the ultra-comfortable chair.

"What happened?"

"Nothing. I just went off the rails a bit. If you're not calling about that debacle, what's up?"

Drake picked up the e-reader in his free hand and turned it on.

With a sigh, he said, "I got another story... Part III was delivered right to my tablet thingy."

There was a pause. When Chase spoke again, she was no longer breathing heavily, and her voice was muted.

"Seriously? Jesus, Drake, what does it say? Is there another body?"

Drake frowned and turned the reader on by pressing the button that had been hidden until Screech had shown him. He scrolled to the third image of the woman's face, blood smeared across her lips. He clicked on it and read the first few lines out loud.

*"The girl's wrists were tightly bound to the goalpost, her body forming a cross shape. She was naked, and even from a distance, Sergeant Cristin Allan knew that rigor mortis had set in. She reached up and moved a few strands of frozen hair from her face. The woman's eyes were wide, her lips covered in scarlet blood."*

Drake's heart was racing as he read the words.

*Sergeant Cristin Allan... Sergeant Chase Adams.*

"Fuck," Chase whispered. "I—hold on a sec."

Drake heard her hand cover the mouthpiece, then in a muffled voice, she said, "Hey, Officer, any homicides checked in yet? In the last hour or so?"

There was an exchange that he didn't pick up, then Chase spoke again, clearly this time.

"Nothing—no new bodies. Goddammit, does it say where the body is? Goalposts... like at a soccer field? Schoolyard, maybe? It can't be at the barn... I have two officers there day and night, on rotation. And there are no goalposts there. Drake? *Drake?*"

The door to the elevator suddenly pinged, drawing Drake's attention. Ken Smith stepped out, immaculately dressed as always, his silver hair perfectly coiffed. Only he looked different this time, and it took Drake a moment to realize why.

The man was frowning.

"Drake? You still there?"

"I have to go," Drake said quietly into the phone.

"What? What do you mean you have to go? Drake? *Dra—*"

Drake hung up and stood. He finished his drink and put the empty glass on the table beside the chair.

"Detective Drake," Ken said, unsmiling.

Drake scowled.

*I wish you wouldn't call me that.*

"This better be important—I'm a busy man. Tell me you have some good news... a video of the doctor with his manager."

Drake shook his head.

"No. I have everything in place, but—"

Ken's frowned deepened.

"What do you want then?"

Raul, as if responding to the change in pitch of Ken's voice, suddenly appeared at Drake's left.

He instinctively took a step back.

"Everything okay here?" Raul asked in his thick accent.

Ken nodded.

"Fine. Drake was just about to tell me why he's interrupted my afternoon."

Drake decided it was best to just come out with it.

"I need cash. A loan."

Ken's eyes flicked over to Raul for a split-second, and it dawned on him that the man wasn't angry so much as he was surprised.

And his glance over at Raul...

*They're following me,* Drake thought suddenly. *That's why this is a surprise. They've been following me, and they didn't expect me to come here. Not like this, anyway.*

Ken's eyes narrowed.

"What do you need the money for?"

Drake ignored the question.

"I'll get it back to you—it's a loan, not a gift. I just need a few weeks."

An uncomfortable silence ensued, and Drake feared that Ken was going to press him for why he needed the money. And those were details that he didn't feel like getting into with anyone, let alone him.

But, instead, he said, "how much."

"Twenty."

Ken nodded, then turned to Raul.

"Go get him the money."

Raul bowed his head and left through the kitchen and out of sight. When he was gone, Ken focused his eyes on Drake.

"The report on the doctor was a trade for the information I gave you about Craig Sloan, about Dr. Moorfield and the tribunal. The package Raul handed you last time was for the video that you will provide me shortly. But this—"

As if on cue, Raul reappeared in the foyer and handed a plain yellow envelope to Ken, who tapped it against his palm.

"This one is for the Sergeant."

Drake felt his heart rate quicken.

"What about her?"

"The press conference—you need to tell her to keep a wrap on whatever she—whatever *you*—are dealing with… the dead women. Another serial killer, panic in the city, that doesn't work for me. Not now, anyway."

Ken held the envelope out to Drake, who grabbed it. When he tried to pull away, however, Ken held fast.

"Ten is to keep this case, and the Sergeant, under control. The other ten… that's for something else."

Drake raised an eyebrow.

"Something else?"

Ken let go of the envelope, and Drake slipped it into his jacket pocket.

"I'll tell you when I need you again. In the meantime, get the footage of the doctor. Now, if you'll excuse me, I have to go back to work."

With that, the man spun on his heels, then left in the elevator without another word, once again leaving Drake with Raul. Only this time, he was twenty thousand dollars richer.

# Chapter 38

CHASE WAS FURIOUS.

There was another book, another murder, and Drake had the nerve to hang up on her.

*I should never have brought him on board,* she thought.

But it dawned on her that even if she hadn't made Drake a Special Consultant on the case, he would have been involved anyway, given that someone had delivered the mysterious e-reader to him.

*Somebody wants Drake to remain involved with the NYPD. But who? And why?*

Chase shook her head. She had little time for these questions when there was a body out there somewhere, hanging from goalposts.

She hurried out of her office, moving toward the one that she had once shared with Drake, and leaned inside.

Agent Stitts sat in front of his computer, punching away at the keys. She knocked once to get his attention, and he looked up at her, a startled expression on his face. When he realized that it was her, however, his eyes narrowed.

"What's up?"

Chase wasn't sure if it was her body language or something else, but the man somehow knew that this wasn't a social call, that she wasn't going to ask him to grab a late lunch.

"Come with me," she said curtly. "We have to visit Dunbar."

Stitts nodded and stood, making his way to her side without saying a word.

"Drake was sent another book," Chase said quietly as they made their way down the dimly lit staircase toward the Records room.

Agent Stitts stopped and turned to face her, eyes wide. "Already? So soon after Charlotte?"

Chase nodded.

"This—"

"I know," Chase said, cutting him off. She knew what he was going to say, and it would do neither of them any good to say it out loud.

Too many perked ears, even here, in the basement of 62nd precinct.

The killer was moving quickly now, so quickly that he wasn't even waiting for them to find the body before publishing the story—at least to Drake's device.

Which posed a significant problem for Chase and her team: mainly, what might happen if the author, if L. Wiley, suddenly flooded the market with books? How were they to know which ones were real, where they should focus their efforts, and which were just made up?

And if the public found out? If there were suddenly hundreds of books called Scarlet Grin or Maroon Sneer or Crimson Smirk? Then what?

This case, unlike all of the others, had to be solved as soon as possible. They had to catch the killer before he struck again.

"What does it say? Where's the body located?"

Chase shook her head, thinking back to the way that Drake had just suddenly hung up on her. She had brought him on board to help with the case, but so far the only thing he had done is provide them with the stories—which had simply been delivered to him.

Other than that, he had done nothing. Except for being preoccupied, lost in thought like some goddamn middle-aged philosopher.

"Nothing—he had to… he had to go."

Another eyebrow raise from Stitts, but before he could ask for details, Chase deliberately opened the door to Records and stepped inside.

Officer Dunbar was huddled over a computer, his large frame illuminated by the bluish glow from the screen. The walls on one side of the room were lined with cabinets, paper files that had yet to be digitized, while the other was stacked with hard drives and glowing lights.

The old and the new.

Drake and Chase, working together in… *abstraction.*

"Dunbar, we need—" Chase started, but stopped when a flicker of movement caught her eye. She leaned around Dunbar's desk.

A young, thin man with a shaved head looked up at her. He smiled at first, revealing a set of teeth that looked too small for his mouth, but when he saw the expression on her face, he immediately grew serious. His eyes flicked to Stitts and then he jumped to his feet.

"Sergeant Adams, I was just leaving to get a coffee. You want?"

Chase shook her head, and the man, whose name escaped her, fled the room. When he was gone, Stitts closed the door.

"What? What's up?" Dunbar asked nervously.

Chase moved to behind his chair.

"There's been another murder," she said flatly.

Dunbar swallowed hard.

"What? Where?"

"Don't know yet. That's what I'm hoping you can help us with."

*And Drake, too, if he ever decides to call me back.*

Dunbar turned back to the screen and called up L. Wiley's author page on Amazon.

There were three books now, all with the same image of the woman with the bloody lips, all a different shade of red.

"Shit," she swore as her eyes fixed on the third book. Despite what Drake had told her, deep down she had hoped that he was wrong. "It wasn't online an hour ago."

Dunbar clicked the cover and then read book synopsis.

It was only a single sentence.

*Another murder and the police are no closer to finding out who the killer is.*

"He's mocking us," Agent Stitts remarked.

Chase felt her anger rising and she pulled the cell phone from her pocket. She clicked redial, but after a single ring, it went right to voicemail.

She swore.

"We have to read it—we need to find out what's in there. Where the body is. If there are any clues to the killer's identity."

Dunbar chewed his lip.

"We can't buy it."

Chase frowned.

"What? Why not?" A glimmer of hope. "It's not for sale?"

Dunbar took a deep breath before answering.

"Oh, it's for sale, but we can't buy it. I've been reading a little bit about this whole indie publishing scene. Apparently, it's all about visibility. With over 60 million books online, it's not necessarily about the quality of book you write—although that plays a role—but it's about discoverability. People need to see your book to buy it. And every time someone buys the book, it jumps up the ranking a little, gains more exposure."

"So what? Get to the point, Dunbar."

"I noticed a disturbing trend over the last few days. The first book—*Red Smile* Part I—has been trending upward. Not by much, but it's ranked ten thousand spots higher than this morning even."

"What does that mean? How many people have bought it?"

Dunbar shrugged.

"Impossible to know exactly, but I'm guessing it's sold about ten copies a day since its release."

"Which makes what? Fifty total sold?"

"About that."

"So we don't want to buy the damn book because that will push it up the rankings, is that it?"

Dunbar nodded.

"Exactly."

"Then we need Drake's copy," Agent Stitts chimed in.

*Did your intuition tell you that?* Chase thought angrily, but then breathed deeply, trying to keep her cool.

He was just trying to help—they all were. Even Drake, in his own way. At least that was what she hoped.

"Shit."

A silence interrupted only by the mechanical whirring of the hard drives stretched out for several seconds.

"We have to take it down," Chase said at last. "We have to get the books removed before anyone else downloads them."

"I thought you said you didn't want anyone at the eBook vendors to find out about it? That it might be leaked that these books are about actual murders?" Dunbar said.

"We have no choice. Let's hope that if we take the books down, the killer will lose interest, that without a venue for their work, they'll slow down," Chase replied, but even as the words exited mouth, she knew that it was a long shot. Killers didn't tend to slow down between crimes, they sped up.

Her arms suddenly started to itch.

They worked faster, the crimes becoming more gruesome as they sought the feeling of their first kill.

As they fed their addiction.

She turned to Agent Stitts.

"You think we can get the vendors to give up L. Wiley's real name?"

"I can try to put some pressure, but these companies... they're massive. Even with a subpoena, they can tie us up in legal garbage for years."

Chase swore again.

Sometimes the wheels of justice worked so slowly that they were barely moving. Sometimes the wheels of justice were square.

*But Drake, he isn't bound by the same rules... maybe...*

She shook the thought from her head.

"See what you can do on that front. We gotta stem this, and quick."

It was only then that she noticed Dunbar shaking his head. "What now?"

"If we shut down Wiley's account, they can just open another one. Put the book up under another name... L. Wile, maybe, instead of L. Wiley."

Chase felt her frustration rising.

"Then we need to get the vendors to give up his name. Twist their arm, do whatever it takes."

Dunbar's expression soured and he opened his mouth, but then closed it again.

"Just say it," Chase demanded. "Jesus, just say what you're thinking."

"It's just... online, people have been reporting that these pen names are sacred. The bigger vendors guard them very tightly, to the point that there has never been a leak. There's also a case where a judge subpoenaed their records for a specific book that contained a photograph from an armed robbery, a previously unpublished photo that contained critical evidence, and while eventually the book was pulled, the author's real name was never revealed."

"Shit, you're just full of good news today, aren't you?"

Dunbar looked down.

"Sorry, I've just—"

"I can still push, see what happens," Stitts offered.

Chase shut her eyes and breathed deeply. When she opened them again, she found herself focusing on an array of smaller book covers below *Red Smile*.

"What are those?" she asked.

Dunbar followed her finger.

"Also Boughts."

"Also *what*?"

"Boughts—an automatically populated list of other books bought by people who bought *Red Smile*. Supposed to help buyers find other books they might like. Sort of—wait a second."

Suddenly excited, Dunbar whipped his mouse about and hammered at the keyboard. A couple of seconds later, the screen was segmented into three panels, one for each of the books.

He then started to scroll through the Also Boughts, capturing the images of the covers and dropping them in an image processing program.

"What now?" Chase asked.

Dunbar clicked several more times and then brought the image processing screen to center stage.

"These are all the books that the people have bought in addition to *Red Smile*. A lot of authors buy their own books to get the also bought machine started... if L. Wiley has written other books under a different pen name, they might be in this group of eighty or so books."

Chase was nodding now.

They might be onto something.

"Cross reference this with the books that Tanya and Melissa and Charlotte either bought or took out from the library. Maybe this is how he's targeting the victims."

Dunbar opened several files and then the screen became a blur of text. More windows popped up and then disappeared before she could get a good look at them.

"I was already running program to find similarities in the victims's reading patterns, but the number of books that it had to scroll through—especially with Melissa—was immense, and there was a lot of overlap, but—" he clicked a button and then smiled when only three covers showed up on the screen. "Using the Also Boughts, there are only three books in common to all of the vics, and the Also Boughts."

Chase leaned toward the screen so quickly that she almost knocked heads with Dunbar. A frown immediately formed on her face as she read the titles out loud.

"Embracing the Manbeast, Seducing the Manbeast, Enveloping the Manbeast... what the hell kind of shit is this?"

Dunbar blew up the covers, which all had some derivation of a bare-chested man who looked half wolf and a scantily clad woman staring up at him.

"Shifter romance," Dunbar said, sounding almost embarrassed. "It's about—"

"Who cares what it's about," Chase snapped. "Who's the author?"

"R.S. Germaine," Dunbar said.

Chase felt a weight lift from her shoulders.

"Great. Get his—or her—address. Looks like me and you, Stitts, are going to pay the animal porn author a visit."

But, once again, Dunbar shook his head.

"Jesus Christ, what now?"

Dunbar gulped audibly and brought up another screen. It was the author profile for R.S. Germaine.

"You can't."

"And why's that?"

"Because R.S. Germaine is also a pen name."

# Chapter 39

DRAKE COULDN'T BELIEVE THAT he was back at Patty's Diner. He would've chosen any location, any other location in the entire city, except for this place, but the bastard refused to meet anywhere else.

In fact, Drake was surprised that he was willing to see him at all. It had been at least a month since he had visited the dilapidated diner, and he didn't miss it.

It had the same, cracked vinyl booths, the same cloying stench of decades of grease mixed with a hint of bleach, and the same disgruntled staff.

Broomhilda waddled over to him, and if her face wasn't so heavily lined, Drake would have thought she was smirking.

"Yeah?" she said, and Drake couldn't help but shake his head in disgust.

"Just a coffee."

The wannabe smirk turned into a pursed lip grimace, and Broomhilda turned to leave.

Before she returned, the door chimed and a man in a hooded parka stepped in from the cold.

Planting both hands, white from the snow, on the table, he hovered over Drake.

"You have some fucking nerve calling me," he spat.

Drake leaned back in his chair, wondering if this was such a good idea. After all, he had just spent an hour with one person he wanted to punch, but couldn't. But this wasn't Raul, this man…

Drake figured he might be able to get away with giving him a bit of a thrashing.

"Sit down," he ordered coldly.

The man's blue eyes narrowed, but after swiping a long strand of blond hair from his face, he did as instructed.

"I took a huge risk and—"

Drake pulled the envelope from his coat pocket and laid it on the cracked table.

"Well isn't this a change of roles," the man said sourly. His eyes darted to the envelope, which was good, but he didn't reach for it as Drake had hoped.

Screech had done a little research on Ivan Meitzer, and the rumor mill was abuzz with the idea that the man hadn't made many friends over the past year or so. In addition to stepping on everyone's toes, he had also published a rather scathing book about what it was like to work for The New York Times.

Ivan had gone from a relatively unknown reporter to creme of the crop after his exclusive with Drake about the Skeleton King, but had fallen just as hard. Drake had promised an exclusive about Craig Sloan, but hadn't delivered.

And in the world of reporters, your word was your bond and trust was your currency.

"I need you to do something for me," Drake said flatly. "Something that requires discretion."

Again, Ivan's eyes flicked to the envelope.

"Half is repayment for not giving you the Sloan exclusive. The other half is for this job."

This time, the temptation was too great, and Ivan reached for the envelope.

Drake held fast.

"Before you take this, I can't stress how important it is to keep this quiet. No one can know. I mean *no one*."

Ivan raised his eyes to look at Drake, and after a short pause, he nodded.

"What do you need?"

Drake let go of the envelope, and Ivan slipped it into his jacket.

"I need a name," Drake said. "I need the name of an author."

\*\*\*

Drake left the diner ten minutes after Ivan had fled into the cold. He made his way quickly across the parking lot and was in the process of unlocking the door to his Crown Vic when he suddenly got the feeling that he was being watched.

His eyes snapped up, but after looking around, he saw nothing out of the ordinary for a Friday afternoon in New York City.

And yet, when his phone buzzed and he pulled it out of his pocket, he still couldn't shake the feeling that he was being watched.

# Chapter 40

"ABOUT TIME," CHASE SNAPPED at Drake as he stormed into 62nd precinct.

Drake still hadn't fully recovered from what was already turning out to be a very long, and very trying day, and it took all his willpower not to lash out at her.

Instead, he simply nodded and handed over the e-reader. Chase snatched it from him and then passed it to an embarrassed looking Detective Yasiv who was standing at her side.

Yasiv nodded to Drake, then disappeared down the hallway and out of sight.

"Where's Agent Stitts?" Drake asked.

Although still frowning, Chase's eyes softened a little.

"He's trying to shut down the providers of the book. Get them to take it off the market."

Drake raised an eyebrow.

"I thought we couldn't risk—"

Chase spun away from him.

"Things have changed."

She started toward the stairwell, and Drake pulled up beside her.

"What? What's changed?"

Chase said nothing. Her hand shot out and she grabbed the door and pulled it wide.

Drake followed her into the stairs, but once inside, he reached for her arm.

Chase spun around, her body tense.

"Look," Drake began, looking down at her pretty face. "I'm sorry, alright? I'm fucking trying here, Chase. I have no idea what it means to be a 'Special Consultant'. All I know how to do is find murderers—literally, that's it. I have no idea how to run a business, how to keep old ladies happy—although that seems to be easier than I might have thought—and I don't know how to do whatever it is that we're doing here."

Chase's eyes narrowed, and she stared at him for a good while before answering.

"That's the problem, isn't it?"

Her response surprised him; almost as much as his own openness. It had taken him a lot to come clean with his feelings, but now that he had, he was beginning to regret it.

And he felt the walls going back up again. He snaked a hand into his jeans pocket, his fingers searching for the finger bone.

"What do you mean?"

"*You* don't know how to run a business, *you* can't babysit the elderly, *you* don't understand how to be a consultant. It's all about *you* and it's only about *you*. Let me ask you something, Drake. Did you call Beckett? Reach out to him? See how he's doing?"

Drake recoiled as if he had been struck.

"Didn't think so," Chase snapped. "You may be good at finding murderers, I won't argue with that. But you aren't going to find this one on your own. This isn't Dr. Mark Kruk or Craig Sloan. You need to open up, you need to ask for help, and you need to be a team player, Drake." Chase sighed. "I know it sounds like a fucking PSA, but I brought you in to help, and all you've done so far is fucking drag us down. I have no idea why you are getting the books before anyone else, but it does us no good if you are hoarding them, not letting our tech guys have a crack." She pushed her lips together, and when she spoke next, her voice was an octave lower. "You drinking again, Drake?"

This time Drake answered. Sure, he had had a few drinks waiting for Ken Smith, but that could hardly be considered 'drinking'.

"No," he said, his voice even.

Chase tilted her head to one side.

"No? Then where you coming from? And don't lie to me, Drake."

He ground his teeth.

"Patty's."

Chase shook her head.

"That's what I thought. Let's go, we have to get you up to speed," she said, turning toward the stairs.

Drake watched her go. He had seen something on her face, something that hurt him deeply.

A lack of trust.

*** 

"An IP address is basically a way to track a computer on the 'net. And I think I might have found something."

Drake stared at Dunbar's computer screen, trying to take it all in, trying to focus. But his mind continued to wander.

*Was* it all about him?

He had slept with Jasmine, that much was for him. But the rest… he was doing Ken's bidding because he didn't have a choice. Ken had given him Craig Sloan, which in turn had saved Suzan's life. He owed the man. And after taking the 'loan' to pay Ivan to see what he could come up with, he was further indebted to him.

*The second half… that's for something else.*

So why didn't he just tell Chase about Ivan? Why didn't he tell Chase why he was really at Patty's, why he couldn't call her back, why he was late?

Drake shook his head, something that he hoped the both Chase and Dunbar didn't pick up on.

He didn't tell Chase because he knew what she would do if he did: she would go to Ken, confront the man. That's just the way she worked; she would try and protect him, as ironic as that was. And the more time he spent around Ken and his pint-sized henchman, the more dangerous he thought they were.

*And to think, there's a good chance that Ken is going to be the Mayor of New York City soon.*

"Drake? You listening?"

He cleared his throat.

"Yeah, IP addresses. Got it. But I thought you couldn't trace L. Wiley?"

Dunbar turned back to the computer screen.

"We can't. But after compiling and comparing the books that the victims bought, I can confirm that they also have these three books in common."

He pulled up covers that looked to Drake like covers from softcore animal porn.

"I dug even deeper. Not only did our victims buy these books, but all three of the victims posted a review on at least one of them."

Chase suddenly leaned forward, her shoulder brushing up against Drake's.

He was suddenly reminded of his night with Jasmine, and how he had pictured Chase's face instead of hers.

Maybe she was right, maybe he was falling apart.

Again.

*It's like Clay, like the debacle leading to his death. Like that night in the rain.*

And that night had ended badly for everyone.

*I can't let that happen to her, to Chase.*

"What do you mean?" Chase asked.

"They all wrote reviews on a *Manbeast* book. Favorable ones, too."

"This can't be a coincidence," Chase mumbled.

"And who's this guy? This Germaine guy?"

Chase turned to face Drake, a frown on her face.

"Another fucking pen name. Agent Stitts is still trying to track down who these authors really are, but he doubts he will be able to find out."

Drake felt like he had tripped and fallen into some technological rabbit hole.

"Yeah, but," Dunbar continued, "while I couldn't track the IP address of the author of *Red Smile*, I tracked down R.S. Germaine."

Chase's grip on the back of Dunbar's chair tightened.

"What? You found him?"

Dunbar sighed.

"Not exactly."

Drake could feel Chase tense beside her. This was turning out to be more of a black hole than a rabbit hole.

"What do you mean, *not exactly?*"

Dunbar brought up a map of New York City on his screen. A series of red dots, maybe twenty in total, appeared over an area of approximately fifteen square miles.

"It keeps jumping around. Not like L. Wiley in Asia, though; concentrated in this area here," he pointed to the screen. "It's a low-income housing area. Sometimes what people do is set up one router, and then crack it so that everyone in the neighborhood can use it. That way one Internet connection can be used by many people. The IP address keeps resetting, which is why you see so many dots as the old ones are recycled. I mean, usually there aren't as many users as this, and the connection is probably slow as hell, but people will do anything to save a buck. They probably have a couple of routers in parallel."

"So we're sure that someone in this area—what is that, forty houses? Fifty?" Chase asked.

"About that. The resolution is poor."

"Okay, let's say fifty then. So someone in one of these fifty houses is the author of the *wereporn* books. Is that right?"

Dunbar nodded enthusiastically.

"Yeah, but remember these aren't houses. They're apartment buildings. Gotta be ten, twenty units in each."

Drake exhaled loudly. It was a lot of domiciles to search, but at least it was *something*.

"We need to start going apartment to apartment," Chase said.

"To look for what? A guy with a computer? Low income or not, if they have IP addresses, they're going to have computers," Drake replied.

Chase thought about this.

"The profile," she said at last. "We use the profile."

Despite the comment, however, Drake detected apprehension in her voice. He knew about her desire to enroll in the FBI, and how her opinion on profiling had become more favorable since he had first met her, but it was obvious she thought that in this case, it wouldn't be all that helpful.

"I'll get Yasiv to organize a team of uniforms, get them to start canvassing. Dunbar, send the list of addresses to his cell, and mine, too."

Dunbar nodded and went back to the computer. A few computer clicks, he said, "Done."

Chase stood up straight and headed toward the door.

"Good work, Dunbar. Keep plugging away. See if you can narrow it down somehow. Drake, you come with me. I have a job for you."

Drake followed Chase back into the stairwell.

"What about the press conference?" he asked when they were alone again. "Any leads from that?"

He was doubtful, especially given the rash of bullshit calls they had gotten about the Butterfly Killer, but it was worth a shot.

Chase paused mid-step.

"You still didn't see it?"

Drake shook his head.

"Well, we've been getting calls alright, just not about the killer."

Drake's brow furrowed.

"What do you mean?"

"I—"

Chase's phone echoed through the stairwell. She picked up.

"Adams," she said briskly. Drake watched her face as the person on the other end spoke.

It sagged and all of a sudden she looked older than her thirty or so years.

Much older.

"Okay, I'm heading there now. Keep the press away."

When Chase hung up the phone, it looked like she had aged a decade.

"They've found the body, Drake. And this time it's in a public place."

# Chapter 41

THE GIRL WAS NAKED, strung up by her wrists and hanging from a soccer goalpost at Hockley Elementary School. Her head was hung low, her face covered with strings of frozen brown hair.

Even from across the field, Chase didn't need to see the girl's mouth to know that it would be smeared with blood, or to see the gash across her throat to know that it had been slit.

She parked her BMW and got out, her heart pounding. Detective Simmons had beat her to the scene, and he met her as she started to cross the field.

"Who discovered the body?" she asked.

Simmons pointed to one of the brown brick houses that lined the road across from the field.

"Someone from one of those houses. Says they didn't see anyone, just the body."

Drake swore, and Chase looked over at him.

"This the way it was described?"

Drake nodded, ignoring the curious look that Simmons gave him.

"Pretty close."

A horn blared from their right, and Chase turned in that direction. A pickup truck pulled to a stop by the edge of the field, and as she watched, several women piled out.

"What the hell?" she muttered.

They appeared to be unraveling some sort of poster. As she watched, several other cars pulled up behind the pickup, and more people exited their vehicles. It took only a moment for Chase to realize what was happening.

"Cover the scene!" she yelled, breaking into a sprint. "Get a sheet up and cover the damn scene!"

The first poster unrolled at the same time the shouts started.

"They are victims! The women are not to blame!" the chorus rang out, piercing through the frosty air. "Women are not to blame!"

"Get a fucking screen up!" Chase yelled. Several of the uniformed officers looked at her, then the protesters, then the woman hanging from the goalpost. But none of them moved.

Chase grabbed the first officer she reached and spun him around.

"Put a damn screen up!"

The man glared at her.

"CSU isn't here yet. They're stuck in traffic. Going to be at least another twenty before they arrive."

Chase turned her gaze upward.

"Shit!"

She knew that the press conference had been a mistake, and the dozens of calls that the call center had received had proven as much.

But she still hadn't expected such a visceral outcry.

And now, with the body hanging in plain view, it was going to be on every social media site within the hour.

"Go to the body," Drake said from her left. "Gather all of the officers on scene and go to the body. Stand around it. Her hair is in front of her face, but I want you to block all direct views of the body. And then get someone over to the protesters, push them to the other side of the road. This is a goddamn crime scene, not a circus."

Chase breathed more deeply, realizing what Drake was trying to do. He wanted to make a human shield around the body until CSU got here.

She hurried after Drake, moving closer to the body as he instructed. At least a half-dozen police officers did the same, with Drake barking orders to complete the circle. When they were done, it wasn't a perfect cover, but it was better than having the woman's naked body exposed for anyone with a cell phone to snap a photo.

They stood in silence as the shouts continued to bombard them.

*"Women are not to blame! The victims are not to blame! Women are not to blame!"*

Chase hung her head low, her cheeks flushed despite the temperature.

This was her doing.

And it was all wrong.

There was something wrong with the profile, something that didn't feel right. Agent Stitts had told her to use her instincts, her gut, and this was as strong a reaction that she had experienced in years.

"Find this guy, Drake," she said suddenly, aware that all the officers were looking at her, but not caring. Chase looked up, staring her ex-partner directly in the face. "Let's catch this bastard."

# Chapter 42

COLIN HURRIED INTO HIS home, slamming the door behind him. He closed his eyes and tried to catch his breath. His hands were shaking. His heart was pounding. He felt his entire body awash with guilt.

"Dad? You okay?"

Colin opened his eyes to see Colby standing there, her eyes wide.

He offered her a fake smile.

"Fine, honey. Where's your sister?"

"In here!" Juliette hollered from the other room. Colin leaned to one side, peering beyond Colby.

The TV was on, which meant that Ryanne wasn't home. Part of him was glad, while the other half started to become furious.

"You guys okay? Where'd your mother go?"

Juliette shrugged and then turned back to the TV room, eventually plopping herself down on the floor beside her sister.

"Dunno. She just left."

Colin shook his head. Something had to be done about her. Leaving two seven-year old's alone to fend for themselves?

He looked down at his hands, the fingers tensed in the gloves. They were still shaking.

"I'm going to take a shower, okay guys? Then I'll make you some dinner."

He removed his gloves and patted his girls on the head, one after the other.

They didn't look up.

On the way to the shower, he tossed the gloves in the garbage.

His mind was racing and it wasn't until he was fully undressed that he realized he had cut himself. Holding his hand up to the light, he stared at the two-inch-long gash that ran from between his first and second knuckles to the middle of his palm.

"How the hell did this happen?" he muttered. "I was careful... so careful."

His heart skipped a beat, and he rinsed the blood away. He breathed more deeply when he realized that although the cut was long, it wasn't very deep.

Colin stepped into the hot shower, allowing the water to cascade over him. His thoughts went to Ryanne, of seeing her in the bed, her breasts sagging beneath the t-shirt, the landlord behind her, pulling up his underwear.

*In our bed—She slept with him in our bed.*

Out of spite, he tried to conjure images of the girl with the piercings, of her pale ass as he bent her over the desk, but every time he did, it continued to transform into Ryanne. Ryanne looking back at him, smiling, laughing, a cigarette dangling from her lips, but never falling.

*"Come on, big boy, come on Glenn, pump me harder!"*

Colin started to cry.

*What have I done? What in god's name have I done?*

Everything he had done was designed to make him feel better, to give him some semblance of control. But it hadn't worked.

And he hated himself for it.

Colin got out of the shower and quickly toweled himself off. He did so with his eyes closed, too ashamed to even glance in the mirror.

The clothes that he had been wearing were damp from the snow, and the knees of his track pants were dirty with mud.

He found a plastic bag beneath the sink and shoved them inside, then he tied it up.

Throwing on a fresh tracksuit, he made his way back downstairs, trying, and once again failing, to put on a happy face.

He settled for a neutral expression.

"Colby, Juliette, what would you like for dinner?"

No answer.

Colin sighed heavily.

"Girls? Dinner? What would you like?"

Still nothing.

"I'm going to make green peppers and Brussel sprouts if you don't answer me!"

This finally got a response.

"Pizza!" Juliette shouted.

"Burgers!" Colby followed.

"How about pasta?" Colin replied.

He took their silence as acceptance and started to fill a pot of water. After adding a pinch of salt and setting the burner on high, he bent down and searched the cupboard for a box of pasta.

Not immediately noticing one, he pushed several half-open cereal boxes to one side before he eventually found a bag of spaghetti. It was already open, and when he went to pull it out, the noodles slid onto the floor.

"Shit," he grumbled and started to pick them up, trying not to break the individual strands.

A loud bang from behind him caused him to jump to his feet, and he spun around.

Ryanne was standing in the middle of the kitchen, his computer bag sitting in the center of the counter. Her face was red, her hair wet, and her boots were covered with a layer of snow.

"Ryanne? What's wrong?" he said quietly.

*Does she know? Is that why she—*

"I fixed your fucking computer," she spat.

Colin felt relief wash over him, but a bleep from the cartoons in the other room reminded him that the girls were within earshot.

"Ryanne, keep it down—"

Ryanne's eyes bulged.

"Keep it down? *Fucking* keep it down?" she snapped, stepping forward. "I had to walk for three miles in the snow because some asshole slashed Glenn's tires, and all you can tell me to do is keep it down?"

She was within two feet of him now, and Colin couldn't help but glance over at a steak knife in the drying rack.

*How easy would it be? To grab a knife and...*

"It's just that the girls are in the other room, they might—"

Ryanne's eyes narrowed to slits.

"They might what? They might figure out that their father is a no-good hack? Can't even provide for their family because he thinks he can write fucking books?"

Colin felt his cheeks redden and he slid closer to the rack.

"I don't want to fight, anymore, Ryanne."

She ignored him and strode forward.

"That you make your goddamn wife walk in the snow because you can't get a real job and get me a fucking car?"

Ryanne was right up in his face now, and he could see that her lipstick was smudged, that her hair was a mess.

"That you whored me out so that I could fix your piece of shit computer?"

Red flashed across Colin's vision. Without thinking, he lashed out. His fist cracked against the side of Ryanne's jaw, sending her staggering backward.

"I didn't make you do it!" he screamed. His voice was so shrill that he didn't even recognize it as his own. "I didn't make you do anything! You did this! *You did this!*"

Colin moved toward her and as he did, Ryanne fell to the ground, her hand rubbing her jaw where he had hit her.

"You'll be sorry," she said, her eyes blazing. "You're going to be so fucking sorry you did that."

"Fuck you!" he screamed, his hands balling into fists. Any rational thought had fled him. He raised his right hand high above his head, intending to bring it crashing down, not on her jaw this time, but on the smeared lips that had so obviously been wrapped around the landlord's cock less than an hour ago.

But a split-second before he struck her again, a small voice from his left drew his attention.

"Daddy? What are you doing daddy?"

It was Juliette. She was standing with her hands at her sides, her eyes wide. Colby was beside her, a matching expression on her face. They looked so young then, half of their seven years, if that, like baby chicks looking to their mother for sustenance.

And they were terrified.

Colin gasped and lowered his hand.

"What have I done?" he whispered. "I'm sorry."

He grabbed his computer bag from the counter and ran toward the entrance. Even when Ryanne shouted after him, he didn't look back.

"You're going to fucking pay for this! Colin, *you're going to pay!*"

# Chapter 43

CHASE'S BEST GUESS HAD been three hours.

She was wrong: photographs of the body were online in under an hour. To make things worse, there were several of her in the shot, sprinting toward the body that hung nude in the distance. In the photo, her face was almost unrecognizable. *Old.*

"Shit," she grumbled, forcing herself to turn off her computer monitor.

*Another body, another book.*

Chase picked up the phone and dialed down to records.

"Dunbar? Tell me you managed to narrow down the search for the author? For R.S. Germaine?"

Dunbar hesitated before answering, and Chase felt her stomach drop.

"No. Nothing yet. But we have another problem."

Chase frowned.

"What?"

"The book—*Red Smile*? It's rising up the ranks. Jumped up to sub 8k in the last hour."

Chase closed her eyes.

"What does that mean, Dunbar? Speak English."

"It means that it's starting to move. People are buying it."

Chase's eyes snapped open.

This was turning out to be the worst day ever. Starting with the goddamn debacle of a press conference. Before she could reply, there was a heavy knock on her office door.

"Hold on a sec," she told Dunbar as she stood and made her way toward it.

When she opened it, she felt her heart sink all the way to the pit of her stomach.

Less than two months ago, Officers Lincoln and Herd from Internal Affairs had come for Sergeant Rhodes. Today, they were here for her.

# Final Act

## Chapter 44

IMAGES OF THE YOUNG woman hanging from the goalpost, her throat slashed, filled Drake's mind as he drove back to Triple D.

All to the soundtrack of shouting protesters...

Despite Chase's warning, Drake had gone ahead and watched the Sergeant's press conference after all.

And he had cringed the entire time.

*How could she say that? What the hell was going through her mind?*

He knew that Chase meant well, but her phrasing had been... *off*. Insensitive, callous, even. The worst part was that it hadn't sounded like her at all. Truthfully, even to Drake who was about as sensitive to political correctness as a rounded stone, it *did* sound as if she were blaming the victims.

Snow was falling heavily again, and Drake flicked the windshield wipers on high.

When he had been Chase's partner, she had addressed the media several times. And each time, she had been authoritative and showed a level of composure that had impressed him. But that had been with Rhodes watching on, his beady eyes staring at her as much as the crowd. He had been her support mechanism, as much as it pained Drake to say so, and it was apparent that she needed one.

Like Drake, it was beginning to become clear that she was better off behind the scenes instead of in front of the camera lens.

Pulling his Crown Vic into the parking lot, Drake parked but left the car running, and the heater on, as he checked his phone.

There were two missed calls, one from Screech and one from an unlisted number. Neither had left a message, and yet he had a sneaking suspicion that the second call was from Raul.

It was almost as if he could smell the creepy bastard through the phone line.

A shudder ran through him, and he turned off the car and opened the door. The cold hit him like an ice water enema, and Drake tucked his chin down low to protect himself from the brunt of the wind. He hurried across the parking lot and yanked the door to Triple D wide.

"Screech?" he said as he stepped inside. He removed his coat and hat and hung them on the wooden rack beside the door.

"Right here, boss," Screech replied from the bathroom.

Drake sighed. It was like Groundhog Day.

"You ever leave, Screech? You're always—"

The door to the bathroom opened and Screech stepped out. He was wearing a Hawaiian print shirt, cargo shorts, and a straw hat.

Drake gawked.

*This is new…*

"What the hell? Have you lost your mind?"

Screech laughed.

"Probably... working with you will do that to anyone," he moved toward his desk, beside which Drake saw a small suitcase packed and ready to go.

"No, seriously, where are you going?"

Screech picked up his bag and slung it over one shoulder.

"Going on vacation. The weather is shit and your company is as about as much fun as a brooding demon on her rag."

Drake blinked. He was caught off guard, and while his initial reaction was to tell him he couldn't go—they were, in fact, hunting a serial killer—he reminded himself that Screech could do as he pleased.

He was, after all, half owner of Triple D.

"Aaaaaand," Screech continued, clearly noticing Drake's expression, "I've got a Yacht to find. Caught some chatter on the net about a yacht in the Virgin Gorda, one with a very distinctive name. *B-yacht'ch.*"

Drake stared for a moment longer. He *had* told Screech to look after the missing yacht, and if the man got a vacation out of the deal, so what?

Screech deserved it.

"Knock yourself out. Bring back some pirate's booty, would ya?" he said as he made his way toward his office.

Drake expected Screech to nod, maybe come over and shake hands, and then leave, but he didn't. Instead, he just stood there, staring at Drake, a queer expression on his face.

"Honestly? I also wanted to get away before the shit storm rains down diarrhea."

Drake stopped mid-step.

"What?"

"You haven't read the news yet, have you? Jesus, man, what was the point of setting up that fancy phone if you—"

"I've been busy working, Screech. What are you talking about?"

Screech swallowed and his Adam's apple bobbed.

"Yeah, well, you know your favorite books? They just made the top ten list."

Drake screwed up his face.

*Favorite books?*

"*Red Smile,*" Screech specified.

Drake gasped.

"It looks like your buddy Ivan somehow got wind of the whole deal, wrote all about how *Red Smile* is based on real murders, on an active investigation."

Drake's heart migrated from the pit of his stomach to his throat. He actually retched.

"Wh-what?"

Screech shrugged.

"Some asshole leaked the news, apparently. And now the books are selling like mad. Sick fucks, I tell ya. Sick fucks buying it up like crazy."

Drake could hear his blood pounding in his ears like a bass drum line.

Screech swallowed again, then checked a watch that he wasn't wearing.

"*Welp*, looks like I better go, got a plane to catch."

Drake watched the man walk backward towards the door.

"Good luck, Drake," he said, and then his partner was gone.

Drake stood in the main lobby of Triple D for what felt like an hour.

*An asshole leaked the news to him.*

An image of the dead bodies, first those at the barn, buried in hay, then the poor woman hanging from the goalpost flashed.

Everyone was reading about them now; their families, their friends. The killer was probably laughing at them all, most of all him and Chase.

Fury suddenly usurped bewilderment, and Drake reached inside his sport coat pocket. He grabbed the e-reader and pulled it out. Somehow, he must have turned it on, because he found himself staring at the horrible image of the woman with the blood-stained lips.

Without thinking, Drake hurled the e-reader across the room. It struck the wall behind Screech's desk and the screen shattered, raining thousands of tiny pieces of glass or plastic or fucking unobtanium or whatever the screen was made of to the floor.

He cursed loudly, then grit his teeth.

*An asshole leaked the news to Ivan Meitzer. And I'm that asshole.*

*Again.*

# Chapter 45

"GIVE ME ONE MORE day!" Chase pleaded. "Just one more day. I don't give a shit about the images online or what Twitter is saying. I care about the dead women... and the next victim. Because, mark my words, there will be another murder. In fact, I wouldn't be surprised if he's already kidnapped someone."

Officer Herd stared at her for a moment. He was a short, awkward-looking man, with an unusually small space between his nose and upper lip that not even his thick mustache could disguise.

"I'm sorry, Sergeant Adams, but I'm just doing my job. Assistant Deputy Inspector Roger Albright said that you were to be relieved of your duty," his dark eyes softened somewhat. "It's only temporary, until this all blows over."

Chase could read between the lines; Rhodes's suspension was supposed to be temporary, too, but last she heard the bald bastard had become a hermit up in Vermont somewhere.

She shook her head.

"We're close, Officer Herd. Really close. Just take a walk, come back later. Tell Roger you couldn't find me. Anything, just let me solve this case. Please. If we have to start over..." she let her sentence trail off.

For a moment, Officer Herd looked like he might give in to her pleas, but then Officer Lincoln stepped forward.

"Sergeant Adams, I'm sorry, but—"

A fourth person entered the small office just then, and all eyes turned to him.

"You're sorry? For what? Because you interrupted a federal agent in the middle of an investigation? Why? Because some social justice warriors think that she made some sexist remarks?" Agent Stitts said angrily. He strode forward, and Chase thought she saw Herd flinch. "Chase was trying to protect people, women in particular. This isn't some power play or some bullshit political ploy. This is about saving lives. Why don't you take that up with Deputy Inspector Albright? Hmmm?"

Herd's upper lip curled, while Lincoln looked generally confused.

As did Chase.

*Federal Agent? What the hell is he talking about? Is he saying that I'm an agent, or is he speaking about himself?*

"I'll talk to Inspector Albright," Herd said at last.

"Yeah, you do that. In the meantime, let us stop a fucking killer, alright?"

With that, Agent Stitts stepped fully into the room, and the other two officers took their cue to exit.

Chase rose and shut the door behind them, briefly considering locking it in case the men changed their mind.

She left it unlocked.

"What the hell was that?" she asked.

Stitts smirked.

"What? I fudged the truth a little. You know how it is. As soon as I saw the images online of the crime scene, of you running through the snow, I figured this was coming. And then with the Meitzer article..."

Chase's eyes narrowed.

"The what?"

Agent Stitts hesitated before answering.

"You don't know? Shit; it's out, Chase. The cat is out of the proverbial bag."

Chase wasn't sure if it was the cold weather or the shock of almost being suspended, but either way, she wasn't grasping what Stitts was saying.

"Jesus, is this some sort of FBI code that I'm just not getting? I mean—"

"Ivan Meitzer from the Times just posted an online article about the murders and the books... the print version will be in tomorrow's paper. And now *Red Smile* is just flying off the virtual shelves; people just can't get enough. And this is only the beginning."

Chase's heart palpitated in her chest.

"How? What?" she paused for a second, her eyes narrowing. "Did you say *Ivan Meitzer* published the article?"

Agent Stitts nodded.

"You know him?"

Chase swore under her breath.

"I don't, but I know someone who does."

# Chapter 46

"I WAS JUST TRYING to help! You said to do what I can, and that's what I did. Ivan was my contact and he—"

"Every time you try to help, something gets fucked up!" Chase shot back. "Every time!"

Drake shook his head, trying to stem the fury that brewed inside him.

"I thought he could—"

"Keep your voice down," Chase instructed.

"—help, provide some information, use his contacts in the publishing industry to find out who the real author of *Red Smile* is."

Chase shook her head, then looked over at Agent Stitts, who appeared confused.

Confused, and none too happy about the situation. Although the agent had yet to explicitly state his dislike for Drake, it was all over his face.

"Yeah, you heard right. He thought that Ivan Meitzer, the same one who has it out for him, would help solve the investigation. That he wouldn't print what he told him."

"Don't be an asshole, Chase. Speak to me, not to—"

Chase's eyes whipped around.

"Speak to you? Speak to *you*? That's the problem, Drake. You don't fucking listen. Don't you get it? I brought you onboard here, and it's my ass on the line. Not yours. You've got other... shady... business going on, don't you? I mean, I make money, sure, but you know where I get it from. But how about you? Where are you getting the envelopes of cash that you keep dropping off to your dead partner's wife?"

Drake was floored.

*How does she know about that? Is she following me? Is that it?*

"There's nothing shady about Triple D, Chase," he said, trying to skirt the subject. "And I—"

"Uhh, I'd love to sit here and listen to mommy and daddy fight all day," Agent Stitts interrupted, "But we just don't have the time. The book is selling now, but tomorrow when the Times article is out in paper form, it's going to be a real shit-show. We need to get on this now, before we're completely drowned in copyrats and dead-end tips. And before Herd and Lincoln return."

Drake was still fuming, but Agent Stitts level-headed words struck a chord with him.

The man was right; they were going to be overwhelmed starting tomorrow morning. Time was one thing that they just didn't have.

And that said nothing of the killer's next victim.

*How long before he kills again? A day? Two at best?*

Drake took a deep breath, his eyes darting over to Chase. She was pissed, too, but he could also see that she was over her head, and maybe a little scared, too.

She wasn't ready for Sergeant, and perhaps never would be. She was a field agent, and that was where she belonged.

"I'm sorry," he said, attempting to bury the hatchet. "I was trying to help, but I fucked things up. I get that. Nothing I can do about it now will change the facts. Let's just move on, alright?"

Chase bit her lip and looked as if she wanted to say more, to further berate him, but she held back. Eventually, cooler heads prevailed, and she turned to Stitts.

"No luck pulling the books from online retailers, I guess."

Stitts shook his head.

"Not happening. At least not without a court order," he looked over at Drake. "With the news breaking now, it might actually be easier to get one, but it will still take a few days."

Chase frowned.

"Days we don't have. The killer's cooling off period is slowing. Drake, you still have the e-reader? What are the time stamps between the books?"

Drake felt his face flush, remembering how in a fit of rage he had thrown it across the room.

When he had regained control, he had tried to put it back together, but it was impossible.

The screen was completely destroyed.

"I don't have it," he said softly.

"You *what?*"

Drake shrugged.

"I don't—"

The door to the conference room suddenly burst open, and a red-faced Detective Yasiv burst through.

"Chase? Chase?" he asked, his eyes darting.

"You ever hear of knocking?"

Yasiv's face reddened until it was almost purple.

"Sorry, it's just—there's someone here to see you."

"Who? This better be—"

Yasiv swallowed hard.

"It's a woman… and she says she's been raped by your killer—by the author of *Red Smile.*"

# Chapter 47

CHASE STRODE DOWN THE hall with Drake and Agent Stitts at her side, and Detective Yasiv taking up the rear.

She moved briskly, ignoring the stares from everyone in the precinct, knowing that the news of IA coming to her office must have already been going around.

*Raped by the killer!*

It must have been some sort of hoax given that the news of the book had just broken, but given the severity of the accusation, and considering the public outcry at her choice of words at the media address the other day, she wasn't taking any chances.

"Interrogation Room 1, you said?" she asked over her shoulder.

Yasiv hurried to keep up.

"Yes—Room 1. She came in less than an hour ago, said she would only speak to you."

Chase nodded and broke into a walk so fast that it was nearly a jog. Instead of taking the elevator, she opted for the stairs. Taking them two at a time, she quickly found herself outside the door marked INTERROGATION ROOM 1, and was reminded of being here with Tim Jenkins, Drake furious, insisting that this wasn't their guy, that he wasn't the Butterfly Killer.

The last time that she had seen Tim Jenkins alive.

Chase shook her head, clearing her thoughts, then turned to her entourage.

"She said she only wants to talk to me, so I'll go in alone. You guys head into the adjacent room; you can watch and listen on the monitor." Then to Yasiv, she said, "You notify medical? If she's been raped, we should swab her and run the kit as soon as possible. Did she say how long ago the attack happened?"

Yasiv shook his head.

"She said she would only talk to you. Wouldn't even tell us her name. And medical is on their way."

Chase nodded.

"Good. And get Dunbar up here, tell him to watch on the monitor as well. Get him to cross reference anything she says about the low-income area that the IP address pinged, and anything about L. Wiley or R.S. Germaine or the books. Got it?"

The man confirmed that he would.

"Drake, get ready to move. If she reveals anything that you think you can act on, I want you to get out there. Don't hesitate, just go. And Take Stitts with you."

Drake nodded.

It felt strange and maybe even wrong to give Drake the reigns over Stitts, especially given that this whole mess was partially Drake's fault, but Stitts had told her to use her gut.

And her gut was telling her that she still needed Drake, which was why she hadn't told him to fuck off already after his colossal mistake.

Another deep breath, a curt nod, and then she opened the door to the interrogation room.

"My name is Sergeant Chase Adams. Why don't we start with yours?"

# Chapter 48

DRAKE TAPPED HIS FOOT anxiously as he stared through the two-way mirror, waiting for Chase to get through the legal jargon before questioning the woman.

She was in her mid-twenties, he guessed, with a shock of black hair that was shaved on the sides. Her pale face was punctuated by piercings in her nose, eyebrows, and lips.

Drake doubted if they ended there.

"So what happened, Hanna? Why don't you start at the beginning?" Chase said. Her voice was strange coming through the speakers above Drake's head, and there was a slight delay between her lips moving on the other side of the two-way glass and the sound, giving the entire scene a bizarre, ethereal quality.

The woman crossed her arms over her narrow chest.

"I was raped," she said, lips pressing together. "The bastard who wrote those books raped me."

Drake could see Chase struggling to keep her emotions in check, and knew that she was frustrated.

"Hanna, from the beginning. Tell me where you met this man."

Hanna's scowl deepened.

"Why? So you can tell me that I deserved it? That the fact that my clit is pierced means that I deserved to be raped, hmm?"

Drake was caught off guard by the comment, and evidently so was Chase. He had heard this line of speech before, of course, but usually it was in reference to a shirt being too low cut, or a skirt too short.

A clit piercing was a new one for him.

Chase leaned forward.

"I'm here to help, Hanna. And don't forget, you asked for me. Did you come here just to berate me over my comments to the press? Is that it? It's disgusting that you would—"

The woman lowered her eyes and she shook her head.

"No," she said softly, "I was raped. I was raped by *him*."

*She's lying*, Drake thought suddenly. Clit piercing or not, the woman hadn't been raped.

The door to the observation room opened, and Dunbar burst through, open laptop in hand. He offered a curt hello to Stitts and Drake, then set his computer down on the table.

"Did I miss anything?"

"Not yet," Drake said, still staring at Hanna.

She was nervous, a dead give away that she was lying.

"Tell me, then. Tell me what happened."

After a deep, shuddering breath, one that to Drake looked orchestrated, rehearsed even, Hanna started to weave a tale that started with a writer's group, then extended to her asking for help after class. She went on to describe the rape scene in great detail. So much detail, in fact, that at one point Drake found himself cringing.

He looked over to Stitts, who was staring intently at Hanna as he had been moments ago.

Drake wondered if the man was thinking the same thing he was; mainly, that those who undergo a traumatic event, such as rape or violent assault, usually couldn't recall this level of detail. During these horrible acts, the victims are completely overtaken by one of the three main evolutionary precepts: Fight, Flight, or Freeze. Memory, on the other hand, is a distant faculty, and all of the human machinery is rerouted for one of those three acts.

*Too much detail, she's remembering too much.*

Drake looked over at Dunbar next, who appeared oblivious to the graphic account as he punched at his keyboard.

"Writer's group in New York...," he mumbled, presumably to himself. "There are dozens of these things. Need more information."

Drake reached into his pocket, intent on fondling the finger bone.

Only it wasn't there.

Panic overtook him, and he searched his other jean pocket.

When his hands still came up empty, he patted his chest, the inside of his jacket.

Still nothing.

"Drake? You okay?" Agent Stitts asked, sounding far away.

*Where the hell is it? Where is it?*

Drake tried to think back to the last time he had seen it.

*Was it yesterday? Did I have it when I visited Ken and asked for the money? At Patty's? Did I bring it out when Ivan had arrived? After he left?*

"Then where the fuck is it?" he asked out loud.

A hand came down gently on his shoulder, and he glanced up.

"You alright?" Agent Stitts asked, concern on his face.

Drake swallowed and shook the man's hand away.

"I just—"

But he was interrupted by Chase's voice filtering through the intercom.

"Medical will be here in a few minutes to take swabs, Hanna. But before they come, can I just ask you one more thing?"

A dry swallow.

"Yes."

"Do you know the name of this man who did this to you? Did you get his name?"

Hanna's eyes shot up, and Drake saw that they were red from crying.

"Colin… his name was Colin Elliot. And I'm just happy that he didn't kill me like those other poor girls."

# Chapter 49

THERE WERE THREE HARD knocks on the door, and then it opened. A portly nurse in a white gown looked in with a severe expression on her face.

"Medical," she said simply, and Chase rose to her feet.

"Thank you, Hanna," she said to the woman across the table from her. "And we're going to catch this guy. I promise "

Hanna nodded, but said nothing. Her demeanor had completely changed from when Chase had first arrived in the interrogation room.

She remembered what Stitts had said, that in his profile he had stated that the killer was a man who had been emasculated.

And yet none of the other victims had been sexually assaulted.

Chase pushed these feelings aside for the time being. The woman had made a claim, a very vivid and graphic account of a rape, and it wasn't her job to judge her in this moment.

She would make sure that this man... that *Colin Elliot* would be brought in for questioning. And if he did rape her, then...

Chase left the room and headed to the adjacent one.

"Did you get that?" she asked, after entering. She clicked a button and the glass went dark, and the intercom shut off, offering Hanna privacy as she was examined and swabbed.

"Dunbar? Any hit on the name?"

Officer Dunbar didn't look up, he just continued to type furiously.

"Not yet, working on it."

She turned to Drake next.

"Something's not right here," she said absently. Drake was looking particularly pale, almost as if he were going to be ill. "You alright?"

"Fine," he grumbled, even though it was clear that he was anything but fine.

Chase instinctively sniffed the air, trying to pick up the scent of alcohol, even though this was one of the first things she had done when Drake had come down to the precinct.

She smelled nothing, and then considered that this was perhaps that reason why he was acting so strangely, and looked sick.

After her brief addiction to heroin, she knew how bad things could get before they got better.

She swallowed and tried to focus on the task at hand, on Hanna, on her story, on the killer that they so desperately sought.

"What's not right?" Agent Stitts asked, bringing her out of her head.

Chase turned to the now black two-way mirror.

"The rape... the other girls, all four of them... none of them had signs of sexual assault, did they?"

Detective Yasiv shook his head.

"CSU and the ME's office tested them thoroughly. Melissa had had sex recently, as recent as a day or two before she went missing, but her mother confirmed that she was seeing someone. An ex-boyfriend, and he was cleared. Incarcerated when both she and Tanya went missing."

"So why now, then? If this Colin Elliot is our killer, why did he just start raping now?"

"And why did he let her go?" Drake added.

Chase agreed.

"It doesn't make sense. Drake, in the books, was there any mention of rape?"

Drake shook his head.

"No. None. Only about the killing. And us discovering the bodies, of course."

"Then why now?" Chase asked again.

"Maybe it's not—" Drake began, but Dunbar cut him off.

"Got it! Collin Elliot, Elgin Street, Apartment four."

Detective Yasiv grabbed for his coat.

"Elgin Street?" Chase repeated. "Where's that?"

Dunbar finally looked up from his computer screen.

"You're not going to believe this, but it's right in the heart of the area that the IP address that posted the *wereporn* books pinged."

Chase's eyes bulged and she turned to Drake.

"Go! Go grab this guy and bring him in!"

Drake nodded and reached for his own jacket. Then he looked at Stitts.

"You packing?"

Stitts nodded.

"Good. I'll drive. Yasiv, you follow behind with a couple of uniforms."

Chase planted both hands on the table and allowed several deep breaths when it was just her and Dunbar left in the room.

There was something else bugging her, and it wasn't just Hanna's story, or the inconsistencies with the killer's MO.

It had something to do with Agent Stitts's profile. It wasn't right; they were missing something, something big, and yet she couldn't put her finger on it.

"Fuck," she said out loud, and when Dunbar looked over at her, she frowned. "Keep digging, Dunbar. I've got a feeling that this isn't over yet."

And then, to herself, she thought, *it might not even be over when we arrest Colin Elliot.*

# Chapter 50

DRAKE RACED ACROSS THE city, thoughts of the missing finger bone suddenly pushed to the back of his mind.

The only thing he was focusing on now was catching their killer, of arresting Colin Elliot before he raped or killed another woman.

"You and Sergeant Adams go back a ways, don't you?" Agent Stitts asked from the passenger seat. The question took Drake by surprise, as he had just cleared his mind of thoughts not related to the case.

"Huh?" he asked, his eyes still on the road. The snow was coming down heavier now, and he had to squint to make sure he stayed on the road.

"You and Chase. You were partners a while back?"

Drake nodded, but said nothing. Even though the sample size of their interactions had been small, Agent Stitts came off as an introspective person.

"And?"

Drake sighed.

"And what?"

His tone dripped with annoyance, but he didn't go so far as asking the agent to shut up. After all, he knew how badly Chase wanted to be recruited to the FBI, and if he hadn't squandered that already with his Ivan Meitzer fuck up, then he wasn't going to tell this guy off now, ruin her chances.

She deserved better.

"How is she? Stable? Trust-worthy?"

Drake resisted the urge to look over at the man.

*Stable?*

"Chase is no-nonsense, doesn't take shit from anyone, as you saw earlier. Damn fine detective, too. And trust-worthy? Definitely."

Silence fell over the car for a few moments, before Agent Stitts spoke again.

"And there's no sign of her problem? Of a relapse?"

This time Drake couldn't resist the urge. He looked at Stitts, his eyebrows knitted in confusion.

"Relapse? What are you talking about?"

Agent Stitts stared back for a moment before answering "Let me ask you something, Drake. How much do you really know about Chase Adams?"

Drake shrugged, his mind still stuck on the word *relapse*.

"Well, for instance, did you know that she's married?"

Drake said he did, although kept to himself just how long it had taken him to acquire this knowledge.

"What about her son? Did you know she has a son?"

Try as he might, Drake couldn't help but let his surprise show on his face.

It was response enough.

"Didn't think so."

Drake had enough of this intrusive questioning and decided to put an end to it.

"We were partners for one case. That's it."

His thoughts turned to Clay and then to Suzan, and how his ex-partner had intentionally kept the details of the crimes they investigated from her.

And then there was Jasmine...

"She kept some things to herself, but so what? That doesn't make her a bad detective. If you only knew the things we've seen..."

"Oh, I can imagine. And I don't think she's a bad detective—on the contrary, I think she's a fantastic detective. If I didn't, then I would have taken over the investigation the moment she brought me in. What I'm trying to figure out, is whether or not she's a good partner."

Drake turned back to the road and flicked the wipers to maximum. They were ten, fifteen minutes away from Colin Elliot's address with the traffic, and it couldn't come fast enough.

Detective Yasiv had called ahead, and several uniformed officers were already monitoring the place, the roads in and out, but were waiting until they arrived to move in. There might be another woman with him, and the last thing they wanted to do was to force Colin's hand, make him do something rash.

"You're a chatty guy, huh?" he said.

"Just doing my due diligence, Drake. I hope you can appreciate that."

Drake raised an eyebrow.

"Due diligence? She's heading to the FBI?"

All of a sudden, the Chatty Kathy to his right went silent.

"Hmm?"

Stitts took a deep breath and then answered without pretense.

"We're considering her for a profiler role, something mid-level. But several red flags have been raised."

*Relapse,* Drake thought.

"And not all of them have to do with her past," Stitts continued, as if reading his thoughts. "Of a greater concern is her judge of character."

"Judge of character?" Drake repeated harshly. But even before the words were out of his mouth, he regretted saying them. He turned back to the road. "You mean me, don't you?"

Out of the corner of his eye, Drake saw Agent Stitts nod.

"The FBI is not like the NYPD. In New York, Chase is surrounded by men in blue, case and point the uniforms waiting at Colin Elliot's house as we speak. In the FBI, it's usually just the agent and a partner, but as you can see, we occasionally work alone. And not everyone is as inviting as Sergeant Adams, let me tell you."

Stitts's words hung in the air like a foul stench, and they clung to it even as Drake passed the first squad car marking the entrance to the compound that contained Colin Elliot's last known address.

He thought back to how he had tried his best to prevent this very thing from happening, how he had taken all of the blame for the errors made during the investigation of the Butterfly Killer to protect Chase.

And it was all for naught, it seemed.

In the end, he had sullied her reputation, despite his efforts.

"You can't hold my actions against her," Drake said softly. "That's not fair."

"Of course not. But I'm wondering what it says about her judgment that she insisted on bringing you on board."

Drake pulled the car up to the side of the road and parked it behind two police cars whose lights were off.

He reached across and popped the glove box. Agent Stitts leaned out of the way as he pulled a pistol out.

"I thought you said you weren't armed?" Agent Stitts asked, a hint of concern on his tongue.

"I wasn't," Drake grumbled. He was about to open the door, when Stitts's voice drew him back.

"I've known people like you, Drake; people who always try to do the right thing, but can never manage to get it right. And I'll let you in on a secret: things are going to get a lot worse for you and those you love before it gets better."

Stitts opened the car door and a blast of cold air filled the interior.

"If it ever does," he finished as he stepped out into the cold.

# Chapter 51

AFTER THE NURSE LEFT Hanna, Chase turned the two-way glass back on and observed the woman.

She was lying about the rape, of that she was certain, but there were too many coincidences not to think that there was a connection between Colin Elliot and their killer.

He was a writer, and while Hanna didn't know his pen name, she had confirmed that he wrote under one. He also lived in the area that the books, the three *wereporn* novels that the victims had all read and reviewed, had been published, and he fit the physical profile that Agent Stitts had offered.

*The profile that I don't believe.*

As she watched, Hanna pushed a lock of black hair from her face, then smoothed the front of her t-shirt.

She wasn't raped, but there was fear in her eyes. Chase fell short of thinking that this was some sort of ploy by feminists to further out her for her ill-advised comments, and that this was a different animal entirely.

*Is it possible that Colin was their killer and for whatever reason Hanna was someone he had just let go? Maybe they had consensual sex, and he decided that that was it? That that was enough?*

Was it possible for a man who had already killed four women to have a normal-*esque* relationship with a woman and not slit her throat? To not paint her lips red?

Her thoughts turned to some of the most infamous serial killers in American history: The Boston Strangler, Ted Bundy, John Wayne Gacy. They lived normal lives outside of their killing sprees, hadn't they? And the people who knew them in their everyday lives thought that they were kind, charming individuals.

So why did she find it so hard to believe that this murderer, that Colin Elliot could be the same?

*Because the profile is wrong, that's why.*

The radio on her hip crackled and she brought it to her mouth.

"Sergeant Adams?"

"Go ahead."

"We're in position. Just give me the word and we'll serve the arrest warrant."

The quality of the connection was poor, and she couldn't quite make out if it was Detective Yasiv or Drake speaking.

"You're a go. Get this bastard and bring him in," she said.

"Affirmative."

The radio went silent and Chase checked her watch. It was nearing seven, and dark had already settled over New York City.

She reached for her phone next, knowing that she only had a few minutes before the next report came in. Before dialing, however, she turned to Dunbar, who was still busy punching away at his keyboard, his tongue pushed into his cheek like a teenager playing video games.

He probably wouldn't even hear her if she made the call from within the small room, but she decided not to chance it.

"I've got to make a call. I'll be right back," she said.

Dunbar didn't even look up.

Chase went into the hallway, and after looking around briefly and confirming that she was alone, she dialed a number.

Her husband answered on the first ring.

"Hello?" he said. He sounded sleepy.

Chase hesitated. What could she say? What could she say that she hadn't said already? That she was sorry? That this was the last time she would miss dinner? Miss Felix's bedtime?

"Hello?" Brad asked again.

Chase decided that she couldn't lie to him. Not anymore.

"Brad, it's me," she said.

Brad sighed, and Chase knew that she didn't have to say anything; her husband already knew what she was going to say.

"I'm not going to be home for a while, hon. Not until late again."

The only reply was Brad's labored breathing.

*Don't let it get the best of you, don't let it take you over like it did in Seattle*, he had said.

But Chase didn't know any other way of doing her job. She wasn't a manager of a supermarket. If she wanted to catch the vilest members of society that tormented New York City day and night, she was going to have to put everything she had into it.

She had to put as much effort into hunting them that the killers put into honing their craft, of feeding their disease.

"I'll tell Felix you send your love," Brad replied flatly.

"Thanks, Brad. I'm sorry, I really am. And we're going to go on vacation. I promise. We're—"

But Chase realized that the line was already dead.

He had hung up on her.

# Chapter 52

DRAKE LEANED UP AGAINST the wall beside the door and looked over at Stitts, then to Yasiv and the other officers who stood behind him. He adjusted the grip on his pistol, then nodded at Stitts.

Stitts nodded back and then stepped in front of the door.

He knocked three times, haid, then stepped off to one side.

"FBI! Open the door!"

Drake counted to five, as they had discussed, and when there was no reply, indicated for Stitts to knock again. The man did, and repeated his order.

This time, however, they didn't wait.

Drake pushed him aside and delivered a strong kick to the door, just beside the handle. The wood splintered, and on the second such blow, the door swung wide.

Agent Stitts, gun held out in front of him, rushed inside, and Drake followed.

"FBI!" he yelled.

"NYPD! Come out with your hands up!" someone behind Drake shouted.

The entrance was filled with shoes, and Drake had to step over them to avoid stumbling. The interior of the small apartment was dark save an ambient glow coming from a room near the kitchen.

Stitts cleared the first room, while Drake made his way to the second.

"Colin Elliot!" he shouted. "Come out with your hands up!"

A flicker of movement, a shadow in front of the blue light from he realized was a television, caught his eye and Drake strode forward.

His finger tensed on the trigger when a figure stepped out into the hallway.

"Dad?" a sleepy voice asked.

Drake inhaled sharply and lowered his gun. He moved protectively in front of the other officers who streamed into the house behind him, concerned at the prospect of an itchy trigger finger. Then he reached out and grabbed the little girl in his arms, hunching over her protectively.

"Girl! A little girl!" he yelled.

The girl yelped in shock and surprise. She tried to pull away, but Drake held fast.

"It's okay, we're the police," he whispered. He was about to say something else, when another girl, sporting a matching set of flannel pajamas, stepped out of the TV room.

"Another one! There's another kid in here!" he bellowed. Still cradling the first girl, he moved across the hallway to the second, wrapping her protectively in his arms with the other.

His heart was racing in his chest, and his adrenaline surged so greatly that he didn't notice that both of the girls were scratching and clawing at his arms, trying to free themselves.

"Detective Yasiv!" he hollered. A second later, the man was at his side.

"Take them outside! Take them outside, *now!*"

Drake finally let go of the girls, and thrust them at Yasiv, who grabbed them much the way he had and turned back toward the entrance.

"Clear the rest of the lower level," Agent Stitts ordered from his right. "Drake, come with me upstairs."

Drake nodded and hurried toward the stairs.

"Colin Elliot! Come out with your hands up!" Stitts yelled.

When there was no reply, they started up the stairs, side-by-side, each leading with their pistols.

Drake was breathing heavily when they made it to the landing. Stitts looked over at him, then indicated the first door on their left, which was closed, and then the one on the right. Drake, understanding his meaning, went to the door on his left first and threw it wide.

The first thing he noticed was a female figure lying on top of the sheets, sporting only a pair of underwear.

*Another victim*, he couldn't help but think. He stepped into the room, and when he did, he realized that there was someone else in the room.

Someone who was trying to climb out the window.

"Stitts!" he yelled as he leveled his gun at the back of the man's head. "Get the fuck in here!" and then, to the man, he said. "Colin, if you don't step out of the window right now, I'm going to repaint your walls red."

The man hesitated, and Drake rushed him. He tucked the gun in his belt as he did, and then drove his shoulder into the man's spine.

The man's face cracked against the half-open window, sending a spider web of cracks spiraling out from the point of impact.

Colin grunted, and fell backward.

The man was larger, *much* larger, than Drake expected and when he toppled backward, the brunt of the man's weight fell on top of him.

The air was forced from Drake's lungs, and his diaphragm spasmed in protest. Colin tried to struggle to his feet again, but Drake reached out and grabbed a handful of hair.

Colin yelped, and Drake pulled his face down hard, rolling as he did.

Still unable to draw a full breath, Drake suddenly found himself on top of the other man, this time pushing *his* weight down on the man's chest.

Colin stared up at him, his eyes wide, blood spilling from a cut just above his right eyebrow. Drake pulled the gun from his belt and pressed the muzzle against the man's chin.

"You move again," he gasped, "and I'll blow your fucking head off."

Colin fell limp as Agent Stitts ran up beside him. To Drake's surprise, Stitts shoved him off the shirtless man.

Rolling onto his back, he stared at the ceiling with the sound of handcuffs ratcheting in his ears.

"Call Chase," he managed, finally catching his breath. "Call Chase and tell her that we caught the bastard."

# Chapter 53

CHASE TRIED TO IGNORE the shouts of the protesters outside 62nd precinct, spouting their pro-victim rhetoric. She wanted to go up to them, to each and every one of the dozen or so people holding signs, and shake them, scream at them that she was only trying to help, that she was just trying to keep them all safe.

But she did none of the above. Instead, she just watched from the shadows, her breath making puffs of fog, further obscuring her face.

*We got him,* Agent Stitts had told her over the radio, *We've got Colin Elliot in custody. There was a woman with him, but she seems okay. Disoriented and bruised, but alive. EMS is looking at her now, and is going to take her to the hospital when they're done. There were two kids here, too, Chase, but they're fine.*

Chase breathed deeply.

It had been close, *too* close. They had been close to losing another victim. Maybe three.

Several police cars pulled into the lot, honking to clear the crowd. She stepped forward as they made their way to the doors, and in the distance, she heard, and then saw, the rumble of Drake's Crown Vic. She had been doubting her decision to bring him on board, but if they had just caught the man responsible for the heinous murders and the macabre stories, then it had all been worth it.

The door to the lead police car opened, and a uniformed officer stepped out. He acknowledged her, then made his way to the rear door.

"Is his head covered?" Chase asked.

The man nodded.

"Covered, just as you asked."

"Good."

The officer opened the back seat and pulled a man out into the cold. He was wearing a pair of track pants and a t-shirt, and the first thing that struck her was that he was larger than she expected.

Perhaps it was Agent Stitts's profile, or Hanna's description of him, but she hadn't pictured Colin Elliot as a pot-bellied six-foot-two man with a slight hunch to his spine.

"Get him inside. Interrogation Room 6," her thoughts turned to Hanna for a moment, who was still decompressing in Room 1. "Keep him on the second floor, and for no reason are you to pass the rooms on the main floor. Got it?"

The officer said he understood, and then hooked an arm roughly beneath Colin's, and hoisted him from the vehicle.

"Don't let him speak to anyone until I arrive," she added as they headed into the precinct.

Chase slunk back into the shadows, watching Drake's Crown Vic pull into a parking spot near the front of the station. Agent Stitts stepped out first, and then Drake, a scowl on the latter's face.

Concern grew inside of her, and she wondered if it had been such a good idea to put them together.

They walked over to her and she stepped toward them as they neared.

It dawned on her that the crowd must have picked up on the fact that something was happening, something big, as their shouts increased in intensity.

Agent Stitts got to her first.

"I want you to join me in the interrogation room," she instructed. Stitts agreed. Then she turned to Drake. "You wait in the observation room. I'll call you if—*when*—I want you to enter. I want this to be quick; I want to get a confession out of

this bastard and put this case to rest before the news goes
wide tomorrow... before the article gets published in the
Times."

Drake looked uncomfortable.

"What? What is it?"

Drake's eyes darted to Stitts and Chase understood that he
wanted to speak to her alone.

"Agent Stitts, meet me inside. Wait for me before you
interrogate Colin," she instructed.

Stitts nodded and entered the station. When he was gone,
she addressed Drake directly.

"What is it? What's the problem?"

Drake hesitated before answering.

"I have to go," he said with something akin to shame in his
voice.

Chase gawked.

"You *what*? Drake we—"

"I'm sorry," he said, shaking his head. "We caught the
man, and now I have to go. Not for long, but there is
something I need to do first. I'm sorry."

Drake was heading back to his car before she could even
answer.

"Drake!" she shouted after him. "Drake! *Drake!*"

But the man didn't turn, he simply got back into his car and
sped off, barely taking a wide enough berth around the
protesters to avoid running them over.

*What the fuck is going on with him?*

# Chapter 54

THE LAST THING THAT Drake wanted to do was leave Chase with Colin Elliot. They had caught the bastard, and he wanted to be there when he confessed.

And yet the voice on the phone during the car ride back to the station had been direct, unwavering in his demand.

He slammed his hands on the steering wheel.

"Fuck!"

This was the worst possible timing, but what could he do? Did he dare say no to Raul? To Ken?

The answer lay in the fact that he was once again driving across the city to meet them. Only this time it wasn't at Smith, Smith, and Jackson, or at Ken's penthouse apartment. On the contrary, the address that Raul had given him was a new one, one that he didn't recognize.

The GPS on his phone indicated that it was an abandoned building near the port. He had tried to reach out to Screech, to ask him if he could dig up what the place was all about, but the man must have been airborne: his phone went directly to voicemail.

*What could they possibly want now?*

Drake pulled into the empty parking lot the better part of an hour later, with snow swirling in the dark sky like iridescent confetti.

Drake squinted into the night, trying to find another source of life. In the distance, he could hear the beeps of car horns, taxicabs no doubt, and the occasional squeal of air brakes, but nothing else.

As he stepped out of the Crown Vic, he felt his heart rate quicken. It thumped painfully in his chest from the bruising when Colin had fallen on him.

And yet, for some reason, despite the eerie quality to the meeting location, and the strangeness of the meeting itself, Drake knew that nothing would happen to him here. Not, at least, by Ken or Raul's hand.

He was important to them, important enough that Ken had given him twenty-thousand dollars without so much as a hesitation—with conditions, sure, but that was different—and had sent him on his way.

Drake was important to the man who was destined to become mayor.

He just had no idea why.

"Hello?" he called into what looked like a hangar used to maintain large trucks. With two hands, he gripped the side of the corrugated sliding door and shoved. It screamed in protest, but opened wide enough for him to step inside.

But he didn't. Despite his internal assurances that nothing would happen to him here, he wasn't an idiot. He knew better than to walk into a dark building at night at the behest of a strange man that he barely knew.

"Hello?" he said again, trying to keep his voice from wavering.

The only reply was his own echo, and he was surprised by how scared he actually sounded.

Against his better judgment, Drake felt compelled to enter. *I can just go inside, have a quick peek then get the fuck out of here. Fuck Ken and his henchman. I came, I did my part.*

Drake pulled the gun from the back of his jeans and held it out in front of him. With his other hand, he grabbed his cell phone and flicked the flashlight on.

Only then did he enter the hangar.

The glow from his flashlight was weak, but acute, illuminating a cone of about six feet directly in front of him.

"Hello? Raul?" he called into the near darkness. With his limited vision, Drake determined that the hangar was almost completely empty.

*Why the hell did they invite me here?*

Drake took several steps forward, shuffling his feet across the concrete to avoid tripping over anything that might have been left on the floor.

"Raul? I'm going to—"

There was an audible buzz from somewhere above him, and Drake instinctively ducked.

The sound was followed by a loud click, and a bright spotlight suddenly flicked on. Drake shielded his eyes and leaned away from the intense light that erupted from somewhere in front of him.

He swore and made sure that his gun was still level.

Drake expected something to strike him while he was blinded, a bat to the back of the head maybe, or something more subtle like a knife to the liver.

But when he heard only the blood rushing through his ears, he realized that he was becoming accustomed to the light and managed to lower his forearm from his face.

Squinting heavily, he realized that he was no longer alone in the hangar—that he hadn't ever been alone.

Beneath the spotlight, Drake made out the dark outline of a figure slumped over in a chair. The bright specks that flicked across his vision prevented him from making out more details, and against his better judgment, he strode forward to investigate.

"What the fuck?" he whispered.

The man—it was indeed a man, he saw—was collapsed in a cheap wooden chair, the crown of his head pointed at Drake.

It was clear that his hands were bound behind him, and that this was the only thing that kept his body in the chair.

Without thinking, Drake continued to advance. He noticed that the man had long, blond hair obscuring his face, the tips of which were tinged red.

Still blinking rapidly from the bright light off to his left, he pressed the first two fingers of his hand still holding his phone to the man's neck.

*A pulse... he has a pulse.*

Drake slipped the phone into his pocket and then gingerly put a hand on the man's chin, raising his face to look at him.

All of the breath was sucked from his lungs.

Both of the man's eyes were dark, the surrounding area bruised, and blood trickled from his nose, sliding over the ragged piece of duct tape that covered his mouth.

And yet, despite his injuries, Drake recognized the man.

It was Ivan Meitzer.

"I see you've become acquainted," a voice said from behind him, and Drake spun around, leading with the pistol.

# Chapter 55

"I AIN'T TELLING YOU SHIT. I don't gotta even speak to you."

Chase leaned away from the man, a scowl on her face.

"Listen, Colin, you can—"

"I've told you a hundred times already! My name is not Colin! It's Glenn—Glenn Happ! It's on my license," he reached out, but the cord connecting the cuffs on his wrists to the table reached its length, and his arms snapped back.

"Shit! Just look at my wallet! I've got everything in there, Social Security, Driver's License, *everything!*"

Chase's frown deepened.

"If you aren't Colin Elliot, then why were you in his bed? With his wife? That was his wife, correct? Or is this all a misunderstanding? Got the wrong house, maybe? The kids? What about the twin girls who go by the names of Colby and Juliette Elliot?"

The man who claimed not to be Colin threw his head back and swore.

"I'm not *Colin!* I was sleeping with his wife, but I'm not him!"

Chase turned to look at the two-way glass, behind which he knew that both Officer Dunbar and Agent Stitts were watching, and hopefully investigating the man's claims.

"I don't care what your name is, you can call yourself Colin or Glenn or Miss fucking Marple for all I care. You killed those girls, and we're going to prove it in court," Chase sighed, watching the man closely for any hint of fear, of remorse, of anything.

But all she saw was anger in his round features.

"Or you can just cut us all a break, and tell us why you did it, why you killed those girls."

The man pushed his lips together tightly in sheer defiance.

"No? Not ready to man up and admit what you've done?" Chase mock checked her watch. "Fine, it's still early. You've got time. Why don't you start with the books, then? Tell me why you wrote the books. Was it just for money?"

The man's face contorted.

"Books? Look, lady, I don't have no fucking clue what you're talking about. I didn't write no books."

He tried to cross his arms over his chest, but the chains were too short and he ended up just awkwardly crossing his forearms.

"What about Hanna? Tell me about Hanna. You raped her after one of your writing classes."

"What in all hell are you talking about? Hanna? Who the fuck is Hanna? And writing classes? I'm a fucking landlord for Christ's sake."

There was a knock on the door, but Chase ignored it.

"I know you killed those girls, Colin," she whispered, leaning across the table.

Chase hoped that her true suspicions didn't come through in her words. Sure, it could all be an act, but this didn't sound like any writer she knew. Chase had read the first two parts of *Red Smile* on Drake's e-reader, and while the work was far from literary genius, it included several three-syllable words that she would bet a nickel the man across from her wouldn't be able to pronounce, let alone spell.

"I told you, I'm not Colin," the man hissed. Then his pale lips broke into a smile, revealing a chipped front tooth. "And I'll tell you something else, too; that dipshit Colin didn't kill nobody, either. He's as limp-dicked as they come. You're barking up the wrong fucking tree, lady."

Chase felt warmth rise in her cheeks and was about to shout something back, when the knock on the door returned.

She pointed a finger at the man's face.

"This isn't over," she promised.

The man laughed as Chase made her way to the door. Agent Stitts poked his head in and indicated for her to come out.

Chase didn't look back.

Agent Stitts was silent as he led her to the adjacent room.

"What?" Chase asked once the door was firmly closed behind them.

Still, Stitts didn't speak. Instead, he looked over at Dunbar who, with a sour expression etched on his face, turned the laptop around for her to see.

On the screen was a photograph of the man on the other side of the two-way mirror, only younger, with slightly thicker blond hair and a front tooth that had yet to be chipped.

"Yeah, that's him. So what?"

"Look at the name," Stitts said, finally breaking his silence. Chase squinted and took a step forward, her eyes scanning the screen.

"Shit," she whispered, her heart sinking.

The name at the bottom of the photograph read Glenn Happ.

Chase turned and stared at the fat man chained to the table in the other room.

"Jesus Christ, we got the wrong guy."

*And the killer's still out there.*

# Chapter 56

"**WHAT THE FUCK IS** going on, Raul? What is Ivan doing here?" Drake asked, keeping his gun aimed directly at the center of the man's chest.

Raul stepped out of the shadows and into the light. He wasn't wearing his typical butler-*esque* attire, but something more befitting of the locale: loose-fitting track pants, a dark sweatshirt, the hood of which was pulled back revealing his pitch-black hair.

Raul didn't answer. Instead, he continued to walk toward Ivan, keeping a safe distance from Drake.

"Raul, I don't know if your eyes are still fucked from the light, but I've got a gun pointed at your chest. I think it's about time you start answering my questions."

Raul still said nothing, and this time Drake thought he saw a smirk slide out from under his wiry black mustache.

"Raul? I'm not fucking around anymore. I've had one *helluva* a day, and I ain't in the mood for games."

Raul made it to Ivan, and was within half a dozen feet of Drake himself, when he reached down and grabbed a fistful of the man's hair.

Drake saw blood on his knuckles as he yanked Ivan's head back.

"You know Ivan, don't you?"

This time Drake remained silent.

"Of course you do. But *we* know Ivan, as well."

Raul slapped Ivan across the face, and the sound echoed throughout the hangar.

Drake's finger moved from the trigger guard to the trigger itself.

"Hit him again and I'll put a hole in your spine, Raul. I mean it."

Raul ignored him and waited. After several seconds, Ivan's eyes fluttered and then they opened—*wide.*

His gaze jumped from Raul to Drake, and then his mouth started to move behind the duct tape, generating incomprehensible muffled.

"You see, Drake. You weren't the only one to pay Ivan to perform a task," Raul said, his accent suddenly so thick that Drake had a hard time understanding him. "But there's something that you need to know about Ken Smith. He is a man with strong loyalty; he's loyal to his family, his friends, the people he employs, and last, but not least, to the citizens of New York. And this," Raul reared back and slapped Ivan again, this time hard enough for the man's head to snap backward.

"Hey!" Drake shouted, stepping forward and applying pressure to the trigger. "I warned you, Raul, step away—"

But Raul continued as if nothing had happened.

"This prick decided that it was more important to fuck you over than it was to be loyal to Mr. Smith or to New York. Seems like everyone who has read the news think they know you. But what they don't know is that you work for us now. And with that comes a level of respect."

Raul crouched down in front of Ivan, his back now fully turned to Drake.

Drake seized the opportunity and silently moved forward.

"Isn't that right, Ivan?"

Drake was so close to the man now that he could smell his cheap cologne. With his free hand, he reached out and—

His phone in his pocket suddenly buzzed.

The distraction only lasted a fraction of a second, but that was all Raul needed.

Drake glanced down at his pocket, and before he could look up again, Raul had stood, turned, and somehow yanked the gun from his hand, despite his grip. Raul was lightning fast, faster than Drake thought humanly possible.

Drake cried out and instinctively lunged for Raul, but the man easily sidestepped him and held the gun up.

Drake stumbled, landing awkwardly on Ivan's lap. The man grunted and groaned, and Drake pushed him back as he stood.

He glared at Raul, amazed at how quickly their roles had reversed.

"You gonna shoot me now, is that it?" he sneered.

Raul smirked again, an expression that made ice shoot up Drake's spine.

"Is that why you brought me here? To shoot me? Kill me and Ivan so that you and Ken can... can what? Take over the world?"

"No, senor, I'm not here to hurt you," Raul gestured to Ivan with the barrel of the gun. "Ken did this for you. He wanted to show you that he was loyal to you, the way he expects you to be loyal to him."

Drake scoffed.

"For me? Listen, bud, I don't know what kind of fucked up place you were brought up in, but that isn't the way it works here. Not in New York. Shit, not in America."

Raul's cheek twitched.

"Isn't it? It's working now."

Drake scowled, but had no reply.

"You want a shot at him?"

"What? Are you insane?"

Raul shrugged and raised the gun, this time aiming it at Ivan. The man's furious breathing sounded like a jet engine from behind the tape. He started to struggle, but the binds were tight.

"Woah! *Woah!*" Drake said, putting his hands up. "Easy now."

Raul suddenly spun, and for a split second, Drake thought that the gig was up, that Raul was going to pull the trigger and put an end to this whole mess.

But Raul didn't shoot. Instead, he flipped the gun around and held it out to Drake.

Drake lunged forward and snatched it from the man. Raul's other hand snaked into his jacket and once again Drake found himself pointing the gun at him.

Only this time he aimed it at his head instead of his chest.

"Easy!"

Raul's movements slowed, but he continued to reach into the pocket of his sweatshirt.

Sweat beaded on Drake's forehead despite the frigid temperature inside the hangar, but he relaxed when Raul pulled out a yellow envelope.

"Go on, take it," Raul insisted. "It's yours, after all."

Drake eyed it suspiciously, but recognition swept over him and he snatched it from Raul's fingers.

As he did, Raul's sweatshirt pulled up, revealing a strange tattoo on his forearm that looked to Drake like a coiled snake devouring an eyeball.

Raul pulled back, and Drake's eyes focused on the envelope. There was a smear of blood on the corner, but he knew it was the same one he had given Ivan yesterday.

Drake tucked it into the pocket of his jeans.

"What are you going to do to him?" he asked.

Raul shrugged.

"It's already been done. Ivan has learned his lesson. Haven't you, Ivan?"

Ivan, still puffing as if he were on the verge of hyperventilating, nodded violently.

"Good."

Drake's phone buzzed in his pocket again, but this time he resisted the urge to look down.

"You should answer that," Raul suggested. A moment later, the light clicked out, leaving Drake in total darkness.

Survival instincts took over, and Drake spun around, locating the sliver of moonlight that eked in from the open hangar door. Without thinking, he sprinted toward it.

Several seconds later, he found himself in the cold, and a few seconds after that, he was back in the relative safety of his Crown Vic.

*What the hell just happened? What the hell have I gotten myself into?*

His phone buzzed a third time, and with a trembling hand, the other still clutching the pistol tightly, he answered it.

"Drake," he croaked.

"Drake, it's Chase. We fucked up."

Drake shook his head.

"What? What happened?"

"We got the wrong guy. Colin's still out there and we need to find him. We need to find him before this shit blows up tomorrow."

An image of Ivan, his mouth taped, his eyes bruised and blackened flashed in his mind.

"I don't think we need to worry about that anymore," he whispered.

"Why? What's going on?"

Drake shook his head and cleared his throat.

"Nothing. Never mind. Just tell me what you want me to do."

# Chapter 57

CHASE HUNG UP THE phone and then turned back to Agent Stitts.

"I'm going to talk to him again. Just because he isn't Colin Elliot, doesn't mean he isn't our guy," she said, but her voice lacked conviction.

Agent Stitts eyed her suspiciously for a moment.

"What's your gut telling you?"

Chase sneered.

"My gut's telling me that we fucked up."

With that, she headed out of the room and back into Interrogation Room 6.

"Glenn," she said with a sigh. "I've got some questions for you."

The man smirked; he actually *smirked*.

"Did yer boss tell you that I ain't Colin? That I'm not a spineless prick that hit his wife?"

Chase made a mental note of the comment, along with a reminder to speak to Ryanne Elliot after she was through at the hospital.

"How do you know Colin and his wife?"

Glenn pursed his lips, and while he was clearly trying to be defiant, she knew what type of man he was.

She knew that she could get him to talk.

"I told you already, I was sleeping with Ryanne."

"And how did you first meet her?"

Another shrug.

"I'm their landlord," a disgusting smile suddenly appeared on the man's face. "That bastard Colin couldn't pay the rent one month, and Ryanne came to me pleading for an extension. One thing led to another and…"

Glenn brought up two fingers and rammed them into a hole he made with his other hand.

Then he laughed.

"Ya, you know what I'm talkin' about."

Chase tried to keep her emotions in check. The more she spoke to the man, the less likely she thought that he was involved with either the books or the murders. And yet he was a despicable human being if there ever was one.

"Cute," she replied. "Tell me about Colin."

"Like I said, he's a spineless dweeb. Only met him a few times. He let his wife deal with all of the finances. When she spoke about him, she usually just blathered on about how he was trying to write books, about how he didn't even know how to do that good. *Alls* I know is that he couldn't do anything good, including keeping her happy, if you know what I mean."

Chase tapped a finger on the table.

"You know what gets me about this?"

"What?"

"We haul you in, start asking questions, accuse you of murder, and you don't even ask for a lawyer."

Again with the chipped-tooth smile.

"Why do I need a lawyer? I didn't do nothing."

"So you say. But I promise you this: if you had anything to do with the murders, even if you just knew about them and sat back and did nothing, you're going to rot in a cell for a long time. A long, *long* time."

With that, Chase stood and started toward the door. Only now did the smile slide off Glenn's face.

"Hey, where you going?"

Chase knocked on the door.

"Hey, lady, can I go now? I answered your damn questions?"

The door opened, and Agent Stitts stood in the entrance.

"Hey! *Hey!* What do I do now?"

"Get a lawyer," Chase said over her shoulder as she left the room.

# Chapter 58

DRAKE WAS SICK OF being everyone's errand boy, be it Chase, Ivan, or Ken that gave the orders.

And yet he found himself driving into the storm, heading toward another obscure address with instructions that were as vague as those from Raul, which had led him to the hangar in the first place.

*Dunbar found a property on the outskirts of the city, a farm or something that had once been Colin's father's. I want you to go check it out, see if he's there and bring him in. There's an APB out for Colin's arrest, and the police are busy combing the area around his house. If he pops up, we'll grab him.*

As he drove, Drake's mind kept turning back to the scene in the hangar, about his curious decision to leave the place. To not arrest Raul.

And not telling Chase about what had happened.

Then there was the strange tattoo of the snake eating the eye on Raul's forearm.

*When Screech is back from vacation, I'm going to have him look deeper into Raul and Ken Smith, to see what they were all about. About their past.*

When he had first met Ken Smith less than a year ago, it had been in the wake of his son's death. Even then, he knew that Ken Smith wasn't normal, that there was something off about him, something that transcended a man hellbent on acquiring power, on becoming the mayor of New York City. Now, however, he was beginning to think that his radar had been off.

The man wasn't *just* a callous prick, but Drake was beginning to think that he was far, far worse.

And somehow, inexplicably, he found himself working for Ken, indebted to him, even.

"How did this happen?" he asked out loud.

But he knew how. He had been so obsessed with finding the real Skeleton King, with avenging Clay's death, that he had made himself vulnerable. And a man like Ken Smith didn't need an invitation to wield that to his advantage.

The snow was so heavy now that Drake found that even with the wipers set to maximum they were doing a poor job of clearing the windshield. He pulled the wiper stalk, but instead of washer fluid spraying the windshield, all he got for his efforts was a light on the dash indicating that he was out.

"Shit."

Drake was forced to slow to a crawl. Now that he was outside the city, the quality of the roads deteriorated substantially, and he could feel the tires beneath the Crown Vic starting to slide across the surface rather than drive.

*And the bone... the bone that Ivan delivered on behalf of Ken Smith... where the hell is it?*

He racked his brain, trying to remember, but he was drawing a blank.

It had been in his pocket when he had gone to the barn on both occasions, he was sure of it. He was positive, because he distinctly remembered the feeling of the hard surface as he pressed it between thumb and forefinger.

*But after that... where the hell did it go?*

Tail lights suddenly illuminated the snow in front of him, and Drake slammed on the brakes.

The Crown Vic immediately went into a spin and he cried out, yanking the wheel against the rotation.

There was an awful squeal, and he saw the ditch at the side of the road careening toward him.

Someone screamed—it was him, it *had* to be him—and he instinctively let go of the wheel and brought his hands up in front of his face.

# Chapter 59

"**WHAT SHOULD WE DO** with him?" Agent Stitts asked as they stared at Glenn Happ through the glass.

"Let him rot. We can keep him for forty-eight hours without pressing charges. I figure we keep him until the very last second."

Detective Yasiv came into the room, and all eyes immediately went to him.

"Sergeant Adams? I've got practically every beat cop in the city on the lookout for Colin Elliot—they've all been given photographs, and his car has been flagged. If he shows his face tonight, we're going to nab him."

Chase thanked the man.

"And the secondary residence? Elliot's place up north?"

Chase turned back to the now fidgeting landlord.

"Drake's taking care of that."

Out of the corner of her eye, she saw something in Agent Stitts's face change. It was a subtle gesture, a simple tick in his cheek, but Chase's time playing poker made her aware, without doubt, that this was a tell.

*Yeah, he fucked up, fucked up big time, but he was trying to help. And now I need him.*

The NYPD were good, sometimes great, at their job, but other times not so much. Drake, on the other hand, wasn't bound by bureaucracy or strict rules. Which is why she had gone to him in the first place. And, yes, the whole business with Ivan Meitzer and the Times was a direct result of this *flexibility*, but it was a risk she was willing to take… again.

"Sergeant Adams?"

"Hmm?" Chase said, turning back to face Officer Dunbar.

"I said, I found out something about Glenn…"

"Go ahead."

"You know that photo I showed you? That was from a computer engineering course that he took at MIT."

Chase's neck straightened.

"He went to MIT?" she asked, barely believing what she was saying.

*This man with the 'aint's' and 'didn't do nothings' went to MIT?*

Officer Dunbar shook his head.

"Not exactly. Took a course by them. Part of the free online courses that they started offering a while back. Got a certificate in computer programming."

Even the fact that Glenn managed to get a certificate, even in an unaudited course such as the one Dunbar was describing, surprised Chase. And yet as shocking as this fact was, she failed to see the connection.

"And?"

Dunbar glanced around nervously, suddenly less confident than he was a moment ago.

"And remember Drake's e-reader? How the IP was all scrambled... I doubt that Colin, a writer, would be able to do something like that," Dunbar raised a finger and pointed directly at Glenn. "But this man might."

Chase let this sink in for a moment.

"You think—" Detective Yasiv began, but Chase hushed him.

He wasn't the killer, of that she was certain, and her gut told her that he wasn't even involved.

Glenn Happ had no idea what she was talking about when she mentioned the books, let alone the murders.

And yet...

*There's something wrong with the profile... it just doesn't feel right.*

Chase immediately turned to the door and pulled it wide.

*He might not know he's involved, but maybe, just maybe he was manipulated into doing something that he wasn't even aware of.*

And there was only one way a man like Glenn would allow himself to be manipulated in that way.

"Chase?" Agent Stitts asked as she left the room. "You okay?"

Chase didn't answer. Heart racing, she went immediately to the Interrogation Room and stepped inside.

"You're back. I need to... I need to get out of here. I need—"

Chase held her hands up, a gesture so dramatic that Glenn leaned away from her, the chains on his wrists clanging loudly.

She knew what he was going to say—that he was going to ask for a lawyer—and she couldn't let him finish his sentence.

Not right now.

She just had a few more questions.

"Before you say anything, just listen. You answer a few more questions, and I'll let you leave. And not in two days, but now. *Right* now. But if you say anything else, I'll hold you for the entire forty-eight hours permitted by law. Do you understand?"

Glenn opened his mouth to speak, but Chase held a hand up, once again stopping him.

"Just nod if you understand."

Glenn, his jaundiced eyes now wide, nodded several times.

"Okay, good. Now answer this..."

# Chapter 60

DRAKE BLINKED ONCE, TWICE, and then a third time, confirming he had somehow managed *not* to rear end the car that had stopped in front of him.

Breathing heavily, Drake looked around, trying to catch his bearings. When he had jammed on the brakes, his car had spun, and eventually, it had come to a stop perpendicular to the road, just inches from the top of the embankment, and only a few feet from a thick oak tree below.

*That was close.*

Drake patted the dash of his Crown Vic, thanking his lucky stars that it was an old, heavy beast. It wasn't like the newer vehicles made of plastic and foam, light things that would hydroplane on a puddle.

No, his Crown Vic was like him: an old heavy beast.

Drake reached over and unbuckled himself, put his gloves on, and stepped out into the still blowing snow.

"Hello?" he shouted into the storm as he made his way toward the other car. He had seen the taillights, they had been bright enough to make him stop, but now, with the snow coming down, they had degenerated to diffuse glowing red eyes in the night.

"Hello?" he repeated.

Out of habit, he checked to make sure that the gun was still tucked in the back of his pants. Drake quickly pulled out his cell phone, noted that he had only one signal bar, and then slid it back into his pocket.

He didn't think that anything sinister was going on here, but after what had happened with Raul, he wasn't about to take any chances.

Drake slowed as he approached the car. It was still running, and he was confused as to why it had come to a complete stop in the middle of the empty road.

And yet he wasn't angry so much as he was concerned.

*A heart attack, maybe? The driver had a hard attack? A stroke?*

"You okay in there?"

The storm was so loud now that he had to shout to hear his own voice.

When Drake was finally within a few feet of the car, he realized why the driver had stopped. The left rear tire was a spare, a small rubber thing about two-thirds the size of the stock tires.

In fact, Drake realized that both back tires were doughnuts, and to top it off, the front two tires looked flat.

"What the hell?"

The snow at his feet was so thick that it had reached halfway up the bottom of the spare tires.

Drake moved to the front door and tried to peer inside the window.

"Hey, buddy? You alright in there?"

The window was fogged and even by cupping his hands against the glass, he was unable to see inside.

Drake knocked on the glass several times.

"Hey? Hey buddy?"

When there was still no response, Drake reached for the door handle. It was unlocked, and he pulled it open.

Confusion washed over him.

The front seat was empty. The keys were in the ignition, and the car was on, but there was no driver or passenger in sight.

Drake leaned further into the car and peered into the backseat.

*Nothing.*

He pulled his head out and was in the process of straightening when a growl from his left drew his attention.

Drake's eyes went wide and he stumbled backward.

A figure lunged at him wielding what he thought was a tire iron. It was an awkward, ungainly strike that would have missed, had Drake kept his footing.

His heels shot out in front of him, and he fell on his ass. As he went down, the arcing tire iron followed.

It cracked loudly off the top of his head.

The assailant also appeared to stumble in the snow, which was probably the only thing that kept the tire iron from splitting his skull open and sending his brains splattered across the white expanse.

Drake grunted and tried to swear, but the only thing that came out of his mouth was an unintelligible mumble.

The figure fell directly on top of him, forcing the air from his lungs. He tried to push off, but his hands had suddenly become obstinate, stubborn things that refused to listen to his brain.

The white specks of swirling snow suddenly dimmed, becoming gray flakes in an otherwise black void.

A split second before darkness overcame him, Drake caught sight of his attacker's face, which was set deep inside the hood of a winter coat.

Drake tried to speak, to shout, but succumbed to unconsciousness before he could manage a single word.

# Chapter 61

COLIN ELLIOT RAN HIS hand across the top of the door, trying to feel through the thick pad of snow for the key.

When he felt nothing, he swore and removed one of his gloves. As he did, he noticed a small cut on the knuckle of his index finger, and his frustration transitioned into shame.

*I hit her… I hit her and now I'm going to pay.*

He couldn't believe that he had actually done it. It wasn't the first time he had thought about it, of course, but there was a huge difference between thinking something and actually doing it.

*She pushed me… she pushed me too far. Every man has their breaking point, and this was mine.*

With freezing fingers, he searched back and forth for the key.

When he didn't find it, his grimace became a scowl. Colin turned his eyes to the snow around the door, looking to the spot that he had found the key last time he was here.

He was on one knee, rooting through the packed snow when something occurred to him.

Colin whipped his head around to confirm his suspicions. And then, seeing the familiar shape and pattern of footprints, his breath caught in his throat.

*Someone's been here.*

Colin leaped to his feet, giving up on finding the key in the snow, if it was still there.

*I have to get inside, I have to get inside* now!

With a trembling hand, he reached for the doorknob, while at the same time bracing his back foot, readying himself to kick the damn thing down.

To his surprise, the door was unlocked, and he pushed it open.

His eyes scanned the interior of the house, his heart still racing in his chest.

The interior of the small cottage was musty and frigid, but empty.

Everything was exactly the way he had left it that day he had come with Colby and Juliette.

Except that was the problem.

When he had come here, his black notepad had been on the counter, and he had taken it back with him.

Only now it was here again, back in the exact same place as before.

Colin squinted at the notepad as if it might transform into a giant beetle the way the typewriter had in Naked Lunch.

But of course it didn't.

*I took it… I remember coming inside and grabbing it, before heading back out to stop Colby from drowning Juliette in snow.*

After that, he thought he remembered putting it in his computer bag, but couldn't remember opening it since.

*So how the fuck did it get back here?*

Still staring at the notebook, he kicked snow from his boots and entered the cottage. Then he flicked on the lights, which bathed the main room in a dull yellow glow. His steps as he approached the counter were slow, deliberate.

Hesitant.

He was halfway there when he heard a sound.

Colin froze as he listened.

At first, he thought it was mice again, which wouldn't be a surprise considering how old the place was, how many holes and cracks there were in the floorboards.

He had also seen mouse shit in some of the drawers the last time Ryanne had driven him out of the house and he had spent the night here.

But when the sound came again—powerful scratching this time—Colin knew that this was no mouse.

And when the words followed, his heart stopped completely.

"Please? Anyone up there? Please, I'm freezing down here. Please help me."

# Chapter 62

"YEAH," GLENN SAID WITH a hint of pride. "I scrambled the IP. But so what? That ain't a crime last time I checked. In fact, I bet it's part of the Constitution, or some shit. Big brother 'n' all that."

For what might have been the twentieth time, the man tried to cross his arms over his chest and then appeared annoyed when the chain caught.

He was like a child, continuing to check that a live burner on the stove would scald.

Chase shook her head.

"Yeah, it's not a crime. But if you want to get out of here, you're going to tell me *who* you scrambled the IP for."

Glenn squinted at her.

"For Ryanne. What'd you think?" he laughed. "You think I did it for Colin?"

Chase swore and started toward the door.

"Is that it?" Glenn called after her. "Can I go now?"

Chase ignored him and knocked on the door. When it didn't immediately open, she kicked at it with her foot.

Stitts pulled it wide, a stern expression on his face.

"You said I can go! Hey! Lady, you said—"

Chase slammed the door closed behind her.

"What? What'd he say?" Agent Stitts asked as Chase hurried toward the other room. "The intercom was still off."

"He said he scrambled the IP for Ryanne, not Colin," Chase replied as she pulled the door to the observation room open. Inside, she was surprised that another man, one she didn't recognize, had joined Dunbar.

Her first thought was that it was another IA goon, and she instinctively moved a half step behind Agent Stitts.

The man had horseshoe hair and thick glasses hiding beady eyes. He was so short that Chase thought that she might actually be the taller of the two.

In heels, there was no doubt.

"Who's this?" she demanded, her eyes glaring at Dunbar.

Officer Dunbar raised his hands defensively.

"This is the handwriting expert that I sent the books to... is this a bad time or... do you want me to tell him to leave?"

Chase had to think for a moment why Dunbar had reached out to a handwriting expert, but then she remembered that he was analyzing the books from Drake's e-reader.

*Red Smile.*

"Benjamin Laroche," the man said in a nasal voice. He held a hand out in front of him.

Chase eyed him up and down.

"Tell me what you've found," she barked.

Benjamin cleared his throat.

"Well, I came to several conclusions based on the files that were provided to me. I must advise you, however, that this is not my—"

"Get to the point!"

The man's eyes bulged.

"My first conclusion is that the author of the *Manbeast* series, I believe his pen name is R.S. Germaine, is *not* the same person who wrote *Red Smile*. I repeat, R.S. Germaine and L. Wiley are not the same person."

Chase squinted as she processed this information. Things were suddenly starting to fall into place.

"What else?" she asked, the fury suddenly gone from her voice.

But despite her question, Chase knew the answer.

It was the reason why the entire profile felt wrong the moment Agent Stitts had opened his mouth.

"And I can tell you, with 98% certainty, that *Red Smile* Parts I, II, and III weren't written by a man, but by a woman."

# Chapter 63

Colin threw the door to the cold cellar open and stared into the darkness.

*There's someone down here!*

He reached for the light switch, missed, and his hand slammed against the frigid wall.

"Hello?" he called out, his voice wavering. "Hello?"

He ran his hand up and down the wall, searching for the light switch.

*I imagined it... Ryanne's got me so messed up that I just —*

"Please... I'm freezing down here."

Colin's hand finally found the switch and he flicked it on. There was a fizzle and a pop, which was punctuated by a brief flash of light before everything was once again shrouded in darkness.

The woman in the basement screamed and Colin felt his heart flutter in his chest. He turned back to the kitchen, his eyes falling on the drawer that he knew contained a flashlight.

"I'm coming," he said, whispering for some reason. "I'm getting a flashlight and I'll be right back."

The only response was a whimper.

Colin ran toward the drawer, pulling it open so quickly that all of the cutlery smashed against the front and several forks flew over the side.

Ignoring the mess, Colin grabbed the flashlight. As he turned back toward the stairs to the cellar, he instinctively checked his phone even though he knew that there was no signal.

"Shit," he swore.

Nothing that had happened made any sense; not the fact that he had struck Ryanne, that she had slept with that fat bastard Glenn, least of all that there was a woman trapped in the basement of his cottage.

But, for the time being, none of that mattered.

The only thing that held any consequence was the woman freezing in his basement, and that he had to save her.

Colin switched on the flashlight and aimed it into the dank cold cellar opening. His breath was coming in frosty puffs and he shivered.

If the woman had been down there for more than a day, two at most, then he was surprised she hadn't frozen already.

It must be close to ten degrees in the cellar.

"I'm coming. Just wait, I'm—"

Headlights suddenly filled the cottage, and Colin instinctively ducked. The throaty roar of an engine followed next, then, in an instant, both the lights and the sound were gone.

Colin's heart thudded in his chest. He crouched on his haunches, cowering away from the cottage door.

"Hello? Is anyone—"

"*Shh! Shhhh!*" Colin hissed frantically down the stairs.

But the woman didn't hush. Instead, her words grew even more frantic.

"Please, you need to help me!" she screamed. "Help! Help! *Heeeeeeeeeeelp!*"

Colin grit his teeth and shook his head.

"Shhhh!" he pleaded, tears streaking his cheeks now.

It was no use; the woman's words had degenerated into unintelligible screams.

Colin was torn; he didn't know if he should go to the woman as he had initially planned, or hide.

The truth was, he had never been in a situation this fucked up before.

In the end, he elected for the latter. Closing the door to the cellar partway, he moved deeper into the cottage, staying low. He saw a figure approach the door and then pause.

*He's seen my footsteps. He knows I'm inside.*

When the shadow grabbed for the door handle, Colin lay flat on the floor, using the worn, tartan couch as cover. Like a child hearing strange sounds from the closet, he clenched his eyes closed and listened.

The footsteps moved into the cottage, and then seemed to hesitate.

*The book! Did I move the notepad? Did I touch it?*

Colin didn't think that he had grabbed the book, only noticed it, but couldn't be certain.

*Fuck! Fuck!*

The footsteps started again, and Colin felt his grip on the thick handle of the flashlight tighten.

*Go away! Just go away! Please go away!*

But the person didn't go away.

Instead, he heard the footsteps approach the stairs.

"Hello? Is that you again? Are you back?" the woman chattered from the cellar. "I'm… I'm freezing…"

The footfalls suddenly quickened and then the door that Colin had left partially open creaked as it was swung wide.

"I'm going to slit your fucking throat, bitch," a strangled voice rasped. "I'm going to slit your throat."

The woman in the basement started screaming again.

*"Help! Help! Help!"*

More tears squeezed out from between Colin's clenched eyelids.

*Just stay down,* he told himself. *Stay down and when the person—whoever the fuck it is—goes into the basement, make a run for it. Just get into your car, and get the hell out of here. Make it to the main road, then call the police.*

Colin felt himself nodding, his chin scraping uncomfortably against the carpet beneath him.

*Yeah, that's it, just run. Run like you've always done. Run like the spineless bastard that you are.*

It wasn't his own voice in his head this time, but Ryanne's.

Or maybe it was Glenn's.

Before he knew what was happening, Colin rose to his feet. He wiped the tears from his face with the back of his hand and started to move silently toward the figure at the top of the stairs.

*You ain't worth shit. You're nothing but a loser, a fucking child who wants to write books—shitty books that no one wants to read. You have a family to look after, and you can't even pay the bills. I have to whore myself because you can't—*

"I'm going to slit your fucking throat, just like all the others," the figure—it was a woman, Colin realized—spat down the stairs.

—pay the bills. *And the best part? I like it. I like fucking Glenn. I like the way his—*

The floor beneath Colin's foot suddenly creaked and the figure at the top of the stairs spun around.

Colin didn't hesitate. He sprinted toward her, bringing the end of the heavy flashlight down in a sweeping arc.

The bulb blinked out when it smashed against the top of the woman's head, but it stayed lit just long enough for Colin to see her face—before she flew backward down the stairs.

He gasped.

"Ryanne?"

# Chapter 64

"WHAT DO YOU MEAN, she's gone?" Chase demanded, her brow furrowing. Agent Stitts moved toward her, a concerned expression on his face, but she stopped him by holding up a finger. "Detective Simmons, for the love of Christ, tell me you didn't let her leave."

Chase couldn't believe what she was hearing.

"Sergeant Adams, I don't know what happened. She was cleared by the doctors, then she just snuck out."

Chase fought back a curse.

"How long ago was this? How did she leave?"

There was a pause.

"I don't know. An hour, maybe less. I have no idea how she left or where she went."

This time Chase swore.

Loudly.

"Find her, Simmons. For Christ's sake, find her, and arrest her."

"A-arrest her? You mean—"

"Just do it!" she yelled into the phone before hanging up.

Dunbar and Stitts stared at her and she bit her lip, trying to figure out what to do next.

"The kids," she said at last. "Where are the kids?"

"They're with Social," Dunbar replied.

Chase breathed a sigh of relief.

"Give Social Services a call, let them know not to let them leave with either parent."

"They can't leave, they—"

Chase threw up her hands in frustration.

"I know they can't leave, Dunbar! Just like Ryanne Elliot wasn't supposed to leave! Just fucking do it!"

Then to Detective Yasiv, she said, "Call dispatch, tell them to be on the lookout for Ryanne as well as Colin."

A muffled shout from behind the glass drew her attention.

Glenn was looking at them, eyes searching for something he couldn't see, face pale, lips twisted in a frown.

"You promised you'd let me go! Lady! *Lady!*"

Chase's eyes narrowed.

"Find out what car Glenn drives and put out an APB on that, too."

Detective Yasiv nodded and pulled his phone from his pocket as he fled the room, leaving Chase alone with Agent Stitts.

An uncomfortable silence came over them.

"Profiles are never exact, Chase. And I knew that this one— I *told* you that this one, given the strange nature of the deaths, the books, wasn't going to be perfect," Agent Stitts started. The man's words were unapologetic, explanatory, not defensive, which unnerved Chase. "But here's the thing, you *knew* it was wrong, you knew it from the beginning."

The words offered Chase little comfort; the murderer was still at large, as was...

"Drake!" she exclaimed, fumbling for her phone.

"What?"

"Drake's out there... he's on his way to Colin's cabin," Chase said as she started to dial.

# Chapter 65

**D**RAKE SHIVERED HIMSELF AWAKE.

It was cold and dark, and there was no telling how long he was out. Somewhere close to him he heard the sound of a car running, but when he tried to sit up, a flash of pain filled his head.

With a grunt, he managed to roll onto his stomach.

Aside from the pain, Drake realized that he couldn't feel anything. Not his fingers, his toes, or his face. He moved his hands to his left to catch some of the ambient light coming from the still open car door.

His fingers were a stark white.

*I've got to get out of the cold,* he thought. Again, he tried to rise, but his head felt as if it would split in two, and instead of on his feet, he found himself on all fours, breathing heavily, spit dripping from his mouth.

*How could I be so stupid? So careless?*

Instead of trying to stand a third time, he felt around his body with numb fingers, confirming that his cell phone was still in his pocket. It took four tries for him to get it out, and twice that number to actually turn it on.

He squinted as he held it in front of his face, grimacing when he saw that it had no service. As he angled it to try and catch a signal, he felt something hard press into his back just above his hip.

*My gun!*

With his free hand, Drake reached behind his back and let out a sigh when he felt the familiar shape jammed into his belt.

It was still there.

Glancing around, he noticed that while his assailant hadn't taken his pistol, she—*a woman, it was a woman's face tucked into that hood*—had stolen something from him.

There were no longer two cars on the road, but one.

This time Drake fought the dizziness and pain and managed to stand.

"Shit."

His Crown Vic was gone.

Through still squinted eyes, he stared up, then down the road.

All he saw was snow in either direction.

Wincing at the pain in his head that bloomed with each step, Drake slowly moved toward the woman's car and slid inside.

The warm air pumping from the vents was almost orgasmic. Drake held his hands in front of the vent and a shudder ran through his body. A minute later, his fingers started to tingle as feeling returned.

He looked up in the rearview, and then cringed at the sight of his appearance. It wasn't the blood that stained his brown hair or even the burn on his cheek from the fire at Dr. Moorefield's house that gave him pause.

It was his sunken eyes, the dullness of the irises buried deep within.

"I'll live," he said to himself. After allowing just a couple more blissful seconds with his hands in front of the vent, he turned his attention back to his cell phone.

There was still no signal, but the GPS coordinates to the Elliot cottage were still on the screen.

"Seven minutes," he muttered, staring at the directions.

He turned his eyes to the falling snow, grimacing at the way it continued to pile up in the absence of cars on the road.

A light suddenly lit up on the dashboard.

The car was almost out of gas.

*It's now or never.*

With a grunt, Drake pulled himself from the vehicle and started to trudge through the snow. It was slow going, and before long, numbness started to embrace his extremities again.

"Seven minutes my ass."

# Chapter 66

REAL DETECTIVE WORK WASN'T the way it was portrayed in the movies. Most detectives don't spend their time knocking down doors, aggressively confronting suspects. Almost everything happened behind the scenes; there was a whole lot of talk, of profiles, of ideas, of hopes, of relatively useless information, and occasionally a crime scene to analyze. But for long stretches of time, to the outside world, nothing seemed to happen.

Progress was slow, calculated.

The situation that Sergeant Chase Adams currently found herself in, however, was exactly the opposite.

She was in a frantic race against time.

Chase sprinted from the observation room with FBI Agent Stitts in tow.

"Do you think that she would go there? To the Elliot cottage?" Agent Stitts asked, breathing heavily as he struggled to keep up.

Chase, the phone still pressed to her ear as she listened to it ring in perpetuity, fished the keys from her purse and unlocked her BMW.

"I don't know… maybe. With Tanya and Melissa, we know that they were held for some time. Neither Dunbar nor CSU were able to narrow it down to anywhere specific, but the NYPD has already cleared their apartment. None of the victims were ever there. Aerial photographs of the cottage show that it's secluded, tucked away between trees. I know if I was to hold someone against their will, that's the type of place I'd choose." She shook the strange thought from her head. "But it doesn't matter. Drake's out there somewhere and in this storm…"

Chase let her sentence trail off, trying to ignore the flashes of images of Drake sitting in his rusted Crown Vic, huddled over the dash, trying to keep warm.

Trying not to freeze to death.

Agent Stitts nodded and he tapped the dashboard.

"Then let's go," he said.

Chase didn't need any encouragement.

\*\*\*

It took forty minutes to get out of the city, and that was with the cherry flashing on the BMW dashboard.

The entire time, Chase continued to try to reach Drake to no avail.

Outside the city, things didn't get much better: even though traffic was minimal—non-existent in some cases—the roads hadn't been cleared yet. Even with four-wheel drive, it was slow going.

"What's that up ahead?" Agent Stitts asked, peering through the snow.

Chase squinted. She could see what looked like a car parked in the center of the road.

She slowed as she neared, hoping that it wasn't Drake's Crown Vic.

It wasn't.

But this fact did little to appease her concerns. There were thick tire marks in the snow, indicating that another car, a much heavier car, had swerved and nearly gone off the road.

Chase slammed her BMW into park and hopped out.

She went to the abandoned car first and checked the tag number against the ones that Dunbar had forwarded to her phone before it lost service.

"It's Glenn's car," she shouted into the wind.

"What?" Agent Stitts hollered back. He was only a few feet from her, but the storm sucked the words up and spat them somewhere far away.

"I said, *it's Glenn's car!*"

Agent Stitts frowned and then started to investigate the interior of the vehicle.

Chase, on the other hand, crouched down low, inspecting the tire tracks made by the other vehicle that had since vanished into the white.

It was halfway between where Glenn's car was parked and the deepest grooves of what she was now convinced were made by Drake's Crown Vic that she noticed the indentations.

They had no color—other than white—but she had been to enough crime scenes to know what the speckles were.

*Blood... this is where blood had melted the snow.*

"He was here," she said, this time to herself. "Drake was here."

Chase took a deep, hitching breath, and turned her gaze to the road ahead. She tried to put herself in Drake's shoes, to figure out what he would do without cell service and the only car at his disposal one that was useless in the thick snow.

She knew what he would do.

Drake would keep going. Drake would keep on trudging until he caught the killer.

That was just the type of man he was.

Chase turned to Agent Stitts, who had just poked his head out of Glenn's car, a frown etched on his pale face.

"No one's here," he said.

Chase shook her head.

"Forget about it! Let's go!" she yelled. "Let's keep going!"

# Chapter 67

EVERY BREATH DRAKE TOOK singed his nostrils. Even with the directions on his phone, it had been a struggle finding the Elliot cottage.

Eventually, by traipsing through thick snow, he found a small passage through the woods that led him there.

It took several tries just to shut off his phone, with his hands frozen as they were, and he decided that trying to operate his pistol would be akin to an ant trying to wield a flamethrower, and decided against it.

Stealth was the name of the game now.

He still wasn't sure who had brained him, aside from being a woman, but as he came around a large shrub and he spotted his Crown Vic, he knew that it was someone involved with Colin, with this case.

*Which means that there are two of them, and one of me. A frozen me.*

Drake hunkered low as he made his way across the snow-covered lawn.

There was a single light on inside the cottage, casting a bleary, diffuse glow over the interior.

Drake perked his ears and held his breath, trying to pick up any sound from the inside, but the wind was just too damn loud.

With frozen limbs, he managed to manipulate his way up the steps to the porch, and then he sidled up next to the door.

It was ajar, which he thought strange given the weather.

Drake darted his head into the opening for a split second before pulling back.

His breathing became more labored.

*No, not two of them. Three of them, and one of me.*

There were three figures inside the cottage, all of whom appeared to be either lying or sitting on the floor.

He brought his hands to his mouth and breathed on them, trying to bring life back into the digits.

Drake had no idea what they—Colin and the others—were doing on the floor, but he had to be ready to act.

Dropping to one knee, he crawled toward the door, staying low to avoid being seen through the glass pane carved out of the wood.

With his ear near the entrance, he realized that someone inside was speaking.

A male voice. He paused to listen.

"How could you, Ryanne? How could you do this?"

Drake leaned even closer, trying to block out the storm by covering the ear furthest from the opening.

"I never thought..." the man sobbed. "You've ruined everything. My life, your life... the kids..."

The female voice that replied was nasal, as if her nose had been recently broken.

"You're such a fucking pussy... I had to do something, had to make money somehow. You're just pissed that I wrote something in a few hours that sold more than you have in your entire pathetic life."

This was followed by more sobs, and although Drake couldn't see who was crying, he knew it had to be Colin.

*But the third person... who is that? And why aren't they speaking?*

"Why, Ryanne?" Colin whined. "How could you do something like this? You've... you've... *killed* people. Innocent people."

A wild cackle ensued.

"You said it yourself, *'write what you know'*. I stole your stupid notebook, and you didn't even notice. I took notes, wrote every detail about the girls… about how they screamed when I cut them. About how at first, they all tried to be tough. But in the end, they all cried. They all whined and pleaded and begged for their lives. They were pathetic, just like you. And you know what the best part is? When the police come, they're going to come for you. I even mailed the stories to a detective, with your fingerprints all over it. They're going to pin this on you, Colin." More laughter. "What do they call that? Irony, I think. Yeah, irony."

Drake could take it no more. He rose to his feet and then fumbled to pull the gun from the back of his jeans.

They had it wrong; Chase and Agent Stitts had it wrong.

This whole time they were looking for a man, but it was a woman who had committed the horrific murders, written the macabre tales.

The gun felt like a cinder block in his hands, but something in his gut told him that he was running out of time.

He had to act.

Drake pushed the door wide and aggressively strode into the cottage.

"NYPD!" he shouted out of habit. "Don't move!"

He had intended to sound authoritative, but like the rest of him, his vocal chords were frozen and his words came out in a pathetic wheeze.

And yet it did the trick.

All eyes were suddenly on him and his gun.

The scene that unfolded before Drake took what little breath that remained in his frigid lungs away.

Colin was sitting on the floor, his wife's head cradled in his lap. Blood streamed from her nose and mouth, and one eye was bruised so badly that it was completely closed.

Behind them, he spotted a woman he didn't recognize, bound and gagged.

And shivering.

*Part IV*, Drake couldn't help but think. *Red Smile PART IV.*

Colin stared at him with wet eyes.

"I didn't want any of this," he whimpered. "I didn't—"

It was only then that Drake realized Colin was holding the sharp edge of a knife to Ryanne's throat.

"Put the knife down!" he yelled, this time with more gusto. "Put the knife down, Colin, or I'll shoot."

Colin was so lost in his own head that he didn't seem to hear him.

"All I wanted was to be happy, to write books and spend time with my family. I didn't want any of this."

Colin broke into full body sobs, and under normal circumstances, Drake would have seized this opportunity to lunge at him.

But he didn't trust his fatigued and frozen limbs. Instead, he simply waved the gun.

"Colin, if you don't put the knife down, I'll have no choice but to shoot you. Think about what you're doing... you have kids, and you can still spend time with them. If that's what you really want, put the knife down."

This time, Colin took notice.

"It's ruined. Everything's ruined." A small indent appeared on Ryanne's throat as Colin applied more pressure with the knife tip. "She ruined everything."

Drake swallowed hard.

"Colin, please, think—"

"I know how to write a book... I do. I write good books; people like them."

The bound and gagged woman suddenly moaned and started to squirm, drawing Drake's attention.

She was like the others—like Tanya and Melissa and Charlotte and the other girl, the one hanging from the goalpost. She looked exhausted and terrified, her arms marked with crisscrossed scars.

If he hadn't arrived, Drake knew that it wouldn't have been long before her lips were also marked with blood.

"I know what people want!" Colin suddenly shouted. "A twist ending! *Everyone wants a fucking twist ending!*"

"Colin, no!" Drake yelled, but he was too late.

Colin ground his teeth and drove the knife into the soft skin beneath Ryanne's chin.

This time Drake did lunge, but he was too slow. Hot blood sprayed from the wound, coating Colin's hands and forearms.

Ryanne started to thrash and sputter as Drake approached.

He knew that he should fire, that he should take out Colin Elliot before he pulled the knife all the way across his wife's throat, taking with it any chance of saving her life.

But he couldn't bring himself to do it.

As Ryanne's eyes rolled back in her head, he found himself focusing on her face.

She was no longer a person, despite the blood that soaked the floor beneath Drake's feet.

She was something else.

She was Dr. Mark Kruk.

She was Craig Sloan.

Ryanne Elliot was the Skeleton King.

A ruthless, heartless murderer who deserved her fate for what she had done to Clay Cuthbert, to Dr. Eddie Larringer, Dr. Tracey Moorfield, Tanya Farthing, Melissa Green.

To him.

For what the Skeleton King had done to Damien Drake.

# Chapter 68

CHASE NEARLY SLAMMED INTO the back of Drake's Crown Vic as she pulled up to the Elliot cottage.

She hopped out with her gun drawn, and burled through the snow toward the side porch.

Halfway there, she came to a full stop.

"Drake?" she asked, heart pounding. "Drake? You okay?" The man on the porch lifted his head and stared up at her with bleary eyes.

Chase ran to him, and then stopped again when she realized that there was someone resting on his lap. She was so tightly wrapped in blankets, that it was hard to make out her face, but for a split-second, Chase thought that it was Ryanne Elliot in Drake's arms.

"Get away from her!" she cried. "Get away!"

Agent Stitts hurried up the stairs, beating her to the punch.

"It's not her," he said. "It's not Ryanne."

Drake nodded.

"It was her next victim—but he got here just in time."

Agent Stitts bent down and picked up the girl. Drake didn't resist.

"She's alive," Stitts said, as he made his way toward Chase's car. "We have to keep her warm."

Chase nodded and felt relief wash over her. They hadn't even known that another woman was missing, but she was safe now.

Her solace was short-lived, however, when she realized that the killer was still on the loose.

Grasping her pistol with two hands now, Chase bounded past Drake, staying low as she scanned the interior of the cottage.

"She's dead," Drake said at the same moment that her eyes fell on the woman lying in the center of the room, her body surrounded by a pool of blood.

"Oh my god," Chase whispered. "What happened?"

Drake's words echoed in her head.

*He got here just in time... But who's he?*

Drake, with no emotion in his voice, his eyes still locked straight ahead, replied, "I was too late—I got here too late. Colin was already gone."

Chase breathed deeply.

"What? Where is he now?"

Drake shook his head.

"I don't know, but he's gone. I doubt we'll ever find him. But Ryanne's dead, Chase. She was the one writing the books, killing the women."

He pulled a small black notebook from beneath the blankets that were draped over his shoulders and held it out to her.

She took it, noting that his hands were shaking badly.

"We need to get you warm, Drake. You're going to freeze to death out here."

But even before the puffs of warm air that accompanied her words dissipated, a strong feeling suddenly came over her.

A gut instinct that she just couldn't ignore.

*That's what he wants,* Chase thought with horrible sadness. *That's what Drake wants.*

# Chapter 69

DRAKE LOOKED DOWN AT his phone, and stared at the video of Dr. Kildare and his campaign manager, their lips pressed together. The doctor swept the papers off his desk and propped her on top of it. As the video continued to play, Drake raised his eyes to look at the condo building before him. He felt dirty, he felt *wrong*.

Drake was reminded of his night with Jasmine, and thought about how he would feel if someone had caught them on tape. In that moment, he felt a strange kinship with Dr. Kildare, even though they had never met.

The doctor was having an affair, and he had had an affair with Jasmine. It didn't matter that Clay was dead while the doctor's wife was very much alive.

He had broken his friend's trust, his honor.

And this shame ran deep.

"I can't do this," he whispered. And then, before he lost his nerve, he glanced down at his phone again.

The woman was on her back, her shirt open revealing pale breasts while the doctor kissed her hungrily.

Drake felt sick to his stomach.

His thumb hovered over the garbage bin icon, but only for a split-second.

He pressed it, and with that, the video disappeared.

Drake wiped a tear from his cheek, then he left his car and made his way toward the building.

***

"You sure you don't want something to drink, Drake?"
Drake shook his head.

"I'm fine."

Ken Smith nodded.

"And do you have something for me?"

Drake pictured Ivan Meitzer's bruised and battered face and Raul's bloodied knuckles.

*Ken did this for you, Drake.*

"I don't," he said, aware that Raul had crept up behind him as he spoke.

Ken Smith's expression soured as he took another sip of scotch. He paused, swirled the liquid, then looked up at him.

"You sure?"

Drake held the man's gaze.

"I'm sure. If I find anything I'll let you know."

Ken Smith's cheek twitched, but then he turned his attention back to his drink.

Drake's eyes narrowed. He had expected more, outrage perhaps, or, at the very least, to be berated.

And yet, this silence was somehow worse.

"What about our other situation? The Sergeant?" Ken said at last.

Drake felt anger flash inside him, but he forced it away.

"She's good," he said.

Ken raised an eyebrow.

"We won't be having any further issues with her?"

Drake's gaze didn't falter.

"She's good," he repeated.

Ken nodded.

"You can go," he said.

Drake nodded and turned to leave, shoving by Raul in the process.

The elevator opened and he stepped inside.

"We'll be in touch, Drake," Ken Smith said from his chair. "I'll contact you soon."

Drake scowled.

*I bet you will,* he thought as the elevator doors closed.

\*\*\*

"What should we do with him?" Raul asked when Drake was gone.

Ken Smith clipped the end of his cigar, took a dry pull and then struck a match.

As he waited for the sulfur to burn off, he turned his attention to the photographs that Raul had laid on the table in front of him.

His eyes skipped across the images of Drake in Dr. Kildare's campaign office, first looking back as he opened the door, then the zoomed images of him setting up the camera. Then he stared at Drake hovering over Ivan Meitzer's slumped form, his fists furled, the man's face bruised.

Ken scooped up his cell phone next and pressed the play button. Dr. Kildare appeared in the frame, first kissing then caressing his campaign manager.

Drake had given them what they wanted, even if he had gotten cold feet at the last moment. After all, he had set up the camera.

Ken brought the flame to his cigar and watched the wrapper turn a dark gray.

"Should we *deal* with him?" Raul asked.

Ken leaned forward and picked up the finger bone that Raul had retrieved from Dr. Kildare's office, and wrapped it in a tight fist.

"No," he said, without looking up. "We still need him."

With the video that they had procured, the election was as good as won.

Which meant that they were ready to enact stage two of the plan.

"He'll come back to us, and we still need him," Ken said absently. He raised his eyes and stared at Raul. "But I think it's time for you to make some calls. We need to prepare for what's next. We need to think about bringing Dane in."

Raul's mustache twitched.

"You sure? Even before Drake is on board?"

Ken took a long, slow pull on his cigar, and watched the smoke drift toward the ceiling.

"It's time, Raul. Make the call."

Raul nodded and left the room.

*The next stage is upon us*, Ken thought as he brought the cigar to his lips. *And New York City better be ready.*

# Epilogue

DRAKE SIPPED HIS DRINK and then turned to face Chase. She was smiling at him, her pretty face lighting up for the first time in as long as he could remember.

"Why are you so happy?" he said over the obnoxious music pounding from the speakers.

Chase shrugged.

"I wouldn't say I'm happy, not exactly."

"Then what is it?"

"I dunno. I'm just amazed by you, is all."

Drake turned back to the bar, noticing that Mickey, who was pretending to be drying a glass, was looking at him out of the corner of his eye.

"You getting soft on me, boss?"

"No—but you seem to…" she paused. "You just have a round-about way of doing things, you know? But you get there in the end."

An image of the blade slicing across Ryanne's throat came to mind, but he forced it away.

"Not exactly."

This put an end to the line of conversation, and for several minutes Chase and Drake enjoyed their respective drinks without speaking.

"There's an opening as Sergeant at 62nd precinct, you know," Chase said at last.

Drake sputtered.

"You're shitting me, right? I'd rather scoop my eyes out with a rusty spoon than take that job. If they'd have me, of course, which is about as likely as making bacon from pigeon meat."

Chase threw her head back and laughed, and Drake stared at her. She looked beautiful beneath Barney's eclectic lighting. Drake couldn't look away, even when she stopped laughing. She caught him staring, and he flushed.

"What? You going to miss me or something?" she said in a soft tone that was barely audible over the music.

Drake smirked and took a sip of his drink, enjoying the way it burned his throat.

"Something like that, yeah. I can't believe that the FBI is going to take you on, though. *You.* I mean, come on, don't they have standards? Or is this just some feminist outreach program?"

Chase smiled.

"Well, apparently, my skills outweigh my poor decision making—which consists mainly of being friends with you."

With that, she raised her glass and Drake cheersed her.

There was another short silence, before Chase said, "I'm going to miss you, too, Drake. But here's the thing about chasing bad guys; we're bound to come across each other again eventually."

"Touché," Drake said, turning back to Mickey while he finished his drink. The glass felt strange in his frostbitten hand, and the irony of having a burn on his cheek while his hands were frozen was not lost on him.

"Hey, Mickey, you just gonna gawk all day or fill me up?" He turned to Chase, "What's—"

But Chase was no longer there. Her seat was empty and her glass half full.

"—with this guy?"

Drake lifted his eyes in time to see Chase slipping between the two bouncers guarding Barney's entrance.

"Yeah, I'm going to miss you, too," he whispered.

Mickey came over and filled his glass.

"The one that got away," he said with a wry smile.

"The one I never—"

But his phone rang and Drake paused, pulling it from his pocket. When he saw the word UNLISTED on the screen, he frowned. His first instinct was that it was Ken Smith again, who was probably the last person on earth he wanted to speak to right then, but then he thought that it might be Screech calling from the Virgin Islands or wherever the hell he was 'working' from.

In the end, it was neither.

"Hello?" he said.

A quiet, female voice answered.

"Drake? Thank god, I've been trying to reach you for days now."

Drake's spine suddenly straightened.

"Jasmine? Is everything all right? Is Suzan okay?"

The only sound on the other end of the line was heavy breathing.

Drake bolted to his feet.

"Tell me where you are, Jasmine. I'll come to you, just tell me—"

"I've been trying to get a hold of you, Drake. I've' been calling and calling…"

"What's wrong? Goddammit, just tell me—"

"The last thing I wanted is to do this on the phone, but—"

"*Jasmine! Just tell me what's wrong!*"

"What's wrong? Drake… I'm pregnant."

The glass slipped from Drake's frostbitten fingers and smashed to the floor.

"*You're what?*"

# END

# Author's Note

*Damien Drake is best when he's at his worst.*

A fan wrote me this after reading Cause of Death and I couldn't agree more. FBI Agent Jeremy Stitts also tells Drake that things are going to get a whole lot worse for him before they get better.

If they ever do.

The one thing that's certain is that Drake's story is only getting started. But Download Murder also represents a crossroads of sorts. As you might have guessed, Chase is moving on to greener pastures. But before you shed a bucketful of tears, know this: Chase already has her own series brewing, with book one, FROZEN STIFF, due out next month. Her story is deeper, and her past more troubled, than Drake's books can do justice. Besides, the short, feisty detective deserves her own series, don't you think?

Alas, Chase is not the only one who's leaving Drake's world; Dr. Beckett Campbell is also getting his own series. Unlike Drake and Chase, however, Beckett is only just coming into his own, starting to learn who he really is. And it's still up in the air whether or not he likes who, or what, he's becoming.

But enough about that noise... I want to talk about Drake, and about Download Murder.

Much of this book, in particular Agent Stitts's dialogue, was influenced by Gavin de Becker's work, and specifically his book *The Gift of Fear.* I highly recommend checking it out as it deals with real, no bullshit ways of identifying specific precursors to violence and how to protect yourself from it. What his vast experience reveals may surprise you. It certainly surprised me.

Oh, and don't worry, even with Beckett and Chase getting their own series', Drake will be back before the year's out. The fourth book in the Detective Damien Drake chronicles is called SKELETON KING and is available for pre-order. If I have to tell you what it's about at this point in Drake's journey, you kinda missed the boat.

Sorry; grab a life preserver and start again from the beginning.

As always, if you have any questions or just want to chat, drop me a line at patrick@ptlbooks.com. I have an anxiety-inducing number of unread emails (trust me, it'll make your head spin), so if I've missed yours in the past, email me again. And again. Except for you, mom; I'm ignoring you on purpose.

You keep reading, and I'll keep writing.

Patrick

Montreal, 2017

Made in the USA
Monee, IL
06 May 2021